# ENGLISH RIVER

# ENGLISH RIVER

## Amish Horses Series
## Book III

Thomas Nye

CROSSLINK PUBLISHING

English River: Amish Horses Series Book III

CrossLink Publishing
www.crosslinkpublishing.com



This book is a work of fiction. Names, characters, businesses, organizations, places, events and incidents either are the product of the author's imagination or are used fictitiously. Any resemblance to actual persons, living or dead, events, or locales is entirely coincidental.

Library of Congress Control Number: 2016931765



ISBN: 978-1-63357-064-1

# CONTENTS

Chapter 1 Two Pies in a Pod .......... 1

Chapter 2 Leah's Shawl .......... 19

Chapter 3 Checking the Fence .......... 37

Chapter 4 Catching a Sow .......... 59

Chapter 5 Growing Moon .......... 77

Chapter 6 The Bluffs .......... 95

Chapter 7 A Roar in the Woods .......... 107

Chapter 8 Amish Wedding .......... 119

Chapter 9 Hauling Soybeans .......... 135

Chapter 10 Football Party .......... 145

Chapter 11 Taffy Pull .......... 155

Chapter 12 The Last Straw .......... 171

Chapter 13 Penny for Your Thoughts .......... 179

Chapter 14 River City .......... 185

Chapter 15 Windmill .......... 199

Chapter 16 English Wedding .......... 211

Chapter 17 Herbie's Secret .......... 223

Chapter 18 Snow Tunnel .......... 237

Chapter 19 Icing on the Cake .......... 253

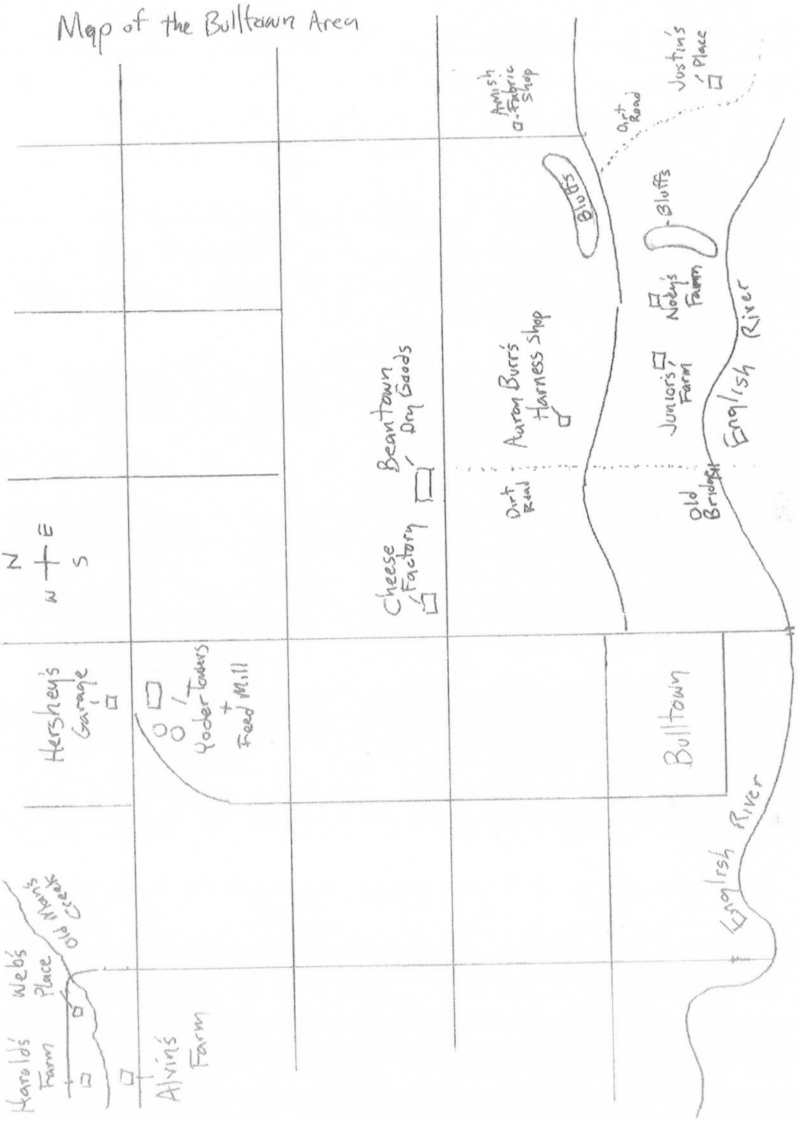
Map of the Bulltown Area
N
W
E
S
Harold's Farm
Web's Place
Old Man's Creek
Alvin's Farm
Hershey's Garage
Yoder Towers + Feed Mill
Cheese Factory
Beantown Dry Goods
Bulltown
Dirt Road
Aaron Burr's Harness Shop
Amish Fabric Shop
Bluffs
Dirt Road
Justin's Place
Bluffs
Noby's Farm
Junior's Farm
Old Bridge
English River
English River

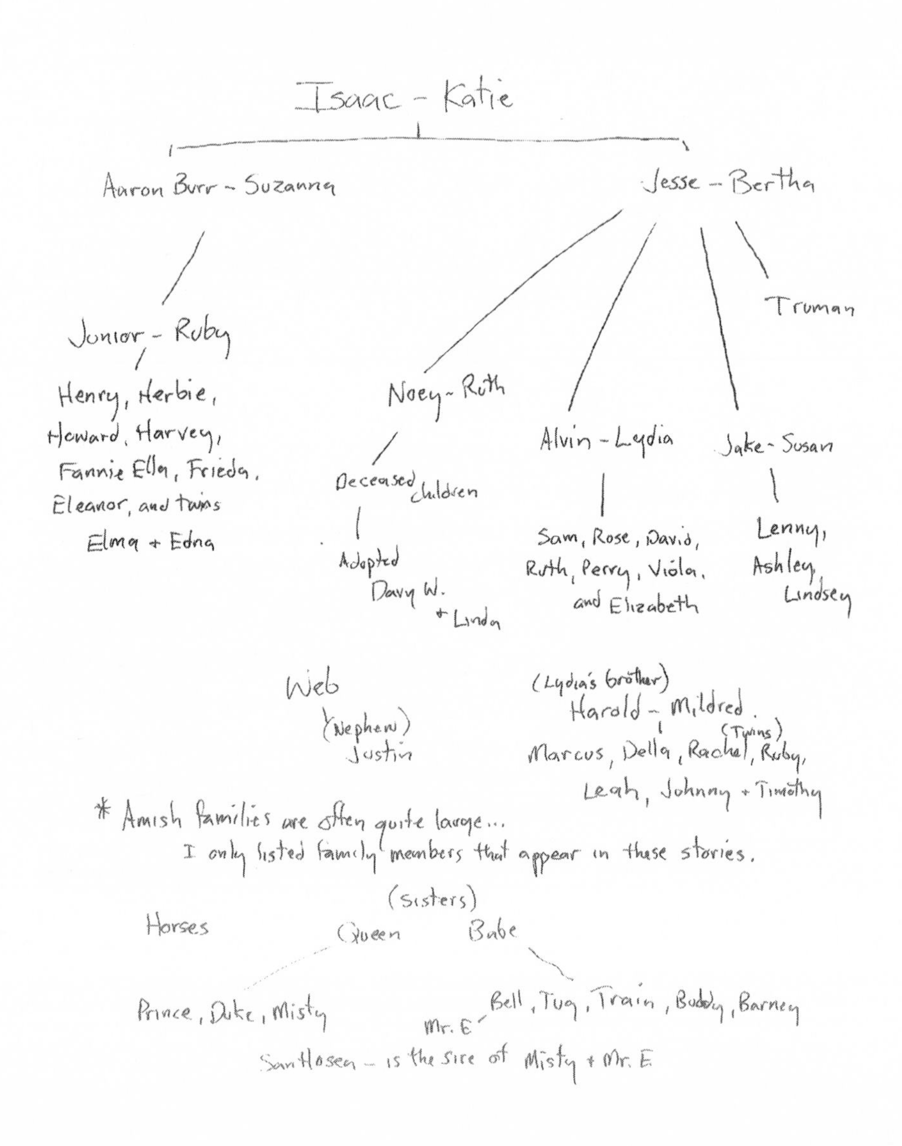
Isaac - Katie
Aaron Burr - Suzanna
Jesse - Bertha
Junior - Ruby
Henry, Herbie, Howard, Harvey, Fannie Ella, Frieda, Eleanor, and twins Elma + Edna
Truman
Noey - Ruth
Deceased children
Adopted Davy W. + Linda
Alvin - Lydia
Sam, Rose, David, Ruth, Perry, Viola, and Elizabeth
Jake - Susan
Lenny, Ashley, Lindsey
Web
(Nephew) Justin
(Lydia's brother)
Harold - Mildred
(Twins)
Marcus, Della, Rachel, Ruby, Leah, Johnny + Timothy
* Amish families are often quite large... I only listed family members that appear in these stories.
Horses
(sisters)
Queen
Babe
Prince, Duke, Misty
Bell, Tug, Train, Buddy, Barney
Mr. E
SanHosea - is the sire of Misty + Mr. E

# Acknowledgments

I want to thank all of my Amish friends for putting up with my "English" perspective of your lifestyle. After years of spending time with Amish friends, my life was so much richer and fuller I had a burning desire to share what I have experienced with the world. Please forgive me if I misrepresent the Amish in any way. My intentions are to show you all in the very best light, which is how you have appeared in my life. The Amish witness to the world is stunning. You have lit the lantern, and I wanted to put that light on a lampstand for my fellow Englishers to see.

Thank you Rick Bates and CrossLink Publishing for patiently transforming these manuscripts into beautiful books.

My wife of thirty-five years, Shari, listened to me read every word of the *Amish Horses Series*. When she smiled, I knew I had something right. My firstborn daughter, Robyn, read each of my books before taking the photographs for book covers, which helped bring them to life. Thank you, Ruby Ellen Photography. My daughter, Lisa, posed in an Amish dress along with her adorable daughters, Lyla and Kinley. They appear on the cover of Whispering to Horses. My daughter, Bethany, was the very first to read *Under the Heavens* and did so while living in Italy. Bethany loves to read, so I sent her each book first. Bethany, you are very insightful and helped make each story better with inventive ideas to make my characters more real. My youngest daughter, Natalie, also posed for book covers in an Amish dress. Yes, that is her beautiful smile on the cover of *Catbird Singing*. My only son, Dallas, wore a straw hat and suspenders for his appearance on the covers of *Under the Heavens* and *English River*. He is so tall my huge horses look smaller. Dallas may be the only guy on an Amish book cover who can also dunk a basketball.

My sister, Twila Lou, spent countless hours helping me rethink sentences that were confusing. Thank you, Sis; you left an imprint on each of my books and I can never repay you for all that you have done.

To my friends, Loren and Gladys Borntrager, who grew up in Amish homes. Thank you for answering my questions and describing an Amish wedding to me in detail. Give the Borntragers credit for what I got right, and blame me for any error. Lue Shetler, also formerly Amish, answered more of my questions and helped with the spelling of *Pennsylvania Dutch* words. She would want to add, "Amish in other areas may say it differently."

To the Harold and Mildred Yoder family: thank you for letting me give your names to Leah's family. Uncle Harold and Aunt Mildred are two of the kindest people I've ever met. Thank you, Holly, at Copyworks, for transferring my drawings into an electronic document. And last, but not least, thank you to my Percheron horses, Karma and Coke, who adorn all of my book covers. Karma and Coke were raised on an Amish farm and taught me much about a very integral part of Amish life, working with horses in harness. To me, you are the best horses in the world.

# CHAPTER 1

## Two Peas in a Pod

Beautiful bird songs twittered through a screen window and drew Lenny out of a deep sleep. He stretched, rubbed his eyes, and opened them just enough to see his little mostly white dog nestled in blankets at his feet. A rooster confirmed it was morning with a, "Cock a doodle do!"

"Russell, I just had a weird dream." The dog stretched from front to back, gave a whining yawn, and then sat up looking at Lenny as though wanting to hear about his dream. "I dreamt that I went back to town. I hated it there; all I could think about is

Leah—oh, and you, too, Russell." Russell cocked his little head and lifted his black ears. "My dream had a really strange ending." Russell tilted his head the opposite way. "I'll tell you about it sometime, but we better get our chores started now."

The wooden floor was smooth on his bare feet as Lenny pulled on his Broadfall pants, looping suspenders over his shoulders. Russell jumped off the bed and followed him downstairs, passing by Aunt Ruth, who was already working in the kitchen. Uncle Noey was tying on his work shoes in the washroom. Russell sat in front of the older man until Noey scratched him behind the ears. Lenny read a plaque on the wall behind his uncle.

"May the Words of my Mouth and the Meditation of my Heart be Pleasing in Your Sight, O Lord, my Rock and my Redeemer." Psalm 19:14

They all headed outside as a red sun pulled itself up over the horizon, painting a blazing mural behind the pasture trees. Crisp morning air had a chill in it that urged Lenny to hurry to his horse barn. He scooped molasses-coated grain into feed bunks, slid open a large wooden door, and shivered while he whistled. A line of tall horses clomped inside.

"Good morning Stone, Jim, Jack, Mack, Big Red, Smoky, Nelly, Misty, and you, too, Mr. E."

Body heat rose like steam off the massive horses, warming Lenny as he tied them and began his morning ritual of currying their sleek coats. Haze rolled in through the doorway like a miniature indoor cloud. Lenny admired his stable full of horses while he brushed them all thoroughly. He spent extra time currying his own horses, Smoky, Mr. E, and Misty. Their glossy coats reflected all the attention they were getting, and all three showed signs of being fed too much. Grain-munching sounds echoed off a stone wall just beyond their roughhewn feed bunks. Lenny set thick leather horse collars on Mr. and Misty's arched necks and harnessed both of them.

"It's your turn today, Mr. and Misty. After we feed the cattle, we have some manure to haul."

Lenny stepped out under the foreshoot looking toward the English River. He had made a habit of looking at the sky every morning, to try and determine what the day's weather would be. "Sunny and warm, with a slight chance of an afternoon storm," he announced his forecast to Russell. Heavy vines clung to tree trunks, adding foliage to a woods that was already thick with undergrowth. There arose a faint hissing sound through the trees. Lenny concluded he was hearing river water snaking its way through the lowest part of the English valley. Something moved in the woods and caught Lenny's attention. Russell sat on his haunches beside him, as though trying to see what his master was looking at. "I wish Noey's place wasn't so close to the river. I wonder what mysterious thing will come out of that woods next." While the young man and his dog were staring into dark foliage, they heard a growl. Lenny would have thought that he had imagined it if Russell hadn't stood up and let out a low growl of his own. He bent down and picked up his dog, holding him tight.

"No, Russell, you're not going out there after some wild creature." Russell's chest vibrated with more low growls.

Suddenly, there was movement in the underbrush. Weeds parted and a lone housecat emerged calmly out of the shadows. Russell lunged free of Lenny's arms and charged at it. The calico feline didn't take off, like most, but stood its ground with back arched. Russell kept up his pace, obviously expecting the cat to bolt, and Lenny expected that, too. Instead, the cat spit and hissed, throwing a handful of claws at Russell's nose. With a yelp, Russell turned to Lenny as if to ask, *Aren't you gonna help me get rid of this cat?*

Lenny only laughed. "I wonder where this cat came from. Let's take a closer look."

The calico had more than five toes on its front paws, making them look like hands with a thumb, or as if it were wearing mittens. Its face was half-brown, half-black; equally split between the eyes and on down its nose.

"This is an interesting cat, Russell. I don't think we should chase it off."

The calico came up purring while rubbing against Lenny's pant legs.

"Now don't push it too far, Cat. I told Russell we shouldn't chase you off, but that doesn't mean we're best friends."

As they headed up to the house, Lenny looked back into the woods; he knew the cat hadn't made the growl he heard earlier. A shiver tingled up his spine.

## A Close Call

After breakfast, Noey and Lenny cleaned off the concrete floor near the horse barn where manure often piled up. The horses spent most of their free time lounging under the foreshoot near a large water tank. Lenny tried to scoop as fast as possible, to make sure he did more of the hard work than his uncle, knowing that Noey had back troubles.

"You should just as well go get rid of that load," Noey suggested after they had a full load heaped on the manure spreader.

Mr. and Misty strained and walked quickly along the edge of Noey's farm. A steady clickity-clack followed them as fertilizer flailed out behind all the way down to the far fence. Lenny spoke to his team of horses, "Whoa!" They stood calmly under the shady limbs of a massive oak. Mr. E snorted, with the sound a person could make by letting air out through relaxed lips, and then stomped at a fly. Misty took a deep breath, as though preparing herself to rest. Lenny looked out across a sea of soybeans. He took off his straw hat and wiped his brow. He told his horses, "We did it! After that big spring flood, I didn't know if Noey's fields would have any crops, and now look at all those soybeans." He climbed down off his manure spreader, walked around his team of horses, and looked into their eyes. Mr. and Misty both returned his gaze with a friendly look. The young man adjusted their collars, making sure nothing was rubbing. Grandpa had warned that poorly-fit collars could rub sores on a horse, just like shoes on a person. His horses seemed fine. A lone leaf fell from a limb above. Lenny stopped and looked at it and then gazed up into the thickly leafed tree above.

"I hope summer lasts forever."

Misty looked at Lenny with dark eyes, which seemed to be asking a question. Lenny tried to explain himself, "I promised Noey that I'd stay for the summer and help him farm, but I don't know what happens when fall gets here." Both Mr. and Misty stood perfectly still, staring at Lenny while he talked. Their ears twitched, which confirmed that they were listening. He continued, "My horses are here, Leah is here, I even feel like God is here. I know God is everywhere, but I can feel Him here." Another leaf fell and landed by Lenny's feet. He bent over and picked it up, crumpled it in his hands, and blew it away like dust. "I want to stay but I'm not sure that is an option, so I'm hoping that summer lasts forever."

Mr. E snorted again, reminding Lenny to get back to work. His horses were rested and ready to finish unloading manure. He climbed aboard his spreader and clucked. Misty and Mr. leaned into their collars obediently, setting the manure spreader tines into a whirring motion with a clickity-clacking rhythm. A pair of squirrels chased each other playfully until horses almost trampled them. Russell came running when Mr. and Misty stepped into Noey's barn with a clip-clop of hoofbeats. The sound rang out like music within the barn's warm belly. Lenny called, "Whoa!" and they stopped instantly. He took his turn working while they rested, digging into a pile of horse manure with a pitchfork. A pungent horse scent rose up from the heap, circling around them, prompting Mr. E to lift his tail and add a few more horse apples to the pile. Lenny's mind worked as fast as his arms. He filled the manure spreader with fertilizer, and his heart with worries of what his future would hold. Noey came in to help without a word passing between them. Russell watched them closely and opted to follow Noey when they parted ways. The older man resumed his tinkering in the shop and the younger man headed out with his horses to unload manure.

When Aunt Ruth rang the dinner bell, Lenny tied his horses in the barn and tossed them each a flake of hay. Aunt Ruth was hanging clothes on her washline. As Lenny and Russell passed close enough to hear, she spoke without looking away from her work. "Are you two about ready for something to eat?"

Lenny answered, "We're starved!" Russell cocked his head to one side, watching Ruth clicking clothes pins. He looked as if he wanted to try it himself. Ruth surprised Lenny by saying, "I hope, for Noey's sake, you would consider staying on permanently with us." Lenny had assumed it was on Noey and Ruth's mind lately, but this was the first time it had been spoken out loud. He didn't want to hesitate too long to answer her but he didn't want to misspeak either. When he felt he had to answer, or it would get awkward, he choked out, "I love it here."

"Well," Ruth said with a smile, "we hoped you felt that way."

A squirrel came scrambling out of a nearby oak tree and Russell charged after it at full speed. The squirrel screeched to a stop and opened both eyes like a person in horror, before zigzagging away in the nick of time. Ruth and Lenny laughed as Russell attempted to climb the tree behind it. When things quieted down again, Lenny said seriously, "It would be a big decision to make. Would Noey want me to keep farming with him?"

"Of course he would! I've been telling him to talk to you about it, but he has trouble bringing up a big topic like that one." Ruth glanced at Lenny to see if he agreed about her assessment of Noey. Lenny nodded.

"I will bring it up at dinner if you want me to?" Ruth asked, more with her eyes than with her words.

"Okay, but don't put pressure on him. I mean, I understand how he feels about talking about big things."

"You and Noey are two peas in a pod," Ruth said, laughing.

During dinner, everything seemed to be going along as usual. Noey, Ruth and Lenny ate in silence, except for a casual comment here and there about farm-related issues.

"We need to move the stock cows to the dry lot soon," Noey announced. "They will ruin that pasture if they're left on it too long."

Lenny nodded that he understood and said, "I hauled four loads this morning."

Noey seemed pleased and acknowledged Lenny with a nod of his own.

Ruth seized the opportunity to say, "It sure seems you two men work well together."

Lenny knew her comment was the opening she had planned. Noey let out a little grunt and took more potatoes.

Ruth tried again, "Noey, wouldn't it be nice if Leonard stayed on permanently and farmed with us?"

"Let's not pressure him into that," Noey replied.

"How could it be pressure, we haven't even asked him yet?"

Noey continued eating potatoes. Just when he seemed ready to speak, he doused a piece of homemade bread with a generous helping of jam and took a bite. When he finally had it mostly eaten, he said with a loud voice, "Well, it would be okay if you wanted to stay on with us longer anyhow. We'd like it if you wanted to anyway."

"Thanks for making that clear," Ruth scolded.

Russell had been lying on the floor with his jowls on his paws. He jumped up and stood looking at Lenny as though expecting an answer. Lenny took a long drink of garden tea and finally answered, "I think I may consider it, possibly."

"You'd be welcome to, if you might want to, anyhow." Noey seemed pleased with himself for getting the words out.

Ruth let out a sigh, "You are two peas in a pod!"

The colts were all rested up and ready to go when Lenny got back to the barn. He forked manure out of nearby stalls and headed back out along the field's edge. A thumping roar came up the road beside Noey's field. Mr. E and Misty were familiar with Justin's big truck and hardly noticed as it came to a stop beyond the fencerow. Lenny drove his horses closer to see what his buddy had to say. Drumbeats were rattling from the truck, and Lenny recognized the song and sang along. Justin's voice added an off-pitch addition to the lyrics. When the song ended, Justin turned down his radio. "I don't know how you live without modern music!" he shouted.

"I don't. I get a little taste of it every day when you drive by."

Justin laughed. "I'm glad I can help a friend in need."

They both laughed and Lenny asked, "How's your wife and son?"

"They're doing great. Married life is the bomb! When are you going to marry that Amish girl and settle down like me?"

"I've gotta decide if I'm gonna stay Amish first."

"I bet she'd be happy to leave the Amish with you. Who wouldn't want to get away from all of those rules?" Lenny only nodded. Justin spoke excitedly, "Hey, Lenny, I'm gonna have a football party in a couple of weeks! Bring Leah along and watch some football. We take my big flatscreen TV outside and play beanbag toss, listen to music, and party. You and Leah could see Justin Jr. before he starts walking."

"Leah would like to see your new baby. He won't be walking soon, though—he's only two weeks old."

Justin smiled, "He's like his daddy. He'll be running before he can walk, and fighting before he learns to cry!" Lenny laughed but he wasn't sure it was funny. Justin pushed more, "So, are you gonna come to my football party?"

"I'll ask Leah. I bet she will want to see your new baby, and I'd like to see some football!"

"Great, I'll plan on it then!" Justin fired up his monster truck.

"Don't forget, you promised you wouldn't rev your engine. We made a deal, remember?"

"I remember!" Justin yelled and drove slowly until he passed Aaron Burr's shop. Lenny heard the big truck roar and its tires squeal as Justin pulled out onto the paved road almost a mile away. Lenny told his horses, "I'm not sure if I can stay Amish, because I miss my music." Misty shook her mane and Mr. E snorted. Lenny said, "I do like it here with you all, but this lifestyle is all work. If I was still in college with my buddies, we would be messing around all the time. I wouldn't have to grow up and start working, yet." He pulled on his suspenders and said, "Maybe I understand why Davy W. wanted to shake off this work harness."

Lenny climbed back on his manure spreader and clucked. Mr. and Misty stepped into action. The clicking of the spreader gears resumed as fertilizer flung out behind them in a steady spray. A warm sun smiled down on them, making Noey's farm look like a calendar picture. His large white farmhouse stood straight and tall, framed in by four huge oak trees. A tiny "grandpa house" stood near the big one, like a colt next to a mare. Noey had explained that he and Ruth moved into that little home when they got married. Grandpa's dad and mom lived in the big house. They planned to exchange houses when Noey and Ruth had a family, but it never happened. Ruth had given birth several times but each time they had to bury their child before a week had gone by. At last, Grandpa's dad, Isaac, told Noey that it was time to trade houses. Isaac recommended that they adopt children, and that was when Davy W. and his sister joined the family. Isaac died a few years later and his wife, Katie, only a month after him. The grandpa house had sat empty ever since.

They headed out further along a fencerow unloading what seemed dirty in a barn, yet was healthy and life-producing out in a field. A shadow passed over Lenny. He knew a red-tailed hawk was flying overhead by watching the winged shadow sail over the soybeans. Without even looking up, he observed its flight, watching the shadow soar until finally the outstretched wings did bend and flap slowly. Lenny faced the sky and looked up at the hawk. His eyes stung because of how brightly the sun shone behind the bird of prey. He imagined what the view might be like from the heavens: rolling hills full of ripening corn and soybeans, hayfields still lush green, and trees crowding along the English River as it slowly slithered through the lowest contours of the land.

For a moment, Lenny thought about Leah and smiled. The next second he was thinking of what he missed about his old life in town. He was so deep in thought he didn't notice that a cool breeze had picked up, tossing horse manes and tails like whips. These breezes didn't blow straight like a summer wind from the southwest, or a northwest winter gale. Lenny hadn't been out on an Amish farm during autumn and wasn't familiar with fall's circling gusts. Two deer came out of the woods and made a spectacular show, prancing graceful and free. Both deer leapt effortlessly over a four-foot woven wire fence, only fifty yards in front of the horses. Mr. E let out a shrill whinny and rose up on his hind legs. Misty kicked a mighty blow at the wooden double tree she was pulling. Lenny jumped, startled by what he witnessed in his colts. He had never been driving a horse that reared in harness like that, nor had he observed the power of a draft horse kick at such close range. Both young horses attempted to jump into a run, as though they had every intention to follow the deer that ran up through the woods with bushy white tails bobbing.

Lenny remembered to seesaw his driving lines, jerking his colts back to their senses enough to avoid disaster. However, Mr. E's strong neck had arched, snapping a short leather strap that held hames together above his collar. Lenny called his horses to a halt and hurried from his seat up to their heads. He had a firm hold on Mr. E before his harness started to slip down his sides. Misty surprised Lenny by standing calmly while he focused on Mr. E, whose nostrils flared, showing red inside. Mr. E's eyes were lit up like fire, and Lenny wasn't sure what that meant. He spoke gently to his colt, even though he wanted to scold him. Grandpa had taught clearly, "When things fall apart with horses, don't get upset. That never helps. Anger only makes things worse." Those words came to the young man as he held tightly to Mr. E's bit and spoke soft, kind words. Finally, a calmness came over Mr. E, and as quickly as the fire had started, it cooled off.

Lenny slowly unhitched his team, unbuckled the loose hanging harness, and laid it gently on Misty's back on top of her harness. He hung Mr. E's collar on her hame and led his horses back up toward Noey's barn. He used soft tones but explained how disappointed he was. "I thought I could trust you two. You both know better than to question the rules of our farm work. Grandpa taught me that horses will follow a lead horse, or a good master straight into a fire. The rule is that you must trust that I will not ask you to do more than you can, or anything dangerous. All of a horseman's rules keep horse and handler safe, and they must be kept." Mr. and Misty listened quietly as they walked along. Lenny looked back to be sure his harness was riding along safely on Misty, not wanting another mishap. He noticed Mr. E's soft, glassy eyes looking at him innocently. He said to himself out loud, "I'm glad I remembered Grandpa's advice not to get angry." He led them into the barn and tied them in their stalls.

Noey stepped into the barn and asked, "What happened?"

"How did you know that something went wrong?"

"I saw the manure spreader standing out along the fence and I figured something came up."

"A buck chased a doe through our soybeans. I guess that spooked them."

"Let me tell you something, Leonard." His voice and the way he said, "Leonard," sounded exactly like Grandpa. "When you are training colts, it happens that they are interested in what they are learning at first. They are intimidated by you and the older horses in the beginning." Noey sat down on a hay bale, crossed his arms, and pulled on his graying beard before finishing his thought. "Usually, after a while, colts will think, 'I'm not sure if I want to wear all this harness. My life was easier when I was younger. I could run and kick up my heels whenever I wanted. Now, I have to follow rules.'" Noey chuckled out loud. "They saw that pair of deer running free and they wanted to be like that."

"Maybe it's mean of us to take away their freedom?" Lenny asked, and then wondered if it was a dumb thing to say.

Noey laughed a little. "Well, at first glance being free of a master seems better, until hunters come into the woods and nobody is there to protect them. More than that, when winter winds come along, food gets scarce and deer have no shelter provided. A good master is not a bad thing. Like a dad, he may ask for a little work out of you, but a little work is good for people and horses—it keeps them in good health."

Lenny's heart felt lighter instantly. "Thanks for explaining about the colts. I wasn't sure why they acted like that."

Noey stated, "There isn't time to start another project before chores, so you may as well go up to Aaron Burr's and get a strap to replace the one that broke. We are going to need every horse in harness once Junior starts picking corn."

Lenny harnessed up Smoky and hitched him to a two-wheeled cart. His charcoal-gray horse trotted quickly along the road, and up the steep hill toward Aaron's shop.

## Harness Shop

Aaron Burr's shop was deathly quiet. It was dark, as usual, but normally there was a happy tapping of Aaron's treadle sewing machine, or a rubber mallet thumping a punch through leather. Lenny stood looking at sparkling silver bits and other harness parts for a moment. A door creaked open and Aaron Burr came in with a smile.

"My wife told me that I had a customer out here."

"Yes, I had a little mishap with my young team today."

"What happened?"

"A couple of deer bounded past us, and Mr. and Misty wanted to run off with them. Somehow Mr. E broke his hame strap." Lenny handed the broken leather piece to the blind harness maker. The old man rolled it in his weathered hands for a moment and laid it down. He maneuvered his way to the opposite end of his shop by running his fingers along his workbench. He picked up a rubber mallet and began punching holes in a strap as though he could think better while working.

"Horses—especially colts—feel what their handler is thinking." Aaron Burr was quiet for a moment, and Lenny wondered if old Amish men could also tell what a young man was thinking. Aaron coughed and spoke again, "Be mindful of yourself as you are working with young horses. If you are levelheaded, focused, and alert, they will take that from you. If their handler gets careless and his thoughts' drift, they can feel that you're not checking them with the lines. With older, more experienced horses, you can get away with that, but not with colts." Aaron added, "This strap that broke wasn't a new one. It was a piece off an old harness that I used to save money for Noey. I have to wonder if that was a mistake; sometimes it's better to be safe than sorry."

He handed Lenny the new strap he had been punching holes into.

"Your harness is all new now, except for your driving lines. Noey told me that he had a spare set, so I didn't make lines for your new harness. Maybe you should take a close look at them when you get home, to be sure they don't have cracks or weak spots in them?"

"Okay." Lenny answered quietly and Aaron Burr smiled.

"You're a good horseman, Leonard. I'm not scolding you. I am just passing on something my dad, Isaac, said after a set of colts ran off with me years ago. Your great-granddad, Isaac Gingerich, was quite a horseman. He taught your granddad and me what his dad had taught him about breaking colts. You have a heritage behind you, so take advantage of what us old Amishmen have to teach you about horses. That is one thing we can help you with." Aaron laughed in a good-natured way and Lenny's heart felt light again. He wondered if there was any way he could let the old man know how much it meant to him. While he was thinking about what to say, Aaron spoke again.

"Leonard, my wife was going to run over to Beantown for a few things. If you would be willing to run that errand for her, I'd buy you a Bulltown bar. We are getting older by the minute and it's not so easy for her to hitch a horse and go."

"I'd be happy to run her errand, but you don't need to buy ice cream for me."

"Leonard, I haven't had a Bulltown bar for some time, and I think ice cream would make us both feel better. Would you be willing to take that fine horse, Smoky, over to Beantown, pick up her items, and two Bulltown bars?" He tapped his cash register and it let out a ding. He laid two twenty-dollar bills on his counter. "Suzanna will give you her list."

"Thanks, Aaron!" Lenny took the money and hurried out the door. He stopped at the house. Suzanna came to the door before he knocked. "Aaron asked me to get the list of items you want at Beantown. I'm gonna run the errand for you."

She smiled. "Was that his idea?"

"Yes, but we are going to have a Bulltown bar as part of the deal," Lenny said, laughing.

"Aaron hasn't lost his appetite for ice cream."

"Should I get one for you, too, Suzanna?" She shook her head, "No, it hurts my teeth."

Lenny unsnapped Smoky's lead rope and hopped onto his two-wheeled cart. They charged down out of Aaron's lane and headed on a dirt road leading to the dry goods store. Lenny knew Leah would be there and he was happy to have an excuse to see her. As Smoky trotted merrily along, Lenny surveyed a soybean field through a woven-wire fence, comparing it to Noey's. He noticed the center of the green field was yellow.

"Smoky, do you know if yellow in a bean field is from bugs, or is that a sign of fall?" Smoky turned his head and looked at the field, yet never slowed his steady hoofbeats.

Lenny entered Beantown Grocery, walking up one isle and down another as though looking for the things on Suzanna's list, but he was hunting Leah. He came around a corner and almost ran her over.

"Hi, Leonard," she whispered. "What's up?" Her expression was always so calm, with a wide-eyed innocent look—the very thing that had attracted him to her when they first met.

"I had a little mishap with my colts today," he whispered back. "I went for a new strap at Aaron Burr's shop, he asked me to run an errand for Suzanna."

She smiled and then frowned. "What happened with Mr. and Misty?"

"Nothing really; they saw a buck chasing a doe and wanted to jump and run, too."

"Did you have a runaway?"

"No, but they tried it and broke a strap."

Leah smiled. "They're good colts, but they thought it was time for Rumshpringa."

Lenny laughed, knowing the Dutch words meant "Running around," a time of courting for Amish teens. He smiled at her and said, "Well, I hope Mr. and Misty realize that I'm the bishop as far as they're concerned, and I don't allow any Rumshpringa."

She giggled at his joke, and then told him, "My sisters and I plan to be at Joe Hochstetler's for the Singing tomorrow night."

"Really—I'll see you there?" He stood for a moment and looked into Leah's eyes. Whenever he did, everything seemed perfect in the world again.

He gathered the things on Suzanna's list and his Bulltown bars, hurrying out to Smoky. As his buggy wheels rolled over the few hills between Beantown and Aaron Burr's harness shop, Lenny hummed to himself. When they could see Aaron's shop, Lenny told Smoky, "Aaron Burr knew what I needed to cheer up. I wonder if he knows that Leah works at Beantown."

### A Warning

When Lenny came back into Aaron Burr's shop, the older man didn't speak right away. He worked at his sewing machine, pumping the treadle. All at once, he stopped his foot tapping and reached for his Bulltown bar. While he ate, he told a story.

"A few years back, a group of young men were fishing on the English River not far from here. One of the boys fell in and he couldn't swim. His friend jumped in to save him, even though he couldn't swim either, and then two more boys dove after them. One by one they all began to drown. If you ever get into a situation like that, it's better to find a way to reach someone without falling in yourself."

Lenny listened quietly, not sure how to reply. The old man seemed to be staring out his window. Lenny reminded himself that his great-uncle was blind.

Aaron coughed and added to his story. "You know, Leonard, rivers like the English can be very dangerous. They have strong currents that swirl and create washouts."

"What's a washout?"

"When you look at a river's surface, it's impossible to know what is underneath. If you watch the water flowing, you will see currents that are continually spinning in certain areas creating holes. Over time those holes get deeper and produce an undercurrent that will draw you in and keep you under. That is called an undertow. Rivers look peaceful and there are long sections that are shallow. A person can walk along for quite a while and think, 'I can handle this' and then, before they know what is happening, they slip into a washout and can't get out."

"I see." Lenny replied, not sure why Aaron Burr brought up that story out of the blue.

On his way back home, Lenny told Smoky, "I know I want to marry Leah. My problem is that I don't want to see her leave the Amish and I don't think I can stay Amish forever."

# CHAPTER 2

## Leah's Shawl

Lenny and Russell stepped into the barn for a shortened Sunday version of chores. They found the stray cat was still around. Russell charged at it, fully expecting to intimidate, but it didn't happen. The calico didn't even bother to slap Russell. This time it merely acted annoyed at the dog. Russell seemed surprised that he had lost his secret power of intimidation. Lenny laughed.

"Russell, I'm telling you this is a special cat. I don't think you want it to be your enemy, but a friend."

The little white dog sat on his haunches listening to Lenny carefully. He yawned nervously and then licked his lips.

A whole line of horses clip-clopped into their stalls. They brought in a sweet horse scent that drifted in on breezes created by their trotting forms. The sound of hooves echoed off stone walls. They each knew their own place in the barn and wasted no time getting to the grain Lenny had poured into their feed bunks. One stall remained empty—Nelly's. Lenny hurried outside to see where she was.

"Nelly! Where are you, girl?" He called and quickly surveyed the small horse pasture. He saw her lying on her side by the far fence. "Nelly, are you okay?" he called as he ran over to her .

Nelly calmly looked at her master, with eyes full of trust.

"How did you get your feet caught in that woven-wire fence, girl?" She lay still, waiting to be rescued.

Russell sniffed her mane while Lenny carefully bent the wires enough to pull her thick hooves back through. "Well, it's obvious you lay down here to roll and caught your hooves in this fence. But Nelly, you're one of the only horses I've ever seen that will just stay put until you get help; most horses would thrash and kick until they hurt themselves." By that time her hooves were out of the fence and she calmly rose up on all fours, shook like a dog, and trotted into the barn for her share of the grain and hay.

Russell and the cat sat side-by-side watching Lenny brush his horses and listened to him singing hymns. Between songs, Lenny told the calico, "I might call you mittens, because of those extra toes you have."

The cat licked one of its oddly shaped front paws and began using it to wash behind the ears. Its face was so evenly divided in color that when it turned to the right it looked like it had a black face, and when it turned left, it was brown.

"I'm surprised you aren't in the milk shed with all the other cats. They all wait for Noey to share a little of Grace's milk with them."

The cat rubbed against Russell and didn't seem concerned about food. Lenny let all of his horses back out to pasture, except Big Red, who he harnessed in Sunday leather.

## Amish Church

Lenny listened as the minister read a Bible passage. The words were German, not in the Pennsylvania Dutch that Noey and Ruth spoke at home. Handmade wooden benches filled the rooms of Joe Hochstetler's house. Amish men were crammed into neat rows, shoulder to shoulder, Lenny in the middle. He couldn't lean back, not being against a wall; he couldn't lean forward because an older man was right in front of him. All he could do was sit straight up and listen. Someone near him smelled of smoke from a wood-burning stove, another of eggs and bacon. There arose among them a general scent of males, young and old. That rugged aroma of men who work hard and don't wear cologne. A few really old men wheezed heavily, including one very large, overweight fellow just in front and to the left. Lenny sat quietly, bored because he couldn't understand much of what was being said.

There was movement, and Lenny noticed a daddy-long-legs spider crawling on a man in front of him. The spider's legs moved one at a time as it slowly made its way from the man's shoulder to his hair. The guy was balding and the spider looked like it was crawling through tall grass. Lenny wasn't sure if he should try to pick it off the guy's head or just wait to see what would happen. He was struggling to hold in a snicker until he realized that David and the young man on the other side of him were also watching daddy-long-legs. The other guys smirked, which forced

Lenny to fake a sneeze or everyone would have known that he was laughing.

All of a sudden, the man with a spider on his head flung one hand up and sent the critter spinning over onto another older man's head. The young men writhed on the church bench, trying to contain their laughter. Daddy-long-legs sat still for a short time and seemed to be regaining his bearings on the world. One leg at a time, it labored to cross another jungle. This man had a lot of hair, which made more work for the spider but also kept him from being noticed. At least until his eight legs began to touch the back of the man's clean-shaven neck. This man reached back and smashed his hand against his neck. His thick fingers squeezed on his catch and he pulled it off his neck and examined it closely.

Lenny could feel the church bench shaking under the weight of a row of young men all trying to contain their sense of humor that had been tickled to the breaking point. Just when everything seemed calm again, Lenny felt the bench shake again. Just knowing another guy was laughing made Lenny remember how funny the spider had looked, and he writhed in gut-wrenching pain again as he tried to contain laughter. Fortunately, the minister said something funny and everyone in the room laughed for a moment. That short moment of unrestrained laughter seemed to cure the young men. After that they were able to focus on what was being said again.

There was a short break as one minister sat down and another stood to preach. Lenny was glad when he saw that it was Ruben James, his favorite minister to listen to. He was young, with a sharp face, intelligent eyes, and a neatly combed dark-black beard. His voice was smooth as honey. The words seeped into Lenny's heart, even though he didn't understand all of them. There was nothing else to do but to listen, so, Lenny made an intense effort to decipher what he said, like some kind of mystical code.

Overseer must be above reproach, the husband of but one wife, temperate, self-controlled, respectable, hospitable, able to teach, not given to drunkenness, not violent but gentle, not quarrelsome, not a lover of money. He must manage his own family well and see that his children obey him with respect. If anyone does not know how to manage his own family, how can he take care of God's Church? 1 Timothy 3:2–5

These were sentences Lenny picked out and put together like a puzzle. Finally, concluding that a new minister was going to be chosen. At one point, every baptized member, male and female, lined up and walked single file into a small room nearby. David, who sat next to Lenny, whispered in his cousin's ear.

"This is a *shtimma*. Each member goes in and votes, naming someone they feel fits the requirements to become a minister. Our bishop and the visiting ministers write down any name that gets mentioned more than once."

When this long process was complete, the ministers came back into the room with all soberness and brought in a Bible for each of those selected by members. One of the names rang out clearly—Alvin Gingerich. The other names were familiar but when his uncle's name was spoken, Lenny instantly felt a knot in his stomach. David seemed moved as well. Lenny searched the faces of all the men in the room looking for his uncle. He finally located Alvin, recognizing his salt-n-pepper beard. Alvin's eyes had a look Lenny couldn't quite place. After analyzing for a long time, Lenny decided that it was the look of humbleness. An expression a person may have when given a very meaningful compliment they didn't quite feel worthy of.

The Bibles were placed on a table in the center of the room. Everyone joined in singing a long slow song and one by one the men who had been named stood and went forward, and each took a Bible from the table.

David whispered, "Some Amish districts use songbooks; we use Bibles. One of the Bibles will have a piece of paper with a passage from First Timothy slipped in at Acts chapter one. Whoever picks up the Bible with that paper is the one God has chosen to become a minister." When the time came, each opened the Bible they had picked up. A slip of paper fell onto Alvin's lap.

Alvin took out his hanky, wiped his cheeks, and blew his nose. Aunt Lydia was in a nearby room but Lenny could see her wiping tears from her cheeks. David sniffled beside Lenny. This was more emotion than Lenny ever remembered seeing in all of his time among the Amish.

## Frog

After church ended, the men gathered under a long foreshoot of the barn all visiting in hushed tones. Lenny made his way through the crowd and found Alvin near a wooden gate at the end of the barn. His eyes were not completely visible because of his glasses, but even so, Lenny thought they looked red. They stood together in silence for an unmarked period of time before Lenny had the courage to speak.

"I'm not surprised that the Lord chose you. I would have said your name if I had been asked to name who I thought fit the description given in the Bible."

Alvin pulled out his hanky, took off his glasses, and wiped his eyes. He slowly put his glasses back on. After a few moments he cleared his throat and said quietly. "Leonard, I hope you make the choice to become a member. You are like a frog."

Lenny knew his uncle wasn't trying to be funny, but it was all he could do to keep from laughing as he asked. "What do you mean a frog?"

"Frogs are amphibious; they can live underwater or on land. Very few people could fit in both in the English world and in the

Amish one. I believe you have the opportunity to choose either, and I hope you decide to live an Amish life."

Lenny looked his uncle in the eyes and nodded that he understood. He wanted to give Alvin a hug, but he knew that wasn't done among the Amish, especially in public. As Lenny looked around, he realized he was surrounded by men he knew and respected. Harold, Leah's dad, was right beside him. Junior was beyond Harold, with Aaron Burr. Uncle Noey was on Lenny's left, and on the other side of Noey were his cousins Sam, David, and Perry. Beyond those cousins were Junior's sons, Lenny's second cousins Henry, Howard, and Harvey. It made Lenny feel so at home and part of everything. Yet, at the same time, it made him miss his friend Herbie all the more. He couldn't imagine why Herbie had left the Amish so suddenly and without telling anyone why.

Lenny knew it wasn't the Amish way to toss around compliments or to give congratulations. However, somehow, without words they communicated how pleased they were that Alvin had been recommended by the church and chosen by God to be a minister.

After everyone had eaten a meal, the young men began to untie and lead out their tall, dark buggy horses. Lenny found Big Red and untied him. His horse greeted him with a warm nicker, which was so deep it could almost be felt more than heard. Big Red followed without being coaxed, and they met up with Noey under the tree, where they had left their black top-buggy. Noey lifted the buggy shaves as Lenny backed his horse into place. They each snapped Big Red in, cooperating without words. Aunt Ruth joined them and spoke.

"We've been invited to stop in and visit with Alvin's family on our way home."

Noey didn't speak but nodded with a smile.

Ruth sat between Lenny and Noey; as usual, she did most of the talking.

"Alvin will make such a fine minister. I can only imagine how pleased Jesse would be." Lenny imagined his grandpa's face and could almost see his blue eyes twinkling. Ruth continued speaking even though the men were silent. "A few years ago Alvin seemed a little too harsh to be a minister. Ever since Jesse's death, he has been more patient and understanding of others." Lenny thought about how Alvin had made him feel unwelcome when he first came to stay in his home. He wanted to say that he noticed a change, too, but thought it might be unwise to speak about that.

Noey grunted and then spoke. "You may not know this, but our dad, Jesse, used to be harsh when we were growing up."

Lenny was stunned. Ruth said what he was thinking. "Jesse, harsh?"

"Yes, I know it is hard to believe. When Alvin, Jake, and I were growing up, Dad made us toe the line. He expected us to keep every rule without question."

"When did that change?" Lenny ventured to ask.

"I'm not sure," Noey answered honestly. "He took it very hard when Jake left the Amish. Not only was he sad, but I think it really hurt his pride that one of his sons would leave. It was almost as if that is what it took for him to realize that he had pride."

The three of them rode along in silence, meditating on what Noey had said.

Noey added, "Pride is a sneaky thing. A man can be so willing to humble himself under the church's rules that he becomes confident in his own humbleness. It is as though pride sneaks in the back door. I know that your grandpa really prayed and asked God to forgive him for his pride after that. I think that was when I really saw him change."

Lenny said, "I only knew Grandpa the way he was at the end. He was the most humble man I ever met."

Big Red pulled their buggy up over the place where the road split two hills and down into Alvin's lane. Lenny told Noey, "I'll take care of Red, you go on inside with Ruth."

Perry walked out to meet them before they even came to a stop, his younger brother, Edwin, following like a shadow. They didn't always unhitch a buggy horse, but there were so many helping hands it was no trouble to put Red in the barn. Perry and Edwin had questions for Lenny about how his soybeans were coming along. Perry asked, "Do you think you may need to borrow Tug and Train to help haul grain?"

"Actually, Noey did say that we will need all of our horses, because we are going to help Junior's family pick corn. I'm sure it would be nice to have Tug and Train around to share the workload."

Perry smiled. "I'll ask my dad about it."

## Grandma

Alvin's family all seemed so happy to have company. They all gathered around the table visiting. Lydia and her daughters brought a large piece of cake for each of them. When they finished their cake, Lydia said, "Leonard, Grandma wasn't able to come over, but she wants you to stop in and see her."

Lenny got up and walked the short way over to her little house. As he walked in, he got choked up, because it made him think about Grandpa. He liked Grandma, but he always had a closer connection with his grandpa. Lenny wished he could talk to Grandpa about what he should do with his future, because he always had wise words and yet never made anyone feel foolish for whatever question they asked.

Grandma spoke to Lenny in Dutch. He knew she was asking how he was doing, and he knew how to reply, "*Tsimlich gut.*" She continued in her own language, asking him how Noey's crops were coming along. Lenny gave the same answer, *"Tsimlich gut."* He knew he couldn't answer every question with "Pretty good," but he was two-for-two. Grandma seemed determined to only speak in Dutch. She asked if he had been to see his parents lately.

Lenny answered in English. "No, but I think I'm going to go see them really soon. I'm trying to make a decision about whether or not I'm going to stay here in this community or go back to the English. I want to see how they feel about it."

Grandma rocked slowly back and forth in her rocking chair. After a few moments she stopped rocking and spoke in Dutch. Lenny wasn't sure exactly what every word meant but he knew she was saying something about, "In the end, you must choose to obey what God has called you to do with your life." She smiled at her grandson and then put her rocking chair back into motion.

Truman had been rocking quietly in his own chair. He echoed his mother in English. "You must choose, Leonard, you must choose." Grandma continued rocking as though Truman had not said anything. Truman followed Lenny when he headed back over to Alvin's big farmhouse. Everything seemed exactly the same as it was when Lenny had stayed in their home several years ago. He noticed the same verse hanging on the kitchen wall.

"The Heavens Declare the Glory of God. Psalm 19:1"

Noey stood up and said, "We better get home and do our evening chores."

Aunt Lydia teased, "Leonard better hurry up with his chores if he wants to go to the Singing this evening."

Lenny headed for the door quickly, to be funny. "Come on, let's go!" Everyone laughed.

## The Singing

Sunday evening was crisp. Lenny harnessed Smoky and stopped by the house to pick up an overcoat before heading to the Singing. Noey and Ruth had walked over to Junior's for Sunday evening popcorn, which left little Russell there alone. Lenny told his buddy, "Russell, will you please stay out of trouble while we're gone?"

The little mostly-white dog snuggled into his nest on the couch, his eyebrows moving from side to side as though he was already guilty of planning something. Lenny hurried out the door with his coat on his arm and hopped onto his two-wheeled cart, clucked, and Smoky lunged out of Noey's lane toward the Singing. As they drew closer to the gathering, other Amish carts began to converge. A young man with a sleek black horse began to catch up to Lenny's cart, but with a simple cluck from his driver, Smoky stepped up his pace and kept ahead. Lenny smiled, remembering how Nelly used to give her best and still get passed by old ladies on their way to the store.

Lenny enjoyed being with his friends and singing. He even joined in when they sang in German, though he was relieved when they turned to the English songbook. He tried to restrain himself from continually looking in Leah's direction so much that he was wore out from his struggle when they were done singing. As soon as the last song ended and boys began to leave, Lenny hurried out to wait for Leah. She was one of the first girls to step outside. Lenny spoke to her quietly in the darkness, and she followed him to his waiting horse. They quickly climbed onto Lenny's two-wheeled cart and Smoky trotted off down a dark gravel road.

"I don't get to talk to you enough, Leah. Sunday evenings don't come around but once a week."

Leah giggled. "We'll have to find some way to see each other more often."

"That reminds me—Justin invited us to come see his new baby."

"Oh, that sounds fun—when?"

"He's having a football party in two weeks."

"What's a football party?" Leah looked at Lenny, her eyes reflecting the moon.

"Justin brings his big TV out into his yard and they play beanbag games, eat food, and probably drink beer."

"We could stop in, see the baby, and visit for a while. We don't have to drink beer."

They laughed and watched Smoky trotting for a few moments in silence. Leah's voice rang out, "I think I should teach you how to speak Dutch and you can help me to learn how to speak English better." She turned her shoulders so she could see Lenny's reaction.

"That would be good if you help me learn Dutch, but you already know English."

Leah smiled. "Thanks, but I know I have an accent. You could help me fix my English so I don't say things backwards." She gave Lenny puppy-dog eyes, as though trying to beg him into helping her.

He tried to keep a straight face, and then all at once he snorted out a laugh.

"Leah, I like how you sound. You don't have that much of an accent." He didn't want to tell her that he loved her accent. Her voice lilted up and down when she spoke English, sounding like music. She said some phrases backwards but that was cute and kept things interesting. The last thing he wanted to do was change that about her. Lenny thought it might be a good time to mention his idea about going to find Herbie. "Leah, I feel so bad for your sister, Ruby. She looks so sad, and she's wasting away?"

"What do you mean, wasting away?"

"She looks like she's losing weight, and she was already thin before." Leah was quiet. Lenny added, "I think I should go to River City and find Herbie. Maybe I could get him to come back."

"No, Lenny, please don't!"

"Why not? I really want to talk to him. Anyway I still don't understand why he left."

"I'm afraid for you to go back there." Leah pulled her black knitted shawl around her shoulders tightly, even though it was a warm fall evening. She didn't look at him, but stared off over the dark rolling farmland. Lenny wasn't sure what she was thinking.

"Leah, does Ruby know why Herbie left?"

"Yes."

"What? Why didn't you tell me? Why did he leave?"

"She knows, but she won't tell me ... she says that she promised Herbie she wouldn't tell anyone." Her words only made Lenny feel more certain that he had to talk to Herbie. He almost forgot Leah was with him for a moment, his mind so preoccupied with what could have happened, to make a guy like Herbie leave the Amish.

Smoky trotted along ahead of them at a steady gait, pulling them down into a low area near the English River. The road had very little gravel, which made for a quiet ride, not having a constant grinding of rock under his two-wheeled cart. Leah spoke up, startling Lenny out of his thoughts.

"Hey, Lenny, turn left here. There is an old bridge that's no longer in use, and it's really fun to walk across."

Lenny pulled lightly on his left driving line and Smoky turned his head, obediently heading toward the bridge. They had been riding through open fields until they turned. Large trees crowded both banks along the English River. It grew darker as Smoky slowed to a walk. Moonlight that had been shining down on them became blocked out by trees that were still full of leaves.

An owl hooted as they climbed down off their cart and tied Smoky to one of the posts, set in the road to keep cars from trying to cross over the ancient bridge. Rushing water sounds added to the already eerie feel that made the young man want to get away from, not walk toward, the English river. Leah seemed unafraid and he didn't want to look like a chicken, so he followed her onto the old bridge. She was almost running ahead of him.

"Come on, Lenny!" she called to him.

He looked down at the dark planks he walked on, realizing he could see silvery water of the English between boards that were obviously really old.

"Leah, slow down! Are you sure it's okay to walk on this old bridge?"

"Yes, my sisters and I have walked across it a hundred times!" she replied, her voice echoing in the long hallway of river that divided woods on both banks.

The old bridge was a massive steel structure with a latticework of rusty metal that rose high above them. Analyzing how it must have been constructed and not paying attention to his feet, Lenny stumbled on a loose board. While on his belly, he looked down between the planks, watching river water rush under him.

"Lenny, where are you?" Leah called back, sounding nervous for the first time.

"Don't worry, I just thought I'd lay down here for a minute."

She laughed and came back, offering him a hand to help him back to his feet.

"What happened?" she asked, her voice revealing that she was smiling.

"I just took a little tumble on a loose board, that's all."

She held onto his hand, pulling him toward the other end of the bridge. "Let's get some leaves. When we were little girls, my sisters and I liked to drop leaves in and see whose first goes to the other side."

Lenny laughed at her accent and Dutch phrasing but didn't tell her why he was laughing.

"Okay, that sounds kinda fun, I guess."

He followed her out under trees on the far bank. It wasn't difficult to gather up a handful of big, flat leaves, under a canopy of trees. They went back onto the bridge a short way and Leah said, "Here, hold these leaves for a moment." She took off her knitted shawl and neatly hung it on the bridge railing. "All right, pick out your leaf and let's race!" she said, her cute voice echoing again.

"Okay, but I'm gonna beat you," he teased.

She quickly said, "Ready, set … go!"

They each dropped a leaf and hurried to the other rail to watch for their leaf floating under the bridge. The river was wide enough that trees leaning over both banks still didn't reach each other in the middle. Moonlight gleamed through that open area and reflected off the water. Leah leaned over the opposite railing watching for their leaves.

Lenny scolded her, "Leah, please be careful. I don't want to have to jump in that cold water to save you."

"I'm not gonna fall in there," she said, giggling. "Here they come!" He could see her pointing even though it was really dark. "That's my leaf ahead of yours," she teased.

"Awh, come on, let's try it again," Lenny said and hurried back to the other side.

She ran over to join him but when she leaned on her shawl, it slipped off the railing, into the water.

"Oh, Lenny, I just dropped my shawl into the river!" Before he could say anything, he realized she was running off the bridge. He followed as fast as his eyes would let him in the darkness. Her shadowy figure rounded the far side of the bridge and down the bank. "Here it comes!" she called.

"Leah, be careful!" His voice echoed as he slid down the bank and bumped her as she leaned out trying to grab her shawl. Her arms opened wide as she tried to catch her balance but still toppled into the river with a splash. Moonlight made the English River glow enough that he could see her dark Amish dress disappear into the water. Without a moment's hesitation, Lenny dove after her, but as he did his racing thoughts replayed Aaron Burr's warning about not going in a river after someone. It was too late.

Lenny felt Leah's leg and took hold of her ankle as soon as he hit the water. He held onto it with all his might, until he realized he was in shallow water and she was standing upright beside him. He came up out of the cold water to the sound of her laughing.

"Well, I got my shawl!"

"That's not funny," Lenny said. Then they both laughed heartily as they waded out of the knee-deep water, drenched.

Lenny always carried a lap blanket in his cart, like any ordinary Amish person. He pulled it up over Leah's shoulders, to keep her warm on the way back to her place. She suggested, "There would be enough blanket for you to get under this with me." Lenny gave her a glance, and as though she knew what he was thinking, she said, "If someone comes along, we'll take it off your shoulders."

He smiled. "Okay." He didn't hurry Smoky as much after that. Lenny told Leah, "Noey offered to let me become a partner with him in farming."

"He did?" Leah sat up so quickly the blanket slipped off them both. Lenny caught it and they cooperated to get it over their shoulders again. "So what did you tell him?" Leah's voice was full of enthusiasm.

"Well, I didn't think I should jump into a big decision like that without thinking it through."

"Haven't you already been thinking about it?" Leah almost sounded put out that he didn't know the answer right off.

Lenny didn't answer her, but it made him realize he had been avoiding thinking about the future. He was happy in the present, and it seemed so difficult to think through what it would mean to join the Amish. They came to her lane before he could try to explain himself. He quietly tied Smoky and followed her inside.

## Eating Pie

Leah lit a lantern, turning it so low the flame flickered. "I'm going to go get one of my dad's shirts for you to wear, since yours is still wet and you may catch your death of cold before today's end."

"I'll be okay. I don't want to use your dad's shirt, he may need it."

"Don't be silly, I'll get an old work shirt. He has plenty." She tiptoed into the other room. Lenny sat quietly looking around the Yoder's kitchen, the flickering lantern light casting a golden hue. A scripture verse hung on the wall opposite him.

The Commands of the Lord are Radiant,
Giving Light to the Eyes Psalm 19:8

Leah slipped back into the room while Lenny was thinking about the verse. She handed him the shirt and he stepped around the corner into the darkness of the living room to put it on, and hurried back. Leah cut a massive piece of apple pie, laying down the saucer as quietly as possible on her kitchen table. She poured a glass of milk and set it down beside his plate of pie, handing him a fork.

"Aren't you gonna have any?" Lenny whispered. She shook her head as she sat down across from him. He cut into his pie and took a bite. She watched him closely, her face glowing in the golden light of that small flame.

"Oh, Leah, that is so good!" he whispered as loudly as he dared. She didn't say anything, but her dimple sunk in deeply. He took a sip of milk and cut out another large bite, self-consciously loading his mouth with a beautiful girl staring at him. Her eyes sparkled as the flame flickered and cast shadows highlighting each of her pretty features one at time. "Seriously, this is the best apple pie I've ever had. It is so thick—how many apples did you put in here?"

Her smile widened and her dimple sank in even deeper. "You better give me a taste," she said, opening her mouth as he lifted up another forkful. Lenny reached it over to her, watching her pretty lips as he directed the bite into her mouth. He wasn't used to feeding anyone, and a little pie filling smudged on her cheek. She used the back of her hand to wipe off her cheek, giggling. "It's really good, isn't it?" Lenny asked.

"Needed more salt probably, didn't it?" she spoke with a completely serious face.

"Ugh, you have to be kidding—it's perfect!"

"Sshhhh...," she said, putting a finger to her smiling lips. Her eyes sparkled with a flickering lantern flame. After he took another huge mouthful, Leah said, "Give me another taste."

Lenny loaded his fork and this time tried to smear pie filling on her upper lip as he put it to her mouth. She almost laughed out loud, wiping her lip with her finger and then smearing it on his cheek. They both laughed. Lenny whispered, "I better go before we wake everyone up."

She walked him to the door. In a dim light he noticed she had a pouty face. "What's the matter?"

"Aren't you even going to give me a kiss?"

"You have your prayer covering on, I didn't think I should."

"Oops," she giggled and quickly took it off. Lenny kissed her and headed home.

# CHAPTER 3

## Checking the Fence

Over the next number of days, Noey's bean fields began to turn light green. Birds that had been flying solo all summer gathered into small clusters. Their flight was synchronized, winging in one direction and then changing course at exactly the same instant. Leaves in a few trees turned a light yellow. Lenny stood in the cool morning air and thought about the changes taking place, worrying about his future. Strange sounds came up out of the woods. Trees were thick near the English River and spread out along the river valley, including part of Noey's land. Bluffs rose up from flatlands in a stark contrast; however, trees that grew along rivers also climbed the steep hills.

Noey had fenced in his section of bluffs for grazing cattle, as there wasn't any other use for such rough land. Lenny was standing there wishing Noey's farm wasn't so close to a river or wooded bluffs. A loud clunk and a thump coming from within the barn behind him made him jump. He didn't think much of it, assuming the new cat had jumped off a ledge or tipped something over. He looked through the double doors. Two little Amish girls were climbing up onto the stone ledge.

"Edna and Elma, what are you two up to?"

They jabbered in Dutch and Lenny made out the words "two" and "face." They were trying to get a cat that was just beyond their reach in the windowsill. The calico cat, silhouetted in the window, watched the little girls with what looked like a smile on its face.

"Here, let me get that cat down where you girls can see it better."

"Two face," Edna said in English. Elma repeated her, "Two face."

Lenny pushed the big cat out of its pose and it jumped down between the twins. Both little girls giggled and squatted down on either side of the cat in their miniature Amish dresses, petting and jabbering. Lenny couldn't help but chuckle at them.

*"Du basa gebscht aucht."* Lenny tried telling them to be careful, in Dutch.

They didn't seem to notice him or fear the cat. They repeated themselves, "Two face," and little Elma pointed to where the cat had a line down its nose, dividing its face into two equal halves, one brown and the other black.

"I was going to name this cat Mittens. Do you girls see these paws? This cat has an extra toe on each front paw, making it look like it is wearing mittens."

The little Amish girls looked closely at the cat's front paws and then both looked Lenny in the eyes and said, "Two-Face."

"Okay, girls, Two-Face it is!"

Fannie Ella's voice carried on a gentle breeze into the barn. "Elma, Edna, where are you girls?"

"They're in here with me!" Lenny called and headed out through the big doors just as Fannie Ella came walking in. They collided and Lenny apologized. "Sorry about that. Your little sisters are in here petting a stray cat."

"That's fine," she said. "Mom sent me over to borrow something from Ruth and they wanted to come along over." The twins came teetering out.

Fannie Ella asked, "Where is your cat, girls?" They didn't respond but headed on past their older sister. It seemed they were finished with the cat and wanted to go see Ruth. Lenny and Fannie Ella watched them scamper over to where Ruth was busily clearing off what remained of her garden, their little bare feet pitter-pattering.

Lenny said, "I'm just finishing up my chores. I need to turn out a few horses, do you want to help?"

"Sure!" She followed him back inside.

He told her, "We are going to leave Misty and Jim tied this morning. All the others can be turned out."

"Why Misty and Jim?"

"I had a little trouble with Mr. E and Misty last Saturday. Noey had the idea that we ought to use Jim with Misty and Stone with Mr. E for the next while. Our older geldings are broke so soundly they can teach Mr. and Misty some good manners."

"Well, that's a good idea, but Mr. E and Misty look so nice together." Fannie Ella gave a frown as she said it.

Lenny answered, "I know, but it won't be for long—just until harvest is finished."

Fannie Ella unsnapped Stone's halter and let the massive dapple horse loose. When he left his stall, the young woman stayed beside Jim and brushed his mane over to one side slowly. She asked, "So how long are you planning to stay here?"

On the other side of Jim, Lenny stood on his tiptoes to see her over the tall horse's back. "Noey and Ruth offered to let me stay on as a partner." He saw Fannie Ella's face light up with a smile before his tiptoe stance gave out and he sank down flat-footed again.

Fannie Ella quickly ducked under Jim's neck and came up smiling. "So, you told them yes?"

"Well, not yet." He looked at her just as her face turned sober. "It's a big decision to decide to stay Amish. I need to think it through."

"Does Leah know that they offered you a partnership?" she asked.

"Yeah, I told her on Sunday night."

"I bet she was hurt that you didn't know the answer right off."

Lenny scowled at her, "Why would you guess that?"

"I'm right, aren't I?" She smirked and then added, "She was probably hoping that you were waiting for them to offer it so that you could ask her...." She stopped her words short and gave an ornery look.

"I guess I should have asked you for advice sooner, since you seem to know everything," he teased.

She shot right back. "If you weren't such a sophomore, you would know that you need advice from a woman about a woman."

"Okay then, tell me how I can explain to Leah that it's not about how much I like her. It's about making a tough choice for my future?"

"If you really care about her, being Amish is a small price to pay. Is it that bad here that you'd be willing to give up Leah to have your radio and TV?"

"Ouch, that hurt, Fannie Ella!"

"Well, that is how Leah probably took it." Fannie Ella's voice was not teasing anymore. She seemed really serious and sad, which reminded him that her family was struggling with the fact that her brother Herbie had left home for the English life.

Lenny leaned on Jim and the big horse didn't budge. He said quietly, "I think I should go back to River City to find Herbie and talk him into coming back home. Plus, it would be a good chance for me to think everything through and talk to my parents about my future."

She didn't look up at Lenny as she answered quietly. "How can you talk Herbie into coming back if you want the English lifestyle yourself?" She headed for the doorway with her small shoulders slumping. Lenny wanted to say something positive to encourage her, but he couldn't think of anything.

During breakfast, Aunt Ruth spoke quietly. "I'm worried about our neighbors. Junior's family all seem so sad these days, and they always were such happy people. Fannie Ella is really taking it hard that Herbie left. The poor little thing just lost her good pony and then her brother disappears like that."

Uncle Noey nodded in agreement. Russell was on a small rug near the sink with his head on his paws watching them eat. Lenny slowly chewed on a piece of bacon and suddenly thought to say, "Maybe I should go to River City and see if I can find Herbie and talk him into coming back?"

Noey's eyes brightened and he said, "That may be a good idea."

"No!" Ruth answered immediately, and then gathered herself and said less emphatically, "I doubt that is a good plan."

Lenny was unsure why she responded so abruptly. He thought he ought to ask Fannie Ella to explain it.

Uncle Noey changed the topic. "Leonard, would you walk our fences this forenoon? We haven't walked them lately and I don't want our cattle getting out."

"Sure. Russell and I could do that." Russell stood up when he heard his name and his tail wagged happily.

## Checking Fence

Lenny and Russell headed through the woods to check on fences. They strolled together quietly under a canopy of leaves as brightly colored birds flew back and forth in branches over their heads. Blue jay calls sounded very similar to crows cawing. Cardinals flashed their bright red feathers and equally brilliant cry. A redheaded woodpecker thumped on a tree trunk, but when Lenny and his dog walked past, it let out an exotic sound and flew away. Noey's cattle stood still, watching the duo as if curious about what they wanted out this far in the woods. Lenny caught a glimpse of something following them and turned to see what it was. A fern-type plant flapped as though something had brushed against it, but he couldn't see anything. A sweet earthen smell filled the forest that had slightly changed color, but mostly it was still green. There were a few fallen trees here and there, some of them partially decomposed. Those rotting trees actually seemed to emanate a sweet, almost pumpkin-pie aroma.

They followed the old fencerow deeper into the woods.

"Well, our fences all look pretty good, Russell, except for this low spot where cattle have been leaning over trying to find greener pastures."

Lenny pulled the wire with his fencing tool and stretched it as he drove a staple into the wooden post, holding everything tight. He told his dog, "We came out this far, we might as well go down to look at the English River."

Russell trotted on ahead as though he was already planning to go before his master suggested it. Leaves rustled in massive cottonwood trees sounding like rushing water. A squirrel bounded from limb to limb way up over their heads. Russell barked a short sharp sound at it and the squirrel chattered a scolding reply. Lenny saw movement behind him again and this time stood perfectly still, staring at the path he and his dog had just come down. A small creature moved in the shadows of underbrush heading toward them. Lenny glanced around to see if there was a tree he could climb if he needed to. Suddenly the creature came out into a lit up section and Lenny laughed. Two-Face was heading up the trail after them with what looked like a smile.

"Since when does a cat follow a man the way a dog does?" Lenny teased his new friend. "Come on, then, if you are going with us you'll have to walk faster." Russell trotted ahead sniffing the ground with Lenny right behind. Their cat seemed content to follow about thirty yards behind them. The river didn't seem nearly as scary to Lenny ever since he jumped in to keep Leah from drowning and caught her in knee-deep water. When he saw the black water rushing past, he couldn't restrain a shudder.

Sunlight glinted through branches and shot down in rays, lighting up little patches on the forest floor. Russell sat on the bank staring at the swirling waters below. Lenny was gawking up at a cardinal that cried above him. All at once, there was a loud splash. Lenny turned to where Russell had been sitting a moment before and he was nowhere to be seen. He looked at the surface of the river and there were large circles growing out of a center spot.

"Russell!" Lenny called, looking around him to be sure the little white dog hadn't slipped off into the woods.

Just then, with a splash Russell emerged and climbed out from the river. He shook his coat, splattering water everywhere.

"Russell, quit it, you're getting me wet! How did you end up in the river anyway? Don't tell me you jumped in there on purpose?" The little Jack Russell terrier trotted back to his perch on the bank and stared into the water again, his head cocked to one side.

"What are you doing, ya little goof? Are you looking at your own reflection and then jumping in to catch that little ornery dog you see in there?" Russell was so focused he didn't seem to even hear what Lenny had said. "Well, I sure hope you've learned your lesson."

Those words barely were spoken before there was another mighty splash. Lenny was helpless as he watched his little friend dive fearlessly into the swirling dark river. He ran to the edge and looked closely to see if his buddy was okay. He could see a white shadow moving below the shifting and choppy surface. The young man thought about diving in to save his dog as he had for his girlfriend, but he remembered Aaron Burr's advice. He looked around for a stick or something that he could use as a rescue tool. He grabbed a limb and watched carefully as the white form pushed toward the bank. Russell broke through the surface, dragging a long gray object in his teeth. It wriggled and tried to get away, but Russell had a firm grip on its tail, pulling it onto the shore and into grass. Two-Face came right over and began to lick Russell's catch. A great big catfish lay on the bank, with long black whiskers moving from side to side above a gaping mouth. Lenny snatched it up by the tail.

"Good dog, Russell! Let's take this home to Ruth. We'll have a catfish fry this evening!" Russell sat up on his haunches and yawned with a whine, then licked his lips.

The young man set off through the woods carrying a big catfish, followed by his tricolored dog and calico cat. They were almost to the barnyard when a deep growl came rumbling up from the river. Lenny stopped in his tracks and looked back through the woods. Everything was silent, even birds hushed their calls for a moment. A few leaves floated slowly toward the ground.

## Noey's theology

"What have you got there?" Noey's voice surprised Lenny as he climbed over the last gate. "You'll never believe this—Russell dove into the river and pulled out this big catfish!"

Noey looked at his dog and called him by name. "Russell, maybe you are finally going to earn your keep around here after all!" Russell wagged his tail and jumped into Noey's arms as though he knew he deserved to petted and praised. Noey scratched Russell thoroughly behind the ears and then let him jump down. "How did the fences look, Leonard?"

"All pretty good. There were a few spots where we needed to pull up the wires and staple them higher on the fence posts. For some reason our cattle think the grass looks greener on the other side of the fence."

Noey chuckled and said, "Cattle and people always seem to think that."

Noey and Lenny stood quietly watching their cattle grazing in the pasture. Dairy cows were grazing in Junior's fields, just beyond the dividing fencerow.

Noey pulled on his salt and pepper beard and spoke. "You know, Leonard, fences are a good thing."

Lenny turned and looked at Noey to be sure he heard correctly. Noey smiled and glanced at his nephew for a moment and then repeated his words. "Fences are a good thing. If we didn't have fences, our cattle would be all over the place getting into trouble. They would eat too much corn or go into the road and get hit by a car." Lenny looked at his uncle sideways. Noey explained himself. "It's kind of like being Amish, with our boundaries that keep us from wandering. Those lines are drawn up to help us stay away from things that only cause trouble. The cows on one side of the fence are Junior's and on this side are our cows. A cow can't be half on one side of a fence and half on the other. We sometimes say about certain Amish young folks, 'They're riding the fence.' Do you know what that means?"

"That they are pushing the rules to the limits?"

"Something like that." Noey nodded. "They are thinking about jumping the fence, because they think the grass looks greener on the other side. But, like cows, if they keep leaning on the fence they will weaken it and other cattle will get out. That is why our bishops sometimes shun a person like Davy W. The idea of shunning is to force a person to make a choice. A young man like Davy needs to decide if he is going to belong in this pasture or in that one. He couldn't put off his decision forever."

"Will the bishop shun me if I don't decide about whether or not I'm going to stay Amish soon?"

"Probably not soon, because you are doing a good job of keeping the rules."

Noey changed the subject. "Speaking of Davy W—I was just thinking about something that happened when he was a boy." Noey smiled and looked far off, as though he could see what he remembered in the clouds.

"When Davy W. was only around ten or so, a dog appeared at our place. It was a friendly, chubby Dalmatian. Davy hit it off with that dog immediately, forming a tight bond. I told him that we had to put an ad in the paper saying that we found a lost dog, and he wasn't happy because he wanted to keep it. I told him that someone is probably really sad because their good dog is missing. Sure enough after the ad came out in the paper, someone showed up one day looking for their dog. In fact, you may know the man—that Web fellow that is a neighbor to Alvin's family."

"Yeah, I know him. So that was his dog, huh?"

"Yes. He came and called his dog by name and the dog ran to him. That old Web didn't seem to notice Davy's tears, he just took his dog and left. I always felt bad that I didn't buy Davy another Dalmatian."

## Just Before Lunch

Lenny was checking the mailbox when he heard a rumble and a beat. He knew without looking that Justin was coming up the road in his big red truck. It growled to a stop, and music thumped out of his open window.

"Hey, Lenny, did you ask Leah about coming over for my football party?"

"Yeah, I did. She wants to come see your little boy."

"Okay, that sounds great." He looked down at Lenny's clothes. "So, do you get tired of wearing those suspenders?"

"I guess so." Lenny shrugged.

"What I'd hate about being Amish is those clothes. I would be okay with the food and farming and everything, but don't you just hate those clothes?"

Lenny laughed. "Yeah, I guess so."

"Well, maybe you can borrow some of my clothes when you come to my football party," he said, laughing.

Lenny said, "Thanks, but I wouldn't want to wear other clothes with Leah around."

"Are you kidding? She'd probably think you looked cool in normal clothes," Justin said confidently. With that, the English guy revved up his truck and music and took off with his wheels spinning and kicking up rocks.

## Later that Day

Noey told Lenny, "Alvin's are going to have church at their place soon, so we are all going over tomorrow to help them clean. The church bench wagon is over at Joe Hochstetler's farm. Will you take Misty and Jim over there with our forecart and haul it to Alvin's?"

Lenny started dragging harness over to throw on Jim before he even replied, "Does Joe know that I'm coming over for the bench wagon?"

"He knows that someone is coming by for it. If nobody is around, just hook onto it and go—they know who you are and won't be surprised if they see you hauling it away." Noey helped Lenny harness the team.

As soon as Misty and Jim were ready, Lenny followed Noey inside.

Ruth seemed chipper, scurrying around her kitchen humming a hymn. Russell benefited from her good mood, snatching up a piece of ham she dropped "by accident." Ruth loaded up Lenny's plate with fried potatoes and ham. It seemed she could hardly sit still while the men ate their fill.

"Leonard, I talked to Lydia today at a quilting. She said that if you bring the bench wagon to them, you could spend the night. They would like your help with chores in the morning. You could take Russell along with you for company if you want."

Misty and Jim clip-clopped along a gravel road while Lenny sang a song that he had stuck in his head from the last young-folks' Singing. He happened to notice an Amish phone shed that stood near a fence. He tied his horses at the hitching rack and took Russell with him into the shed. He called his home phone number and his sister answered.

"Hello, Ashley, it's Lenny. Has school started back up yet?"

He listened to Ashley talk about her volleyball team for a while before she asked, "So, are you going back to college or staying Amish?"

"Good question. Actually, that is why I'm calling. I want to talk to Mom or Dad about that."

"Okay, I'll get Mom. Dad is at work."

"Hello, Leonard, how are things going there?"

"Great, Mom. Uncle Noey needs my help with fall harvest, so I think I should stay on till that's done."

"What about college, Leonard? You already canceled the fall semester, you need to think about what you're going to do next spring."

"Noey has offered for me to stay on permanently as his partner. You know I have a special friend and I'm trying to decide what my future holds."

"You mean a girlfriend?"

"Yeah, we call it a special friend."

"If you stay there we will never see you, Leonard. I think you should think long and hard before deciding to become Amish."

Lenny nodded as though she could see him and looked down at his feet. "I think I'll come home as soon as we finish harvest and you, me, and Dad can talk about it. Oh, and I want to find Herbie and talk to him, too!"

"We see Herbie at church sometimes!"

"You do?" Lenny's face got a smile on it. "Good, tell him that I said 'Hi.'"

"Okay, I will."

"All right, Mom, I have to go, but I will come home as soon as harvest is done. I love you, and tell Dad that I said 'Hi.'"

"I love you, too, Leonard. And I will be praying for you to make the right decision. It's a big one."

"Thanks, Mom—bye."

"Bye."

After pulling his team into Joe Hostetler's lane, Lenny could see the church wagon sitting near the house. He backed his horses and hooked them. Nobody came around, so he clomped up the steps and knocked on the door. After a few minutes he decided to go ahead and leave with the wagon, even though he felt funny taking something from a farm without talking to anyone. Jim and Misty clip-clopped out of the lane and Lenny saw a young Amish man walking up the road toward him. He was trying to think how to explain who he was and why he had taken the church wagon when he realized it was Perry.

"Where are you walking to, Perry?"

"I was told to walk up here and wait for you. Noey and Ruth passed by the Hershberger farm and saw me leaving with my brothers. They told me to walk over here and keep you company since you were coming to our place anyway!"

"That was so nice of them. You're lucky, though, because I was going to turn left up here and go past Beantown. If you would've been a few minutes later I would have turned and missed you."

"Whew, that was lucky! Why would you go past Beantown? That is at least a mile out of your way." His eyes met Lenny's and he said, "Never mind, I can almost guess. Why don't we go that way? I sure could use a Bulltown bar right now!"

"Well, if you insist." Lenny clucked and sent his horses lunging toward Beantown.

Perry asked, "Why do you have Jim hitched with Misty instead of Mr. E?"

"Cause Mr. E and Misty tried running off with me the other day. A couple of deer jumped and ran through our beans and they tried to follow them."

Perry laughed. "Better than driving old plug horses that you can't get moving."

They pulled into Beantown's parking lot and tied Misty and Jim next to a tall, black buggy horse.

Perry said, "That is Junior's horse, Beauty."

"I know," Lenny nodded. "I wonder which of Junior's family is in here?"

"Don't worry, Lenny, I'll tell them it was my idea to stop by Beantown. I am the one that suggested we stop in for a Bulltown bar."

"It won't matter, they will guess it was for my benefit anyway." They walked inside and immediately saw Fannie Ella and her mother talking to Leah.

"Oh, great…!" Lenny muttered to Perry.

"Leonard and Perry, what brings you to Beantown this time of day?" Fannie Ella acted as if it was an innocent question, but Lenny knew she said it to put him on the spot in front of her mother.

Perry tried to cover, "We are bringing the church bench wagon to my place and I told Lenny that I was hungry for a Bulltown bar."

"Wasn't the bench wagon at the Hochstetler farm? That is pretty nice of Lenny going over a mile out of the way just to get his buddy an ice cream bar."

Lenny felt his cheeks heating up and noticed Leah was squirming as well. Fannie Ella's mom, Ruby, was kind and said with a smile, "I don't blame you boys for stopping in, it's awful warm for this time of year."

Lenny smirked at Fannie Ella, but she rolled her eyes at him and walked away. The boys got their ice cream bars and took their time getting to the register, but Leah was so busy helping other customers they didn't even get a chance to talk to her.

They rode in silence for a while busily eating their Bulltown bars. Perry broke the silence, "Sorry you didn't even get to talk to Leah."

"It's okay, I'm happy just to get a chance to look at her!" They both laughed good and hard. "What do you think of Fannie Ella?" Lenny asked.

"Ornery, that is what I think!"

"Yeah, she is a little ornery, but all of Junior's children are ornery, in a good way. I like them all and Fannie Ella is about my favorite, except for Herbie. Don't you think she would be a fun girl to date someday?"

"Well, she's my second cousin." Perry stated it as though he thought that ended the conversation.

"She told me that she asked her mom, and her mom said people can marry a second cousin."

Perry took off his hat and slapped his leg with it. "Did she ask that about me?"

"Eh, maybe not." Lenny realized he put himself in an awkward spot by bringing it up.

"Oh, she asked that about you?" He grinned.

"Well, now that I'm no longer available, it would also apply to you!" They both had another good laugh.

They were still laughing when they heard a man calling, "Perry, is that you?" Lenny pulled up his team.

"Yeah, me and my cousin Leonard," Perry answered.

"Whose horses are these?" He climbed the fence and looked at Jim and Misty. "This dapple is our Uncle Noey's horse, Jim. This younger mare is mine," Lenny explained.

"That's a nice-looking mare, where did you get her?"

"I bought her from Junior, she is out of his old mare, Queen."

"You were smart buying that horse," the man told Lenny. "I'd be happy to have any colt that Queen raised. Is she old enough to pull something heavy?"

"Maybe, with Jim's help anyway. What needs pulling?"

The man pointed down in a ravine. "I've got a load of hay stuck down there. My tractor wheels are spinning and I don't have a heavy team."

"Let's have a look at it," Lenny said, grinning.

They unhooked the church bench wagon and drove Jim and Misty down the hill. They all three looked over the situation. Perry suggested, "Let's unhook the tractor and pull the wagon out from one end and the tractor from the other."

"Good idea," the older man nodded.

"Yeah, I like that," Lenny agreed. "I'll drop a link on Jim's tugs and we'll make him pull more of the load than Misty. If it gets rough, I may pull her up, though. I don't want to ruin her."

Perry and the older man smiled at Lenny. He wasn't sure what it meant but didn't ask. Lenny talked to Jim as they started pulling. "Get up, Jim! Get up, Jim!"

The big gray squatted and dug in deep. Misty didn't crouch as much. She stepped forward willingly and did her part. They had the load of hay pulled up onto a level place within a few minutes.

"I doubt that tractor will come out of there as easy as this wagon did," Lenny said.

"You sure have a nice young mare there, son," the stranger told him. "She is gonna be something in a few years."

Lenny looked at Misty and nodded. They hooked onto the tractor and tried pulling it in the opposite direction. It rolled forward a foot and then slipped back.

"Ooh, I didn't like that!" Lenny winced.

The older man pulled on his beard. "I think we ought to try backing this tractor out the way we pulled that wagon. Sometimes a tractor can back out of a hole just as well. For one thing, there's a set of ruts heading that direction that we made coming in here."

"Okay. I didn't want to ask Misty to try that last pull again anyway." Lenny drove his team around the other way and they rehooked. The man put his tractor in reverse and gave Lenny a nod. Lenny called on his older horse again. "Get Jim, get up, Jim!"

Jim crouched low and Misty acted like she was imitating her older teammate chugging forward. Muscles rippled in her haunches and she didn't let up even after the tractor's wheels stopped slipping and started moving its own weight. Lenny had to call her off. "Whoa, Misty, whoa!" She almost seemed proud of herself as Lenny rubbed his hand on her arched neck.

The older man stood beside Lenny and examined Misty up close. "If you ever want to sell this mare, check with me first."

"I'll keep that in mind, but I can't imagine that I'd ever be willing to sell her," he stated with a pat on her hip.

"We better get going, Lenny. It gets dark a lot earlier these days," Perry reminded him.

"Thanks for your help!" the older man called as they drove off.

They hooked their church bench wagon back on and headed toward Perry's home. Fog hung in valleys and shadows grew longer. It was really hard to see when they passed through a wooded area.

Misty snorted and pranced as they drove past a large modern farmhouse.

"I wonder what is going on with Misty." Lenny looked at Perry to see if he had any ideas. Misty began sidestepping, to go along with her prancing. Jim seemed indifferent to her antics, continuing on his way as though she wasn't even there.

Perry whispered, "This is Laidlaw's place. I bet his big horse is nearby."

The orb of a dark moon with a slice of it lit up, hung just over a row of trees near Laidlaw's stables. As they passed by, moonlight glistened on a massive Percheron horse in a corral alone. Lenny knew instantly that this was Laidlaw's famous stallion. Misty nickered and got a deep response from the huge horse, which pranced gracefully back and forth within his little fenced lot.

"Misty must have noticed him," Perry concluded out loud, and Lenny nodded. It was all Lenny could do to hold Misty in line as they passed by the big horse and on into shadows further up the road.

Perry chuckled in the darkness and Lenny asked, "What?"

"Oh, nothing ... I just was thinking that we should unhitch Misty and lead her back near that horse and see if that is what has her upset."

It was too dark for Lenny to see his cousin's expression, so he wasn't sure if Perry was serious or not. Lenny asked, "What good would that do? I mean, why would we want to know that?"

"Well, I just thought that may explain why she tried to run off on you the other day."

Lenny turned his team into a wooded area near the road and called, "Whoa!"

Perry laughed. "So I take it you are curious, too?"

The young men quietly tied Jim to a stout tree and unhitched Misty. They slipped like shadows across an open field, Little Russell trotting quietly at their heels. Lenny led his young mare until they got closer, and she began leading him. He wanted to scold her but they were getting near Laidlaw's house. Suddenly, she pulled her lead rope out of his hands and trotted over to where the massive horse stood leaning over his board fence, nickering to her in a deep belly sound. They touched noses, both horses' thick necks arched gracefully in the moonlight. Misty let out a short squeal, and the big horse nickered deeply again. Just then, Misty crowded next to the fence.

Perry rushed up and grabbed her lead rope. "Yep, it is that big horse that has her upset. We better get her outta here!" He pulled on her rope but she braced her front feet. Perry was focused on Misty, whispering to her and scolding in a quiet voice.

Lenny told his cousin, "I think it's too late; the fence didn't keep them apart."

The cousins ran back across the field leading Misty under cover of darkness. Lights came on in Laidlaw's house and a dog came running out barking. Both young men were laughing as they hitched Misty back onto their wagon. They could still hear Laidlaw's dog barking as the horses set off trotting down the gravel road. Russell stood on the bench wagon growling at Laidlaw's dog, until the barking faded.

Lenny said, "I wish I could have seen that horse better—he looked like a dandy!"

"Oh, he is!" Perry responded, and they both laughed out loud under the golden moon.

## Alvin's Farm

A fire was glowing as they came over the last hill toward Alvin's. Lenny assumed they were burning trash and asked Perry, "That fire isn't where your burn barrel usually is, is it?"

"No, it looks like they are having a bonfire to me."

Perry helped Lenny unharness and brush his horses quickly, and then hustled out to where they had noticed a fire. Alvin's whole family sat in lawn chairs staring at blazing flames. Their faces were glowing in the firelight, and shadows danced as flames flickered. It was hard for Lenny to see their expressions, but everyone seemed to be relaxed and almost falling asleep as they gazed at the fire.

Aunt Lydia asked, "What took so long?"

"We went past Ruben Hershberger's place and he asked us to help him pull out a tractor and wagon that were stuck down in a low spot."

"Really? How'd Misty do?" Alvin asked, looking at Lenny.

"She did fine."

"She did more than fine," Perry said, laughing. "She pulled like she enjoyed it!"

"How did it happen that you were driving past the Hershberger's place?" Aunt Lydia wanted to know.

"We decided to stop by Beantown for ice cream bars." Perry explained.

Lydia asked, "Do you want to roast some marshmallows?" She handed Perry a stick already loaded with two marshmallows.

"Sure!" Lenny said, and Perry handed him the stick. Aunt Lydia loaded two more on another stick for Perry.

Viola and Little E sang hymns while Perry and Lenny toasted and ate their marshmallows. Lenny looked around the fire at Alvin's large family; they all seemed so happy. One by one everyone headed in to bed.

Russell rode upstairs in Lenny's shirt. The house went silent as soon as the lanterns were turned down.

Lenny couldn't quit thinking about Alvin's large family and typical Amish home. He whispered, "Hey, Perry, are you still awake?"

"Yeah."

"I was just thinking about Noey and Ruth. Your parents have a big happy family and Noey's seem so lonely."

Perry was quiet for a few minutes and Lenny wondered if he fell asleep. Then Perry whispered, "Maybe if you farm with them and you have a family someday, Ruth and Noey could be like grandparents to your children."

Lenny drifted off to sleep thinking about what Perry had said.

# CHAPTER 4

## Catching a Sow

Everyone stood up when the rooster crowed. They hurried through chores and worked all day cleaning Alvin's farm even though it was already immaculate. Lenny helped fork out every horses' stall and pen in Alvin's huge barn. Perry and Lenny hauled manure. Lenny drove Misty and Jim, and Perry drove Babe and Bell on steel-wheeled manure spreaders. Sam, David, and Truman helped fork manure as fast as they could go, sending both teams out with full loads. Lenny followed his younger cousin out to the field and tried to keep his line of black fertilizer right next to Perry's.

Leah's whole family came over to help. Perry told Lenny, "It seems funny that you and Leah are both my cousins, yet you aren't related to each other."

"I'm sure glad we're not!" They both laughed. "This is one time I wish Leah didn't work at Beantown. Her whole family is here but she is at work."

Perry agreed. "I bet she's disappointed that she can't be here helping."

Everyone took part in washing dairy parlor windows, cleansing them of flyspecks that looked like freckles and stuck on like tar. When they were finished, Lenny stood near Harold and Mildred, Leah's parents, and they visited with him for a short time.

Mildred asked, "Leonard, did you drive over separately from Noey and Ruth?"

"Yes, I brought the church bench wagon with a big team."

"Good, maybe you would be willing to stop over at our place for supper this evening? Harold and I haven't had a chance to visit with you lately, and our whole family would enjoy hearing about your summer."

Before Lenny had a chance to reply, Aunt Ruth answered for him. "That's a really good idea. It's not often that he is over this way, and I know a certain girl that will be sad if he goes home before she gets off work." The women smiled at each other knowingly and Lenny felt his face get hot.

Aunt Ruth told Lenny quietly, "We will take care of your chores this evening, so don't feel like you need to hurry home." She smiled as she said it. Ruth never talked straight out about it, but he felt her nudging him in Leah's direction at every turn.

Noey and Ruth left as chore time drew near. Harold's family walked as a group between the fencerows, leading toward the timber between Alvin's and the Yoder farm. Lenny watched them go and had to smile about how nice it looked to see a large family walking through a field together.

Perry interrupted Lenny's thoughts. "Hey, Lenny, my dad and Noey decided that you should take Tug and Train back home. Noey says that you are going to need a lot of horsepower to haul grain this fall. He told us that you are planning to buy corn from Junior's and that you'll be hauling that home with horses, too."

"I'd love to have them, but I know you would miss them here."

"I wouldn't want anyone else to borrow them but you," he said, smiling. His face reminded Lenny of Grandpa.

A pickup pulling a horse trailer rumbled into Alvin's lane. Everyone stopped their work to see what was going on. Perry told Lenny, "That's the Randall's trailer. They have horses and sometimes bring them here to have us work with them a little. They don't use their horses that often, so they get a little green."

"Green?" Edwin asked.

Perry explained, "That just means they forget their manners, because they haven't been used enough."

Lenny and Perry headed over to see what was going on. A man stumbled out of his truck and stood visiting with Alvin about horses while Sam and David listened. Perry looked into the trailer and Lenny joined him, peering through slats. There was a riding horse inside and a nice-looking brown pony.

The visitor spoke loudly, "I was wondering if you could have someone ride our horse a few times. My wife tried to ride him the other day and he was so stubborn she couldn't make him do anything. He just trotted in circles and she about fell off." Alvin and his sons didn't say anything but chuckled.

"Oh, yeah, and I brought a pony along. My kids are getting too old for her and never did ride her much anyway. She hasn't been used in a long time. Maybe you could work with her, too. I'd like to get her tuned up so I could sell her at the fall horse sale. That is, unless you know someone that wants to buy her?"

Perry whispered, "Maybe that'd be a good pony for Fannie Ella."

Lenny nodded and headed over to talk to the man. "How much are you asking for that pony?"

"I don't know, but I'd be happy if I could find a good home for her. I'm a little afraid that if I take her to the sale barn, she won't bring much anyway. What would you give me for her?"

Lenny didn't know what to offer. He asked, "Could we get her out of the trailer so I can take a look?"

"Sure!" he said as he unlatched the door. He brought out both the horse and pony.

Lenny took the pony's lead rope and instantly liked her. Her big dark-brown eyes seemed kind, and she followed him without hesitation. "Is she a good riding pony?"

"Well, my kids never rode her that much, but the guy we bought her off said that he broke her to ride and drive. We never tried driving her. My kids complained that she was hard to hold back. She always wanted to run off."

"She doesn't kick or bite or anything like that, does she?" Lenny asked.

"Oh, no, nothing like that! She was just a little more pony than my kids could handle."

"I know a young girl who is really good with horses and ponies, but her pony got hit on the road and killed. I'm sure she would like this pony, but I don't know what to offer you for her." By that time, his wife had walked out around the truck and was listening.

The man said, "Three hundred dollars would be enough, I suppose."

Lenny was just ready to say okay, when the wife growled. "No, just give her that pony!"

"I'd be glad to give you something for her. I know my little friend will love her!"

"Well, all right—a hundred and fifty," the man said.

"George!" his wife scolded.

"No, really, ma'am, that's a good price. I'll take her." Lenny got out his checkbook and asked, "Can I write a check?"

"Sure!" The man grinned as his wife scowled at him.

She told Lenny, "Her name is Penny!"

## Heading to Harold's

Perry helped Lenny harness and hook all four horses onto his little forecart, and they tied Penny onto the hitch under his seat. Tug, Train, Misty, and Jim trotted briskly through the woods leading down to Old Man's Creek. Lenny listened to the sound of their large hooves thumping on the ground, Penny's rapid hoofbeats following behind. The sound changed as they crossed wooden planks that spanned the small bridge. Clip-clops rang out and echoed over the creek water. As they neared Web's place, a thin man hobbled across his yard.

"Is that you, Will?" the man yelled as the huge row of draft horses trotted closer. The man sounded like Web but he looked about half his size. His bib overhauls hung on him as he walked toward the horses.

"Going up to see your little Amish girlfriend?" he cackled. It was clear to Lenny that it was Web by his teasing and laugh.

"Yeah, I guess you could call her that." Lenny laughed even though he didn't like Web teasing him about Leah. He eyed the older man, wondering why he looked so thin and sickly, yet he didn't feel that he could ask.

Web teased, "You must have got a kiss from that Amish girl—looks like you've gone Amish after all! And it looks like you bought a pony for her, too!"

Lenny didn't feel like laughing but chuckled in order to be polite. Web's face was drawn in and wrinkled, his skin ashen.

"How have you been, Web?"

"Not too good. Didn't you hear about me having cancer?"

"Well, Perry did say that you had been sick, but he didn't tell me it was cancer."

Web coughed. "I guess all my rough living finally caught up with me." Lenny didn't know how to respond. He sat looking at his horses, trying to think of something to say. Web changed the subject. "So, you live with your uncle Noah nowadays?"

"Yeah, I guess you know Noey, huh?"

Web coughed for a bit, then spit on the ground. "I knew him when he was my neighbor, but he moved over to Isaac's place years ago and I haven't seen him much since then. I did go over to his farm one time when my dog ran off and ended up there."

"Oh, yeah, Noey told me about that. He said that Davy W. hit it right off with that Dalmatian and really wanted to keep him." Lenny grinned, until he saw that Web's face grew even more ashen than before. "Are you all right, Web?"

"Oh, I am fine, except that I'm dying," he half-coughed, half-laughed. "If you see Davy, tell him that I'm sorry about taking his dog away from him. I should've let him keep old Coach."

Lenny nodded that he would. He wished he had something good to say to Web—or that there would be something he could do for him. For the past couple years Lenny had harbored bad feelings about the guy; now that he was dying, Lenny was ashamed of himself for not seeing how sad and lonely Web was.

"Web, I haven't always done everything I should have either, but I've found that if you mention it to God, you feel much better."

Lenny almost wished he hadn't said it, until he saw Web nod and say, "Maybe I should try that."

He turned to head up toward his house and Lenny called, "I'll pray for ya, Web!" The thin old man didn't turn around but started a coughing fit as he climbed his steps.

All four horses lunged forward when they heard their driver cluck. They easily pulled the little cart and pony uphill and into the Yoder's farm lane.

It was a beautiful afternoon, and Harold and Mildred's farm seemed to Lenny as though it was right out of a fairytale. The straight white house stood on top of a big hill, next to a towering windmill. Harold's barns were weathered, yet neat and clean. Every tree on his place was beginning to turn red or golden. Even leaves on the ground were pretty colors. A cornfield beyond the house was partly picked and stood in straight squares of brown stalks, some showing part of their golden cobs where dry husks had fallen off.

The house door swung open and Harold's little boys romped out barefoot, running up toward Lenny. They rattled out Dutch phrases so quickly it was hard to tell what they were saying even for a person who knew the language. Being older, Johnny must have remembered that his guest didn't speak Dutch well, so he changed his words to English. He held onto his straw hat with one hand, even though it was already on his head.

"One of our sows had pigs down in the lower pasture and it looks like she has at least eight of them with her, or maybe even more!"

His little brother, Timothy, continued speaking his lightning-quick Dutch. The littler brother didn't have on a hat, and his suspenders looked like they were too small even for his little body and, as a result, his pants were hiked up to his chest. Lenny smiled and nodded, assuming Timothy was adding more to the baby pig story. Soon Harold's daughters had joined them, and Leah fixed Timothy's suspenders and chided him in Dutch. The little boy sprinted off toward the house, his little legs going so fast they were a blur. He came running back out holding a straw hat on his head with both hands.

Harold and Mildred appeared out of nowhere and stood smiling while the older girls asked about Lenny's big hitch of horses.

"I'm gonna borrow Tug and Train to help haul beans. We have a lot of soybeans in our fields, plus we are going to help Junior haul corn, too."

Harold teased, "Is this little pony gonna help haul corn and beans, too?"

"Oh, no!" Lenny replied, laughing. "Junior's family lost their pony. Did you know about their Dusty getting hit by a truck?"

"Yes, we heard about that."

"Well, a man stopped into Alvin's place trying to sell this pony, so I decided to buy it for them."

Mildred said, "That is really nice of you, Leonard. I'm sure that will make Junior's family happy to have a nice pony like this one."

"I hope so."

Harold leaned toward Lenny and said, "Leonard, you might as well put all those big horses in the barn, since you'll be here for the evening."

## Hog Wild

While they were tying horses, Harold asked, "Leonard, will you go to our lower pasture with my girls? One of our sows had a litter of pigs down there and we need to bring them up to our farrowing house before it gets cold."

"Is it tough to get 'em?"

The girls laughed at his question.

Harold replied, "Leah and my twins will show you how we go about catching them."

Ruby was already starting up a tractor before Harold even finished his sentence. Leah and Rachel climbed up and sat down on one fender and pointed for Lenny to follow suit. Russell jumped into Lenny's arms and they climbed up onto the other fender. He held his little dog tight, hoping to keep him out of trouble.

Harold's steel-wheeled John Deere tractor rumbled as Ruby drove downhill toward the pasture, and it let out a random pop every so often. Leah was smiling as she tried to talk over the engine roar.

"When we get down there, we need to catch a baby pig! When we snag one, we'll jump into the hog tote and make it squeal. Mama will come running, and whoever is holding that pig better jump out of there quick." Lenny tried to imagine what she was describing.

They pulled into the pasture and little baby pigs could be seen rooting around in leaves. They all stopped what they were doing and eyed the tractor. When they got closer, the babies all ran toward their mama, huddling under her massive body. She had her mouth open in what looked like a big smile, until Ruby turned off her tractor. Lenny realized the mama was grunting a warning.

Ruby explained, "A mama sow is maybe the most dangerous animal on a farm. When anything threatens their babies, those sows act like a mama bear."

"So, what's the plan?" Lenny wondered aloud.

"I'll drive the tractor at the mama and try to scatter her babies. When we catch one, we'll give it to Leah and she will get in that hog tote and make the baby squeal. When Mama comes, Leah will jump out and we'll shut the gate. Then, we will catch the rest of the babies and haul them all back up to our hog barn.

"I will do that part, not Leah."

"No, Lenny, I can do it," Leah told him.

"I'm not sitting here watching you take that chance. I'll catch a pig and make it squeal."

Leah laughed. "No, Lenny, I've done this a hundred times before."

"You're wearing a dress, Leah, I don't think you should climb outa there with a boy around."

"Let's catch a pig first," Ruby told them.

She started up the old John Deere with a pop and headed at the sow and babies. At first the piglets all stayed right under the sow and ran wherever she went, but finally they got separated. Half of the pigs stayed with their mother and the other half were on Leah's side of the tractor. Mama stayed with the babies she could see.

Leah snagged a baby and started to climb over the wire rack on the back of the tractor, but Lenny called out, "Whoa, I said I'm gonna do that!" He passed Russell to Rachel and told her, "Hang onto him tight!"

Lenny climbed into the tote and took the baby out of Leah's hands. Ruby shut off the tractor that had been muffling the baby's cries. Once the mama sow heard her baby squealing, she came running, grunting loudly. In only seconds flat, she made her way to the wire rack and was jumping on. Lenny didn't expect her to be able to move so fast, as fat as she was. He dropped her pig and scrambled to climb out. He felt a tug on his shirt and realized it was caught on a sharp edge of the wire tote. The sow's grunting was getting louder as she climbed up rushing toward him, mouth open. Lenny never saw Russell jumping free of Rachel's grip, but he was happy when he heard his dog barking and saw him biting the sow's hind legs. The angry mama turned her attention on Russell for a moment, giving Lenny a little more time. He pulled frantically on his shirt, until he heard Leah's scream over the angry sow's grunts.

"Lenny, look out!"

Time stopped when Lenny saw the sow coming with her mouth open. He rolled his body over the top of the wire tote just as the sow got there. His shirt stuck and he felt it ripping off his back as he went to the ground without it. Leah slammed the gate shut behind the sow. Lenny felt himself let out a "Humph!" and time resumed its normal ticking. He shook his head and staggered to his feet, shirtless.

Leah and her sisters stared at him in shock, and then all turned away, giggling. He looked down at his own white chest and farmer's tan. He pulled his suspenders back up over his shoulders, as if that made him more clothed. He tried to hide himself behind the tractor.

Leah pointed out, "Lenny, that sow has your shirt."

They all laughed as the sow shook his shirt in her teeth, taking her anger out on it.

"I guess I'm glad that's my shirt and not me in there."

The girls all laughed again and Leah said, "Come on up to the house, we'll get one of my dad's shirts for you to wear."

Lenny stayed behind the tractor hiding his bare chest. "No, you go up and get me a shirt. I'm not going up there like this!" He trotted over behind a tree and the girls laughed louder.

Leah and her sisters gathered the rest of the pigs, returning them to their mama, a few of them squealing while the old sow held her big jowls open with echoing grunts. She nosed around at her brood, as though doing a head count to make sure every baby was accounted for. All the girls climbed onboard and headed uphill, steel-wheeled tractor popping. Leah held little Russell in her arms and Lenny thought he could hear the sisters still laughing as the tractor climbed over the ridge. He stood behind a tree arms folded waiting for help to arrive. Suddenly, a pony popped over the top of the hill galloping down toward him. Johnny was grinning as he pulled up his little horse and handed over a shirt.

"Thanks, Johnny!"

"Sure! Do you want to ride double up to the barn?"

"I think my feet would be dragging if I got on that little guy." Lenny buttoned up his borrowed white shirt. It was a little tight, but he felt much better finally covered up again.

Johnny laughed. "Maybe your feet would drag, but Charlie is stout—he could easy carry us both!"

"I bet you're right, but I'll walk. It won't be as hard on my shoes, if they don't drag all the way up that hill, I already lost a shirt today."

Johnny laughed a deep belly laugh.

When they got to the barn, Lenny asked Leah, "Where's Russell?"

"You won't believe it. We threw your old ripped up shirt in a rag pile over there and look!" Russell was all curled up on top of the shirt, looking from person to person as they all laughed at him.

Leah and her sisters headed inside to get supper on the table, while Lenny helped the little boys and Harold finish their chores. After they were done milking, Johnny and Timothy turned the cows out. Leah's dad leaned on a gate near Lenny. He could see Leah on the porch and wanted to go join her, but he hesitated to see if Harold intended to say something to him. Harold's eyes wrinkled in the corners with his usual friendly smile.

"I hear that you're thinking about staying Amish, Leonard."

"Yeah, I'm thinking about it."

Harold smiled and said, "You know, I've heard talk about time machines." He looked at Lenny for a moment, as if calculating how much he should say, then continued, "I've always kinda thought of us Amish as living in a different time zone than the rest of the world. When someone leaves the Amish, it's almost as if they get in a time machine and travel into the future. A person has to choose which time frame they are going to live in. You can't live in both at once; you have to decide if you are going to live in the modern day or our Amish time zone." He laughed softly at his own comparison.

Lenny wanted to hear more, so he said, "I think I see what you mean," and furrowed his brow.

Harold continued with his analogy, "You know, Leonard, people were Christians in the old days." They met eyes; Lenny squinted as he tried to focus on what Harold was saying. The older man explained, "Well, some people seem to think that we Amish aren't Christians, because we follow so many strict rules. They say that we are following the law instead of faith, but I like to think of us as just living in a different time. Did you know that a hundred years ago all people dressed the way we do? Some were Christians, some weren't. They drove buggies and farmed with horses, but that didn't make them Christians or not, it was just how they lived. There was a lot good about those days, and we Amish have just tried to keep those good things a part of who we are."

Lenny nodded his head to show Harold that he was agreeing with him.

"Leonard, you stepped back in time when you came to our community, but you will have to decide if you want to stay in the old days with us or go back to the future. I believe that you can be a Christian either way."

Lenny looked into Harold's kind, honest eyes. "Thank you, Harold. You have no idea how much that helped."

The older man smiled and walked away. Leah, watching from the porch, appeared to be worried about what her dad might be saying.

Ruby came out to the barn and announced, "Time to eat!"

## Supper Time

Lenny had been nervous that it might be awkward to eat with Leah's whole family. Once he was seated at the table and smelling the food, he forgot all of that. Steam rose from fried chicken and mashed potatoes, making his mouth water during the prayer. The potatoes were creamy and so delicious he couldn't get enough. Leah and her sisters seemed to enjoy seeing how much chicken he could eat. They kept passing the platter to him and saying, "Have more if you like it!" While he ate, Lenny noticed a verse on Mildred's kitchen wall.

The Commands of the Lord are Radiant,
Giving Light to the Eyes. Psalm 19:8

They topped the meal off with a freshly baked apple pie. Lenny took a bite and said, "Yum, Mildred, you make the best pies ever!"

Everyone laughed until Lenny asked, "What's funny?"

Mildred explained, "Leah is my pie maker."

Leah looked aside coyly and blushed, which brought out more laughter. After the last bite, they paused to thank the Lord for what they had eaten.

Harold cleared his voice and said, "Let's all go out on the porch. Fall is upon us—we only have a few good evenings left for porch sitting."

They took his advice and sat quietly visiting. Harold said something in Dutch that Lenny didn't understand. He knew that Harold asked his daughters to go get something from the house, but he wasn't sure what. Rachel jumped up and ran inside, even though Leah begged her not to. Rachel came back out carrying several harmonicas and passed them to her sisters.

Leah pleaded with them, "No, I don't want to play harmonica right now."

Mildred scolded her with a smile, "Leah, Leonard will enjoy hearing you girls play, won't you?"

"Oh yeah, please, Leah."

She looked at him to see if he was serious. He nodded and gave her his best puppy-dog eyes. She still looked disgusted that her family had embarrassed her. She rubbed her harmonica with her palm, wiped her pretty lips with the back of her hand, and said, begrudgingly, "Okay."

Suddenly, the soft evening air was humming with sweet sounds of old hymns. Lenny never remembered hearing such beautiful music. They played cords while each sister took turns producing the melody. Lenny looked beyond the porch at a grove of trees not far away. The harmonicas created an old sound that echoed off the trees and house and resounded deeply in his soul. For a short period of time, everything in the world was perfect. He looked around at each member of Leah's happy family. They all seemed peacefully content in their old-fashioned world. Harold's daughters were serenading them with bright notes, while his little boys watched quietly, drinking in the sounds. Lenny felt sad that life couldn't stay the same forever. He knew that Harold's girls would marry and move away one by one.

Harold asked, "Leonard, is there a certain song you would like to hear?"

"Can you girls play '*Gott ist die liebe*'?" Lenny responded with his own question.

"You really like that song, don't you, Lenny?" Leah asked.

He nodded. "It's the only German song I know the words to, because I know the English version of 'God is Love.'"

The Amish girls played his song choice through perfectly. When the last note faded, Mildred said, "Let's sing that through once."

Harold sang a low note and his daughters all chimed in singing beautiful harmonies. Lenny, Johnny, and Timothy trailed behind, struggling to fit in.

| | |
|---|---|
| *Gott ist die Liebe,* | For God so loved us, |
| *last mich erlosen.* | he sent the Savior. |
| *Gott ist die Liebe,* | For God so loved us, |
| *er liebt auch mich.* | Loves even me. |
| *Drum sag ich noch einmal:* | Love so unending: |
| *Gott ist die Liebe,* | For God so loved us, |
| *Gott ist die Liebe,* | For God so loved us, |
| *Er liebt auch mich.* | Loves even me. |

When they finished the chorus, they all sat quietly. No one spoke for a long time—as if they, like Lenny, hoped the perfect moment would never end. An owl hooting finally broke the silence.

Harold said, "Leonard, you better hitch up that big team and head home before it gets too late."

"Yes, you're right." Lenny made his way to the barn to get his horses. Leah followed and helped him untie and hitch his four huge horses. "Why didn't you want to play harmonica for me?" Lenny asked.

"I was afraid you would think it was old-fashioned and dumb."

"Leah, that was the most beautiful music I've ever heard! There wasn't anything dumb about it."

Leah's eyes sparkled in the twilight. She smiled coyly and looked down at her own bare feet. "Good night," she whispered.

"Good night," Lenny answered and then clucked, propelling his massive horses into a trot.

As he turned out onto the road, Lenny looked back and saw Leah following him on foot. She cut across the field and ran through the trees, lifting her long apron off to one side to keep from tripping on it. Lenny smiled at the sight as he turned down toward Web's place. He stopped his horses as their paths crossed.

"What's up?"

"I just wanted to say good night, again." She looked up toward her parents' home, now hidden by the hill. She quickly took straight pins out of her covering and took it off.

Lenny stepped off his cart and gave her a quick kiss.

She looked him in the eyes and said, "Good night," and immediately turned and ran, barefoot, with apron in one hand again, hurrying back up through the woods toward her home. Her apron strings flailed under a bow tied at her waist.

When he couldn't see her anymore, he clucked and his horses trotted off into the silent night. Lenny stared at the brightly lit starry sky with a smile on his face. He told his horses, "I want to marry that girl! My problem is that I couldn't take it to see her leave her family behind, and I don't know if I have what it takes to stay Amish." His four huge horses clomped along the dark gravel roads, their ears twitched as they listened to their master.

Lenny's steel-wheeled cart creaked out a tune of its own. The new pony tied to Lenny's cart seat had to trot quickly to keep up with the bigger horses. She seemed to enjoy being part of a big hitch and every once in a while she touched Lenny's arm with her soft nose.

Lenny told her, "Penny, I know a really nice girl who loves horses and ponies. I'm gonna get you two together. She needs a good pony as much as you need a little girl."

Penny's ears twitched and she touched Lenny's elbow with her soft muzzle again, and he could feel her warm breath.

# CHAPTER 5

## Growing Moon

Mornings were a little cooler each day. Fresh, fall air dried leaves like socks on a clothesline, and they fell everywhere, heaping up in piles. Lenny was happy to have Tug and Train in his barn. He spent extra time brushing them like he did with his own horses, Smoky, Mr. E, and Misty. Lenny talked to Grandpa's horses.

"I wish you guys could tell me what to do. Noey offered to let me stay on and farm with him and I want to ask Leah to marry me, but I'm not sure I'm cut out to be Amish." Tug and Train listened quietly, ears twitching. "I know Grandpa would be happy if I chose to stay here. I'm just afraid that I'll agree to it and then wish I hadn't." Both horses looked at Lenny, their large dark eyes glistening, eyebrows raised as if concerned. Lenny felt ashamed of himself without knowing why.

During chore time, Noey stopped by to talk to Lenny about what work needed to be done. He was laughing as he walked in.

"I was in for a little surprise this morning. I walked past our horse lot and I thought one of our horses had a colt."

Lenny looked at him trying to figure out what he was talking about.

Noey added, "You must have brought home a pony last night?"

"Oh, yeah—that! I almost forgot about Penny. When I was at Alvin's place, a man came by trying to sell this pony and I thought of Junior's family. They have been so sad lately maybe this will help cheer them up"

"It ought to help Fannie Ella at least," Noey said, chuckling.

"I think I'll take her over to Fannie Ella right after breakfast," Lenny decided aloud.

## Breakfast

During breakfast, Noey told Ruth, "Leonard bought a pony for Fannie Ella!"

"Oh, good—where did you find a pony?"

Lenny bit his lip and then answered, "I bought her at Alvin's. Some English guy had her for his children. They were getting too big for a pony, so he was looking for a good home for her. I thought of Junior's family and decided to get her for them."

"Good, Leonard, that is so nice of you. I can't wait to see what Fannie Ella thinks," Ruth stated with a smile. "She is coming over to help me can chicken this morning."

"You won't have to wait long," Noey announced and pointed out the window. "It looks like she is headed this way now!" They bowed their heads for an after meal prayer and Lenny headed out to meet Fannie Ella.

"Come down to the barn with me. There's something I want to show you!" Lenny called as he clomped down the front steps.

Ever since Dusty died and Herbie left home, Fannie Ella walked with her shoulders slumped. She followed Lenny instead of going into the house. On the way out to the barn, the young Amish girl asked a question, "What do you miss most about being English?"

Lenny didn't try to hide his surprise. "What makes you think I miss any of it?"

Fannie Ella looked at Lenny sideways. "You probably miss music you used to listen to?"

"Oh, a little, but I keep busy enough so I usually don't think about it," he explained.

"Is it nice to be in town during the winter?" she asked. Lenny looked at her to see what she was getting at. She added, "It must be nice to be in a cozy little town when it's cold out. When winter gets dark and dreary, you can turn on lights, listen to music, and stay warm."

"Fannie Ella, your family is having a hard enough time with Herbie leaving the Amish. You better not be thinking about it."

"Do you think you will go back?" she asked.

"No, I don't think so." Lenny slid open the barn door and she followed him inside.

Fannie Ella seemed to be deep in thought for a moment. She looked at Lenny seriously and asked, "Does Leah know that you are having second thoughts?"

"Why do you think I'm having second thoughts?"

"I can tell," she replied, smiling. "Don't worry, I won't say anything to her. I understand, because sometimes I think it would be nice to be English."

"Fannie Ella, don't say that! You don't know how good you have it here. People in town are caught up in TV shows, computer stuff, and they're always on their phones. Out here on the farm everyone spends time talking with each other. We work a lot, but we have fun while we are working."

"Why are you thinking about going back then?"

"Ugh, you are a little smarty pants!" he teased.

"I always wear dresses, how could I be a smarty pants?"

"That is an English expression. It means that you always think you know everything."

"I knew what it meant," she retorted.

"See, there you go again being a smarty pants! By the way, Miss Smarty Pants, did you see what I got?" Lenny pulled open the outside barn door and there stood Penny sleek and shiny, with dark brown eyes.

"What do you want with a pony?" Fannie Ella almost sounded annoyed.

"I have a friend who needs a pony," Lenny said with a smile.

"Really—who's that?" she asked with a contorted brow.

By that time, Lenny had brought Penny into the barn and she stood looking at the little Amish girl with wide eyes. Fannie Ella didn't even take a good look at the pony. Instead, she started walking out of the barn. She mumbled as she went, "I hope you weren't thinking of me—I'm getting too old to ride ponies."

Lenny and Penny stood looking at each other. Penny's dark eyes glistened. Lenny rubbed her nose and told her, "That's the girl I was telling you about. Don't get the wrong impression, though; she is a really nice girl and she will take good care of you someday." He turned the pony back out with the draft horses and shut the door.

Fanny Ella and Ruth got busy canning chicken that had been butchered earlier and kept cool until they had time to put it up in jars. Noey and Lenny spent their morning splitting logs they had stacked near the buggy shed last summer. They used a log splitter that ran off the power of a tractor. It was noisy enough that the men couldn't talk much while they worked. Lenny loved the smell of oak and walnut logs as they popped and split into two pieces. Noey ran the splitter and Lenny stacked everything neatly in piles close to where they could drop it through a chute into their basement.

During dinner, Noey announced, "It's time to wean calves; the moon is growing."

"What do you mean 'The moon is growing'?"

"You know that the moon is always changing? It goes from no moon to new moon, and then grows until we have a full moon. My grandpa Isaac always said, 'Wean colts and calves when the moon is growing. Never after the full moon wanes.'"

"Huh, I wonder why that is?" Lenny asked.

"I don't know, but it does seem to help."

Fanny Ella said, "My dad always goes by the moon, too, not only for weaning but some other things like planting certain things and such."

Ruth stated, "Well, Noey and Junior both had Isaac for a grandpa. I guess they both got it from him." Everyone nodded in agreement, and they bowed their heads for silent prayer.

## Weaning Calves

Weaning calves was simple, yet difficult. Noey had set it up for his cows to eat at a large bunk and for calves from a nearby smaller trough. The calf trough was just inside a long white shed.

While they were eating, Noey told Lenny, "Go ahead and shut that sliding door. We have a board we set into the track to keep the door shut."

That was the simple part. It seemed the cows didn't notice right away that their youngsters were behind a closed gate. Once they headed back out into the bigger lot, Noey shut that gate as well.

"Why are you shutting the middle gate?" Lenny asked.

"I've found that it's easier on the mamas and calves if there is a little distance between them. It also helps if they can't see each other."

A short time later, one of the old cows began to moo at the gate. A faint calf moo came from within the shed. Then the difficult part began. Three cows stood at the gate bellowing, and a chorus of muffled moos came from within the shed. By midafternoon the whole herd of cows stood at the gate; their calling had become so constant it became a roar, drowning out the sound of the calves all together.

Lenny wasn't used to weaning livestock and it bothered him. He pitied the poor old cows and hungry babies.

Noey seemed to be aware of Lenny's struggle. He encouraged him, "Don't feel too badly for them, Leonard, it's all part of life. Even humans have to be weaned. There is a time for everything. A time to be born, a time to die, a time to morn, and a time to laugh, a time to be with your mama, and a time to grow up."

Lenny nodded that he understood.

Noey said, "We cut back the cows' feed the last while, so they didn't have as much milk. You can feed the calves extra this evening. It will make you all feel better."

## Noey and Lenny

Lenny and Noey headed back into the horse barn, where things were a little quieter.

Noey cleared his throat. "Ruth would sure be happy if you stayed on," he said.

The older man leaned his forearms on Stone's hip. Lenny could barely see his uncle over the two massive horses that stood between them. Noey seemed more comfortable talking without eye contact, so Lenny stayed where he was and listened.

Noey continued, "We could go ahead and set up a partnership and see how it goes. If you should happen to get married sometime, you could move into our little grandpa house with your wife."

Lenny was glad that Noey couldn't see his smile or his face heating up and no doubt red.

Lenny coughed and answered, "Thanks, Noey, I'd like that ... I mean farming with you and everything. I talked to my mom on the phone a few days ago. I told her that I'm gonna stay and help you finish harvest for sure. I promise that I will make my final decision before winter. Maybe we should go ahead and set things up."

Noey nodded. They listened to a chorus of cattle mooing.

"I thought you said weaning while the moon is growing makes it easier to wean calves?"

"It does. You should see how long this goes on if the moon is shrinking."

Once he had a full load of manure, Lenny climbed on the spreader and clucked his horses into motion. As they headed out of the barnyard, Lenny looked back at the grandpa house. It was a cute crackerbox of a house, painted white, with a little porch. Lenny hadn't noticed that there was a porch swing hanging there. Mr. E and Stone wanted to trot, but Lenny held them to a walk while he stared at the little house and imagined Leah waving to him from the porch swing. That earned a big smile from him and he wanted to let out a whoop.

All afternoon, Lenny couldn't quit thinking about what Noey had said. He kept imagining Leah inside that little grandpa house baking a pie, or out in the garden with Ruth. He had never thought about how nice it would be to have a wife. He felt all grown up just thinking about it. When he was loading manure, he stopped and told Stone, "I've been pretty happy to have Leah as my special friend, but it would be even better to have her as a wife."

Stone nodded his big head and snorted, shaking his harness and making it jingle.

The minute they stepped back inside the big barn, Lenny heard a squeaking sound coming from the oats bin. He figured a rat must have made a nest and had babies in there. He picked up a shovel and snuck over quietly. Russell followed and Lenny whispered, "Now you don't jump in there until I slap the nest. If one comes climbing out, you get 'em." He slowly pulled open the door and prepared to slam a nest of rats. He stopped his shovel just before he smashed a litter of kittens. Russell jumped into the oats and Lenny yelled, "No, Russell!" It would have been too late to stop the dog from killing them if he would have wanted to.

"Russell, did you know about these kittens?"

Russell stood in the oats looking over the babies as if they were his own. A little yellow kitty squeaked an infant cat meow and tumbled out away from his littermates. Russell nudged it back into the rags that had become a nest in the corner of the oats bin. A half purr, half meow came through an open barn door. Two-Face appeared, trotting toward them with a smile on her cat face. Russell and Lenny backed away from her kittens, and she jumped in, looked them over closely, and nestled down and proceeded to give them a tongue bath while they nursed.

"We'll, I wasn't sure if you were a boy or a girl cat, but I guess now I know."

Lenny and Russell stood and watched the tiny babies eat.

## The Grandpa House

Lenny looked for Ruth to tell her about the kittens and found her washing windows on the little grandpa house.

"Guess what? One of our cats had a litter of kittens out in the oats bin," Lenny announced as he walked up beside her.

"Late in the summer for kittens, but they might make it if they are in a warm place like an oats bin." She smiled at her nephew and then asked, "Have you ever looked inside our little grandpa house?"

"I don't think so."

He followed her inside. A slice of light came through the little window over the kitchen sink and beamed across an empty rocking chair. Lenny stood and looked at dust particles swirling through light around the bent hickory rocker.

"Huh, something seems familiar about this room. I remember seeing an old man sitting in that chair."

Ruth folded her arms in thought. "Your great-grandpa Isaac Gingerich used to live here, but I didn't know that you ever came to see him here."

"Was Isaac my grandpa Jesse's dad?"

"Yes."

"I think I remember coming in here to see him one time. He had blue eyes like my grandpa, didn't he?"

"Yes, Isaac and Jesse did both have those same blue eyes. And I guess Noey has them, too," she said, smiling.

Lenny nodded. He looked around at the little house. It held a tiny kitchen on one side and a small living room on the other half. He could see a closet-sized bathroom between two bedrooms.

"Noey and I lived here when we first got married," Ruth said, letting out a sigh. "Grandpa and Grandma lived in the bigger house with their two youngest daughters at that time. We weren't sure if we were going to stay on this farm. We thought maybe

Aaron Burr or your grandpa Jesse, or one of the other brothers, may come back and take over the farm. It just worked out that Noey and Isaac got along great." She laughed as she reminisced, looking out of the kitchen window as if she could still see them through the glass. "Noey and Isaac connected through their love of horses. I guess that runs in the family."

Ruth opened the door.

"I'd have to say the front porch was always my favorite part of this little house. I still remember sitting out here on cool summer evenings during that first year Noey and I were married." She stood for a moment with one hand on her cheek, staring at the porch swing that swayed in a gentle breeze.

Lenny looked at Ruth and could almost imagine her as a newly married Amish woman, fully anticipating a large family. For whatever reason, that didn't happen.

Ruth looked at Lenny. "Noey is the happiest he has been in years. He really enjoys having someone around who appreciates horses as much as he does. We don't mean to pressure you, Leonard, but we feel really good about having you here."

"Thank you, Ruth. It's hard to make a big decision like this, but I want you to know that you and Noey have made me feel at home here. I told Noey that I will decide before winter comes."

"We understand. Take your time and think it through."

## Fanny Ella Knows

Lenny stepped out of the Grandpa house and heard a roar coming up through the woods. He shuddered so strongly that he ended it by shaking his arms and flapping his lips like he was cold. As he turned to walk away, he almost tripped over Fannie Ella.

Lenny asked, "Did you hear that?"

"What?"

"It sounds like there is some wild creature living in the woods along the English river, because I keep hearing a roar." He watched Fannie Ella's expression change from concern to amusement. He scolded her, "Why are you laughing at me? I know I heard a roar echoing up the river."

"No, Lenny, you did. Didn't you know that there is a guy from River City who has an animal preserve a mile up the river?"

"An animal preserve? What kind of animals does he have?"

"He is some kind of retired professor from the university. He takes in wild animals that are injured, or that the police take from people who are keeping them illegally. Someone had this lion and the police took it. The professor is keeping it until they can find the right zoo."

"Huh, why didn't you tell me this sooner? I almost moved back to town just to get away from that terrible roar," he said, grinning.

Fanny Ella rolled her eyes and headed in to help Ruth wash windows.

Lenny climbed into the haymow to toss bales down for his cattle. He lifted a bale and noticed something coiled up under it. He jumped and hurried away, tripping over a bale he had already pushed into the walkway. He got up and peered through the dark insides of the haymow. The massive coil lay perfectly still.

"Oh, I guess that's just a big thick rope!" He laughed at himself and walked back to examine it.

Russell watched as Lenny pulled it out full length.

"Hey, Russell, this would make a great rope swing!"

The little white dog turned his head sideways as he sat watching his master. Lenny started winding the rope back into its coil and then stopped.

"You know what I should do? I think I'll make a rope swing for this haymow and bring Leah in here for a ride. Then, when she is spinning, I'll ask her to marry me!"

Russell stood up and barked.

Lenny laughed. "I'll tell her that I won't stop spinning her until she says, 'Yes!'"

Russell barked again, louder this time.

The young man climbed a ladder made of hay bales. He stacked them into a pyramid shape until they were high enough he could loop one end of his rope over a rafter. He tied two half hitches in his rope and used it to help balance as he made his way back down the man-made mountain of hay. Before he had gone far, his bales gave way into an avalanche, tumbling out from under his feet. Lenny held tightly onto his rope and swung out over the tumbling bales. Russell yelped as he scrambled away from a bale that rolled like a boulder toward him.

"This is fun, Russell, you have to try it!"

There were two large stacks of hay on either side of the large haymow. In between haystacks was a walkway that looked like a canyon from where Lenny was swinging. He realized he could start on one stack of bales and swing across to the other, over the deep canyon. Lenny got an idea and hurried down the mow ramp and into Noey's shop. He found a board that was about the right size and drilled a hole in the middle, using a hand-cranked drill. He hurried back up into the mow, with Russell at his heels. He pushed the end of his rope through the hole and tied a large knot about where he thought it would be easy to sit.

"This is the kind of seat they have at Uncle Alvin's place," Lenny explained to Russell, who continued cocking his head to one side, watching closely.

With a seat to ride on it was easier, and Lenny decided he could hold Russell with one hand and his rope with the other. Russell didn't jump into Lenny's arms, but he didn't run off either. They managed to get going and swung out across the canyon, between mountains of hay. They took a second ride. This time Lenny got a running start and they swung way up on either side, and then down into the lowest part of their arch between haystacks. They were just climbing up on the other side when there was a loud "POP!"

Lenny couldn't grasp what had happened at first, until he felt the seat disappear from under him. He concluded that his board broke into two pieces as he was tumbling onto the edge of a haystack. Russell leapt from his arms and landed safely on one pile of bales. Lenny looked into Russell's eyes as he fell backward into the canyon. Russell just kept getting smaller until Lenny felt himself let out a "Humpf!" and then all he could remember was trying to draw in a breath. Russell had somehow made it down the hay and licked Lenny's face as he gasped for air. When he could finally breathe again, he told his dog, "I'm glad that happened to me and not to Leah while I'm asking her to marry me!"

Noey came running up the mow ramp.

"What happened? I heard a loud thump."

"Oh, that was just me. I made a swing in the haymow and my board snapped in two." Lenny lifted up pieces of his swing seat and showed them to his uncle. "Fortunately I landed on some loose hay when I fell."

Noey smiled, eyes twinkling. "I'll show you how to drill a hole that won't weaken your board."

That evening when they finished chores, Noey taught Lenny how to stoke up the wood-burning stove. They loaded a couple logs into a bright red-yellow flame. A sweet smoky scent filled the basement, and it rose up through vents with warmed air.

After supper, Ruth said, "I baked an extra pie for Aaron Burr and Suzanna. Leonard, would you take it over to them before dark?"

"Sure, I'd like to see them anyway."

Lenny headed out to the barn to harness up Smoky. As he slid open the wooden door to get him, Train stepped inside.

"Hello, Train. I guess you think I ought to take you up to Aaron Burr's place. Okay, but I'll have to ride you because we don't have a cart with wide enough shaves for you."

Train stood looking at Lenny as though he understood.

Sliding the wooden door shut, Lenny gathered Train's bridle and snapped a lead rope on each side of his bit. He laid Aunt Ruth's pie up on a tall ledge and climbed a gate to get up onto Train. He coaxed Train close enough to the ledge to grab the pie and set it between his legs. His horse had such a wide back the pie had a nice spot to sit.

"Okay, Train, let's go." Lenny clucked and Train trotted out of the barn down Noey's short lane and onto the road.

Train pranced with his rocking horse motion past Junior's farm and up the hill toward Aaron Burr's home. As they came up the steep incline, Ruth's pie flipped up against Lenny's shirt. He grasped it with one hand and hung on to Train's thick mane with his other hand. Lenny didn't dare pull the pie away until he was able to lean forward and gently lower it back down flat again.

"Whew, I'm glad this apple pie was set up good or it would have all dumped out on my lap."

He drove Train over to Aaron's house porch and reached down and set the pie on the railing.

Suzanna came out of the house.

"Hello, Leonard, what have you here?"

"Ruth baked some apple pies today and she asked me to bring one up here for you and Aaron Burr. I should have brought my cart instead of riding this big horse, because I think I messed up your pie."

"It looks fine to me," Suzanna said as she picked it up, smiling. "Aaron is working in his shop, so you better stop in and visit with him for a few minutes or he'll be disappointed."

"All right, that sounds good."

Lenny slid down off Train and tied him at the hitching rack. Aaron Burr's shop was getting dark as dusk set in. The older man didn't speak until Lenny said, "Hello."

"Is that you, Leonard?"

"Yes, I brought an apple pie my aunt baked today."

"Oh, I didn't recognize the sound of your horse."

Lenny laughed. "I decided to ride my grandpa's big Percheron, Train. It was kind of a silly idea, because I almost dropped your pie."

Aaron answered, "No, I don't think that's a bad idea at all. I used to run errands on Train's great-grandma when I was a boy."

"What, you knew his great-grandma?"

Aaron ran his hand along his workbench and stood near Lenny.

"Yes, your great-grandpa Isaac bought a team of mares when I was a boy. I would have to think about it for a while to figure out how many generations of horses we've had out of those two mares. Train is part of that line, and so is your young team Mr. and Misty."

Lenny's jaw dropped, and he didn't try to stop himself because he knew Aaron couldn't see him. "I guess I never asked about where Babe came from. I knew she is Tug, Train, and Bell's mother, and I guess Fanny Ella told me they were related to Junior's mare, Queen."

Aaron Burr chuckled. "All of those horses came from that team of mares my dad bought many years ago. They weren't that big, but did they ever have heart! My dad said they were the best horses he ever worked with. We raised a lot of colts from old Beauty and Bessy. Queen and Babe were a team at one time, but we split them up when our dad died. Your grandpa got Babe and I took Queen. Often horses go lame or die over the years, but those two are still around by some miracle."

"Thanks for telling me that. I didn't know the whole story of these horses." Things grew quiet for a few moments and Lenny said, "Aaron, can I ask you about something?"

"Of course you can."

"I feel so guilty because I want to go back and talk to my parents about whether or not I should stay Amish. Noey and Ruth are so nice, but I feel like I'm sinning against them by going home." Lenny always looked right at Aaron Burr when they had a conversation. The old man's blindness made him less intimidating to talk to.

Aaron usually worked while talking, but this time he pulled up a stool and sat down. He carefully felt the countertop in front of him. Lenny looked and realized the old man was reading from a braille Bible. He faced straight ahead while he spoke. "Jesus said, 'I did not come to call the righteous, but sinners to repentance.' Do you know what that means?"

"I think I do," Lenny answered, but had no idea what point Aaron Burr might be making.

"Do you know the difference between permission and forgiveness?"

"No, I guess I don't," Lenny answered honestly.

"Think about grade school. If a child is late, the teacher asks, 'What happened?' If the family had a house fire, the teacher concludes that the student is not guilty and gives him permission to be late. But what if a boy says, 'I stopped down by the creek on the way to school and saw a huge fish. I tried to spear it with a stick and I fell in the creek, then I had to go home and change."

Lenny laughed out loud and Aaron Burr grinned.

Aaron continued, "That boy doesn't have permission, so he is guilty." Aaron hesitated and Lenny tried to figure out what the old man was driving at. Aaron faced in Lenny's direction and said, "Many people spend their whole lives trying to convince themselves that they haven't really done anything wrong, that Christ will give them permission to enter heaven. Jesus is explaining that he didn't come and die for people who didn't do anything that bad, or if wasn't their fault. He came to save sinners. He died for people who know that they did something wrong and seek forgiveness."

"Huh, I never really understood that," Lenny said. He was still confused about how that applied to his situation. The young man sat quietly trying to sort it out.

After a few moments, Aaron explained himself. "Leonard, when you first accepted Christ, you knew that you were a sinner and asked him to forgive you. Now, you need to see that wanting to go home to talk to your parents is not a sin, so I'm sure God will give you permission to do that."

"Thank you so much for helping me, Aaron Burr. I really needed your advice."

Aaron laughed. "Now maybe you can give me some advice."

"About what?"

"My harness shop. I'm getting about too old to keep up with my orders and none of my grandsons want to take over my business."

Lenny was happy that Aaron couldn't see him tear up. He looked at the old blind man for a moment and then said, "I wish I could help you, but I have my heart set on farming with horses."

Aaron Burr spoke very quiet and sincerely, "I know that, Leonard. I believe you belong working out in those fields with your horses."

"I better get back home before it gets too dark," Lenny thought out loud.

"Yes, and I better get into the house and have a piece of Ruth's apple pie." They both laughed as they headed out the door.

Outside, Aaron Burr stopped, reached a hand up, and stroked Train's arched neck. He spoke to him in Pennsylvania Dutch.

Lenny didn't know all the words but he knew it was something about his grandpa, because he heard the names Jesse and Leonard.

Train pranced down the road between Aaron Burr's and Noey's homes while Lenny enjoyed his ride. They clip-clopped past Junior's house, and Lenny could see Ruby and her girls working in their kitchen by lantern light. When he got back to the barn, he brushed his horse in the dark and told him, "I'm so happy we are both part of this family. We always have had a lot in common, you and me." Train nickered and Lenny let him back out with the other horses.

Lenny stepped into Ruth's bright kitchen and she asked, "What do you have all over your shirt, Leonard?"

"I don't know," Lenny said as he touched it with his finger and sniffed. "Oh, no, I think it's pie filling! The pie tipped over against me while I rode Train up Aaron Burr's steep drive. Suzanna said the pie looked really good, so I don't think it was messed up."

Ruth laughed out loud. "Suzanna doesn't see that well and Aaron Burr is blind, so I don't suppose it mattered that much." Lenny and Ruth laughed together, and Russell barked. Noey came in from the living room to see what was going on. They told Noey the story and all three of them laughed again while Russell barked.

All through the night cows and calves mooed so loud it was hard to sleep. Lenny pulled his covers over his head to try and muffle the sad sound, but it didn't help.

# CHAPTER 6

## The Bluffs

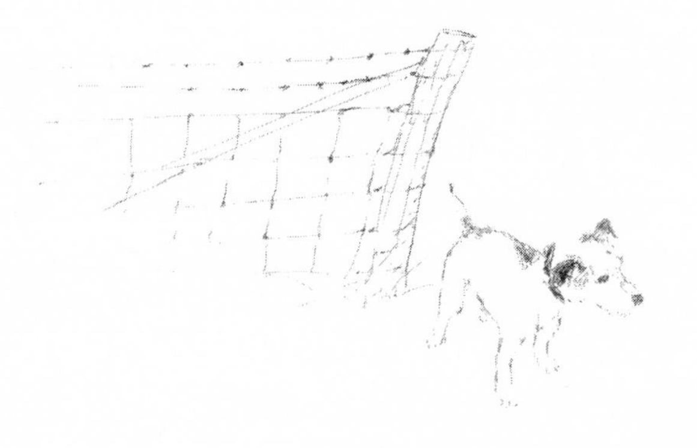

During the next number of days, even birds seemed to be restless; change was happening everywhere. Small birds crowded into branches overhead, fluttering, chirping, and then took flight, bursting out through leaves in small groups. After the little flocks circled around, they came clamoring back into the same boughs they had just left. A full-blown argument ensued in tree limbs above Lenny's head. Part of the troubles seemed to be that whole flocks had moved in from more northern lands, crowding out those that had lived on Noey's farm all summer. Lenny's horses noticed the birds' troubles, too, shaking their manes at all the commotion.

Around the same time birds began to be disturbed, soybean fields began to show yellow patches. Those lighter colored areas spread out further and further until everything turned a brilliant gold. Every breath of air drew crisp. Canada geese flew back and forth across the sky in partially formed V's, not always south, but in every direction. It was clear that it wasn't time for them to leave, yet change was coming.

Lenny sat behind a team of horses with an unsettled feeling in his heart watching the whole thing unfold before him. He told his horses, "Living the Amish lifestyle in autumn is a new experience for me, and winter sounds like a nightmare. Grandpa already told me how brisk weather affects horses, making you all flighty and frisky. Maybe Amish young men look forward to their horses being more lively, but for a guy like me it's downright scary."

Lenny wondered out loud, "Why couldn't summer last forever?"

Misty nodded her head up and down, possibly in an effort to stretch out driving lines that held her bit too tight. Lenny chose to see her head shaking as an agreement with his comment.

"I was dreading fall. Now that I told Noey I would help with harvest and give him an answer before winter, I hope autumn lasts forever."

He clucked and his horses stepped off quickly. Lenny and his team finished feeding cattle. He tossed off hay as the horses circled through the herd.

When they pulled into the barn, Two-Face came inside with a purring meow as she headed across the concrete barn floor. She had a mouse dangling from her smiling mouth. The cat's muffled mews kept up until she dropped her kill into the nest. She sat nearby licking her paws while the baby cats fought over their breakfast. The chubby yellow kitten growled and Lenny teased, "You are quite the lion, aren't you?"

Lenny watched the sight until he was surprised by Noey's voice, "You know, Leonard, only a small section of one field has corn in it. I think we could pick that by hand."

"Oh, really, I thought that only sweetcorn was picked by hand."

"Actually that's the way we used to pick all of our corn when I was your age." Noey pulled on his beard. "I remember one fall my dad had us boys pick corn on our way to school. Our cornfield was east of the home place, the same direction as our schoolhouse. Your grandpa would go along with us and we'd pick to the end of a row. He'd haul back a full wagonload and we would go to class. Our gloves got wet from frost on cornhusks, so we put them near the woodstove and they'd be dry in time for recess. In the afternoons when school let out, Dad would be there with an empty wagon and we would pick our way back home."

"Are you serious?" Lenny looked in Noey's eyes to see if he was joking.

Noey nodded. "And no complaining was allowed either! Later when Ruth and I were first married, we used to pick corn by hand, too. When we finished picking corn in the evenings, we headed in to milk twelve cows by hand. Ruth and I would milk six, and Isaac and his wife would milk six." He chuckled and continued, "Ruth would sit on one side of a cow and I'd sit on the other, and we'd milk her out together and then move on to the next. It was always kind of a race to see which couple would finish milking their cows first. Back in those days, a normal farm had twelve cows and twelve sows. Grandpa Isaac owned six of each and so did I."

"That actually sounds fun," Lenny said, smiling.

"Yes, it's too bad all these modern inventions had to come along and change everything." Noey looked at Lenny with a serious expression, and the younger man had to try and conceal his amusement. Noey said, "I know what you're thinking, but even though Amish life is old-fashioned, a lot has changed over the years."

"I do know what you mean, Noey. I'm actually kind of sad that a lot of Amish in our area don't farm with horses. I'm sure that steel-wheeled tractors look out of date to the rest of the world, but it is a modern convenience that takes away from how sweet things could be. Farming with horses has so much more depth to it. Everything is quiet, so a farmer sees and hears everything around him—birds singing, cows bawling off in the distance, and he gets to know his horses' personalities, too."

"That's exactly what I'm talking about," Noey agreed.

## Picking Corn

After lunch they hitched Stone and Mr. E onto Noey's high-wheeled wagon. Noey attached a tall sideboard on one side of the wagon.

"Do you know what that is for?" he asked his nephew.

"So we can pile corn higher?" Lenny guessed.

"Well, it does serve as a sideboard. It's called a 'bang board' because we toss ear corn against it and into the wagon."

"Oh, yeah, I get it."

They rode out in the wagon. When they were next to their few rows of corn, they climbed out. Noey passed the driving lines through a metal eyehole that stood out from the side of his wagon and tied a knot to keep them from slipping back through.

"This bolt with an eye is on the wagon so we can get to our driving lines quickly, if need be. I'll start picking corn and you hold onto our horses until Mr. E gets comfortable with the sound of corncobs hitting our bang board."

Lenny took hold of the lines and Noey started picking corn. His uncle showed him how to use a husking peg, a blade on a stick to help quickly rip cobs out of husks, and lickety-split he threw them against the board. They made a loud bang and Mr. E jumped. Stone had obviously heard the sound before and stood like a rock.

"I'm throwing the ears harder than usual while you have a hold on the driving lines. I've found that you want to make things worse for a horse when you can control the situation. That way when you can't control what is happening around you, they've seen worse."

"That's a good idea. I usually try to make everything as good as possible for my horses," Lenny explained honestly.

"That is common. Folks try to keep things quiet for a young horse when they are training, not realizing that the time for trouble is in a controlled situation. I like to drive a young team near a loud truck when I have them on a sled or heavy load. That way, when I'm on a forecart and a loud truck passes, they've already been closer to a louder truck. When a young horse is on a busy highway is *not* the time or place to find out about loud trucks." Noey laughed at his own explanation.

In a short time Mr. E seemed relaxed about the banging of corncobs and Lenny was able to start picking corn, too. They threw the cobs against the bang board, but not nearly as hard as Noey had done at first. As they picked corn, leaves along the fencerows began to dance in circles. A few leaves seemed to be chasing each other in a circle and then suddenly lay back down. An instant later they jumped up and swirled again, this time rising as high as a draft horse's head. Long leaves from dried cornstalks floated like strips of crepe paper. Shadows of birds crossed the ground near Lenny's feet, and then he realized he wasn't seeing shadows at all, but low-flying sparrows darting across the field about knee-high. On one such flight, a few of the tiny birds fluttered around in front of the horses and came by so fast one of them flew between Lenny's legs.

Lenny struggled to use the husking peg. It had leather straps to keep it on his hand as he scoured off the silks and husks. He snapped the cobs off their stalks and tossed them as fast as he could go, trying to keep up with his uncle, but Noey made two bangs on the board for every one of his. At the end of a row they stopped and took a rest. Noey leaned on his wagon and took off his hat, wiping his brow.

"This brings back good memories." Noey looked toward the trees as though remembering his past. "It only seems like a few days ago that Ruth and I were young newlyweds. Life goes by so fast even the hard things don't last."

"That's a good saying," Lenny said, smiling.

Noey and Lenny kept at it until they had picked every cob of corn they had raised. They heaped their wagon with a golden mound of cobs.

Noey said, "We overfilled our wagon, but there wasn't enough for two loads. Let Stone and Mr. E take their time so we don't lose any ears on our way back."

"Where are we going with our corn?" Lenny asked.

"We'll put this load in our corncrib. We will be buying more corn from Junior, enough to fill up our crib."

Noey slid open the large doors and Lenny drove his horses into the alley between two cribs. The place brought back memories of Herbie, because it was where he had worked on Lenny's Impala. Lenny couldn't help but think of when he took Herbie and Perry to town in his car and all the fun they had together. He wondered if Herbie was driving the Impala in town at that very moment.

Noey started up a stationary motor that growled as it powered an elevator, hoisting corncobs up into the crib. The two men scooped cobs into a large pan that funneled them into little buckets, which were carried up and over into the bin of wooden slats. When they had partly unloaded, Noey hooked ropes to his wagon's front end. He tugged on a rope attached to a pulley, and it hoisted the front of their wagon up into the air and dumped corncobs out behind.

After they finished unloading, Noey said, "When you haul corn from Junior's, you will unload it just like we did here."

Lenny looked around to try and remember how it all worked.

## Chore Time

Lenny left Mr. E and Stone hitched to the wagon and began his evening chores of hauling hay out to waiting cattle. His horses walked along slowly as he tossed hay off. He was just getting a good start at it when he heard a loud thumping noise. He looked around frantically to see what was happening, and then realized it was Justin coming down the road with his music blaring. The big red truck rumbled to a stop near the fence. Music thumped out of his open windows and brought a grin to Lenny's face as he walked over for a chat.

Justin teased, "I know you are really missing good music like this, Amish boy!"

"Yeah, but like I've said before, I get a little bit of it every time you drive by." They both laughed and Justin turned down his music so they could talk. "So, you're still planning to come to my football party?"

"Yep, Leah is excited to see your baby boy! What time is the game?"

"We start partying early, but the game isn't until 11:00. Come over as soon as you can."

"Leah has to work until noon, so we'll be able to see the second half at least. I'll pick her up from Beantown as soon as she gets off work, but it will take a little while to get there by horse and buggy."

"Don't you get tired of counting on horses to get you everywhere? Think how much faster you could get to my place in a car."

Lenny looked over at his team of horses. They were watching him with their dark, glossy eyes. "I don't mind when they behave like they should. When they give me troubles, I feel like trading them in for a truck like this one!"

Justin laughed really hard. "Why don't you see if that Leah will leave the Amish with you?"

"Well, my uncle asked me to be his partner on this farm. I guess if I agree to it I'll end up being Amish for life."

"Not necessarily," Justin slurred out. "You can put off your decision indefinitely."

"What do you mean by that?"

"Well, you could join up and marry Leah, and then later on you could leave the Amish and sell this farm and you'd have it made."

Lenny shook his head. "I don't think Leah would go along with that."

"You might be surprised. I think most Amish would be happy to leave if they had a half a chance. Why do you think she likes you, anyway?"

"Why?"

"Probably because you're not really Amish. She might think you're her ticket out."

Lenny was quiet for a moment before saying, "I never thought of that."

Justin started up his big truck and music. As he pulled away, he called, "See you at my place on game day!"

Lenny waved and climbed aboard his old wagon. He clucked to his horses and they quietly resumed their cattle-feeding chores.

## Up on the Hill

That evening Lenny was tired and his aching hands were chapped. He decided to take a walk and think about his future. He wandered around Noey's farm for a while and ended up at the base of bluffs that edged Noey's farm. He looked from side to side as he climbed, noticing that trees seemed to be moving. He knew it was an illusion caused by perspective, but it still gave everything an eerie feel. He was glad that Russell stayed with him, knowing his dog would warn him of any danger. A stiff breeze pushed leaves uphill, along with the young man and dog. Leaves seemed to run like little men beside them, until the wind died. When things were still, the little men all lay down and rested, waiting for another gust. When it came, they all jumped up rushing forward, tumbling head over heels.

Branches swayed overhead, moaning and creaking. Russell followed Lenny, sniffing the ground around them, searching for trouble. Two-Face stalked along twenty feet behind them. As he neared the top, Lenny was climbing with his hands as much as his feet. He grabbed a woven wire fence and pulled himself up the last few steps. He looked back down the steep slope, wondering how he would get back down without sliding. Noey's whole farm could be seen from that spot and Lenny was stunned by the view. After gazing at Noey's pretty farm for a while, he climbed over the old fence. He was happy to stand on flat ground again, until he realized he was in the midst of tombstones. He might not have climbed the fence had he known he was climbing into a graveyard.

Tiny white headstones stood in neat little rows, each stone with engraved names and dates. He found one that said Jesse Alvin Gingerich. He said with surprise, "This is Grandpa's grave!" He remembered coming to this cemetery from the road that was on the other side of the bluff. He knelt down for a moment near Grandpa's headstone. "I sure do miss you." He looked at

Grandpa's name for a few minutes and then said, "I know you would be happy if I stayed Amish, but I have to be honest—I'm a little nervous about it."

Russell lay down next to Grandpa's headstone and watched Lenny wipe a tear off his cheek. A row of pines lined the little cemetery on one side. Wind whistled through pine needles sounding like soft words, spoken to comfort. Fallen needles from those trees made a cushion for his knees and added a sweet pine aroma.

All at once Lenny heard a commotion, like a group of people talking loudly. He stood up and looked around for a crowd having a party or an argument. He listened closely and it began to sound more like honking kazoos than voices, and Lenny realized a flock of Canada geese was coming his way. He watched them pass over not far above his head, so close he could have thrown a rock and hit one. The young man spun as the geese flew by, losing his balance and stumbling on a little headstone that was covered with leaves. Lenny bent down and, brushing leaves aside, he read words that were carved into the face of it, "Leonard Noah Gingerich." He brushed more leaves away and said aloud to Russell, "This little boy only lived six days. It says here, 'Son of Noey and Ruth Gingerich.' Imagine that, Noey and Ruth had a baby named Leonard."

The next tomb over had the inscription, "Louise Marie Gingerich." Lenny told Russell, "This little girl must have been stillborn—her birthday is the same as her date of death." Russell sat still and cocked his head to one side, shining dark eyes glistening. Lenny looked back at Grandpa's headstone and Two-Face was sitting on top of it, licking her paws. When the cat saw him looking at her, she stopped washing herself and stared at Lenny. "This is so sad. I knew that Noey and Ruth had lost a few infants at birth, but it was so long ago that it didn't seem real." Lenny brushed leaves off a third grave. "Katie Anne Gingerich" was engraved on the tiny gravestone. A tear fell from Lenny's eye. Noey and Ruth were such kind people he couldn't imagine their grief as they buried their little baby girls and infant son.

"We better get you back to your kittens, Two-Face."

Lenny climbed the fence and lifted Russell over. Two-Face slipped through the fence and followed. The young man slid down carefully on his feet, with one hand on the ground behind him to help keep his balance. Russell partly ran and partly slid down on his hind end. Two-Face slowly picked her way, winding down from one level spot to another.

Lenny was so busy thinking about Noey and Ruth having a son named Leonard he didn't think about how dark the woods were getting. Near the bottom of the hill, he was able to stand up and started walking toward the barn. Suddenly, he heard a roar. Lenny stopped to listen, but Russell took off running toward the barn with his tail between his legs. The roar sounded again, and Lenny scrambled to catch up with his dog. They hurried into Noey's barn and found kittens playing on the floor. There were two calicos, like their mother, a black one, and a tabby yellow. The yellow was Lenny's favorite; he was always off by himself getting into mischief or sneaking up on the calicos. The yellow kitten arched his back as though facing a terrible foe, and then he pounced on his unsuspecting sisters.

"Whelp, we all better get some sleep, morning comes early."

Lenny slid all the barn doors shut and headed up to the house with Russell at his heels. Noey and Ruth were reading evening devotions under a warm glowing lantern. Lenny decided to sit down and listen to his uncle read.

"The law of the Lord is perfect, reviving the soul. The statutes of the Lord are trustworthy, making wise the simple. The precepts of the Lord are right, giving joy to the heart. The commands of the Lord are radiant, giving light to the eyes."

Lenny said, "That is from Psalm 19, isn't it?"

Ruth looked pleased. "Yes, how did you know?"

"That's my favorite Psalm. I love the beginning, 'The heavens declare the glory of God; the skies proclaim the work of His hands....'" Lenny's voice trailed off because his aunt was watching him with a kind smile. He stood up quickly. He couldn't quit thinking about the little graves he had seen. He had to get away before he started crying, and he didn't want to have to explain why.

Ruth asked, "How did you know those verses?"

"Aunt Lydia has it on her kitchen wall. I read it every day when I stayed in their home. You have a couple verses from that psalm in the washroom. And Leah's family has another section on her kitchen wall."

Ruth seemed surprised. "I guess that's right. I never thought about it that we all have a part of Psalm 19 on our walls."

Lenny smiled, but he was fighting to keep back tears. He said, "Come on, Russell, *grauts dich su sbet*."

Noey and Ruth laughed that he had told Russell to "scratch himself to bed" in Dutch.

# CHAPTER 7

## A Roar in the Woods

Noey announced during breakfast, "Today we'll start picking soybeans."

It was easy work for Lenny hauling wagonloads of beans with a team of horses. Noey drove his little steel-wheeled tractor, pulling a small pull-type combine that picked soybeans and dumped them into a wagon. Lenny hurried back and forth with wagons. Winds blew leaves and bean stubble, making an easy job less relaxing. Lenny's hat blew off and he had to run to catch it. He could see Noey watching him with a big smile on his face.

The next time Lenny traded an empty wagon for a full one, Noey called to Lenny, "You may want to wear a *tsipple* cop."

"A what?" Lenny asked.

"A stocking hat. The wind makes it hard to wear a hat with a brim."

## Kittens

Junior's twin daughters seemed to be using more and more English words. They came with Fannie Ella to help Ruth.

After lunch Lenny said, "Edna and Elma, why don't you come out to the barn and see our new kittens?"

They were all excited, jabbering in half-Dutch, half-English, with a few of their own made-up words in the mix.

Lenny told the twins, "Sshhh now, try to be quiet and look in our oats bin. Do you see kittens over in the corner?"

Lenny chuckled as he watched the little Amish girls standing side by side in their tiny dresses peering into the oats bin. They were quiet for a moment as they peeked into the darkness. Then they started giggling and talking about Russell. Lenny peered into the gap and realized that Two-Face wasn't with her babies. Instead of a cat, Russell sat licking the babies as they playfully pounced at him.

The little Amish girls looked Lenny in the eyes and jabbered Dutch words so fast he couldn't even begin to guess what they were saying—except that he continually heard them saying, "Two-Face and Russell."

Fanny Ella came out to see if the twins were getting into mischief.

Lenny asked, "Fannie Ella, what do you think of Perry?"

"Alvin's Perry?" she asked. "He's a nice enough boy I guess—why?"

"I know you are too young to date, but I think you two would make a great match someday." Lenny watched to see her reaction.

She didn't change expression, but stated matter-of-factly, "He's my second cousin."

"Well, you told me that I could take you home from a Singing someday. That was when I figured out that we were second cousins. You said that you asked your mom and she told you that it's okay to date a second cousin."

"That was different—you weren't from around here."

"Whatever, I still think you two would make a good match," he pressed. She didn't seem to enjoy his teasing so Lenny let it go.

Later that afternoon, Alvin stopped by to talk to Noey about something. Everyone gathered around his buggy for a short visit. Russell even sat listening to their friendly conversation, head cocked to one side.

Alvin looked at him and said, "You're quite a Russell."

Little Elma piped up, "He's a Dat now!"

"Really? Did you'ens have some puppies?" Alvin turned his question to Lenny.

Before Lenny could answer, Edna chimed in, talking in Dutch. Fannie Ella interpreted, "She says, 'No, he has kittens. Russell's wife is a cat!'"

Alvin didn't miss a beat, answering, "Oh, I see," eyeing Lenny with a smile.

Lenny explained, "Oh, this noon I showed our new kittens to the twins and it so happened that Russell was in with them instead of their mama."

Alvin laughed. "You are quite a Russell after all."

## The Big Cat

Russell headed out along Noey's fencerow, followed by Lenny in his straw hat and suspenders. About twenty yards behind Lenny, a calico cat tiptoed through leaves. Almost every evening, the three of them walked out to check on their cows. Some trees had turned red; a few looked completely dead, nothing but bare limbs reaching up like wrinkled arms. Most of the woods had turned a brilliant yellow. The forest had been dark all summer; at this point, the leaves seemed to glow golden. Light poked between leaves and flickered on Lenny's face as he walked. When the old wind blew, it pushed like a wave, sending brightly colored leaves to the forest floor. Insects whizzed past in every direction, as though in panic mode. They seemed to know that their time was limited; one hard frost would end their life's work.

"Ya know, Russell, Noey and Ruth are waiting for me to give them an answer about whether I'm gonna stay on or not. Fall is here and I still can't decide what I am going to do."

The little white dog stopped sniffing the ground when he heard his name, and came to Lenny with a look of concern in his brow. Lenny crouched down and scratched his buddy behind his black ears.

"I wish you would tell me what to do, Russell. I want to stay here for Noey and Ruth's sake. I can't even think about leaving Leah behind … or you, Russell. Or you either, Two-Face." Two-Face sat beside Russell licking her paws and then rubbing her head with them. She wasn't like the dog who was completely focused on his master. Lenny looked Russell in his little dark eyes.

"I just don't know if I can commit to staying Amish for the rest of my life. I really need to talk to Herbie. I should at least find out why he left the Amish before I make up my mind." The little white dog cocked his head to one side.

Man, dog, and cat resumed their task of checking fence and cows under a glowing canopy of leaves. In the very corner of their cow pasture, Lenny climbed the fence; his dog and cat slipped through it. Something drew Lenny toward the English River, even though he feared it—like his sore knuckle that he continually pressed even though it hurt. Lenny wasn't as nervous in the woods as he had been earlier, knowing that it was a lion in a cage that he had been hearing growling. When they got close to the gurgling water, Lenny listened for the lion, almost hoping it would roar and send a shiver up his spine.

Each footstep made a crunch. Something hit Lenny on the back and he spun around, searching for an explanation. A walnut rolled passed Two-Face and Lenny laughed at himself for being so afraid. They reached the English River and stood watching its steady current, listening to a constant rushing water sound. With fewer leaves in trees along the banks, the river saw more light, and its water was not quite as dark. Lenny crouched down and picked up small rocks to throw. He tried to make them skip, and Russell and Two-Face sat side-by-side watching rocks make multiple splashes as they bounced.

They enjoyed a quiet moment together on the riverbank, until they heard a roar. Lenny had been hoping to hear that sound, but something seemed different about it. The roar didn't come from as far upstream as usual. It was much louder and came from the wooded area, between where they were and Noey's barns. Lenny's first instinct was to run back home, but as he started off he realized he would be heading toward the sound. He whispered to his pets, "Hey, what was that?"

Two-Face seemed indifferent, but Russell seemed as concerned as Lenny felt. Russell and Lenny headed along the riverbank, stealthily creeping with a vigilant eye searching the woods. Both the dog and young man's ears were perked up, listening for a sound they didn't want to hear. It roared again, deep and vicious, rumbling through the trees and echoing along the English River. Lenny's heart was pounding, almost beating out of his chest. A tingle went up his spine, all the way up to the top of his head, where his hair felt as though it was standing straight up.

Lenny peered through a gap in tree trunks and clearly saw a large tawny-colored lion, strolling through the forest. The young man quickly looked at the river behind him and a thought flashed into his mind. *Cats don't like water; maybe my best bet is to jump into the English and escape*. He would have done it, but the English River's swirling waters scared him almost as much as the beast. He peered around a tree trunk. The lion walked along regally, its massive head covered with a dark reddish-brown mane that completely encircled its big face. As it walked through the woods its tail flailed back and forth, and it let out deep moans from a mouth that hung open, revealing glints of long white fangs. Lenny scrambled up a tree with a low hanging limb. Russell tried to follow, but couldn't. Lenny looked at the big cat. It hadn't seen them yet, so he hurried down and grabbed Russell. When he did, he could see the lion's massive head turn and look at them. His golden eyes were the same color as its coat, except for the piercing black pupils. Lenny stuffed Russell into his shirt and began to scramble up the tree again. The lion roared louder, which seemed to push Lenny like a hand, higher up than he had ever climbed before.

From their perch on a tree limb, Lenny and Russell watched as the lion sauntered over to where they had been standing only a few moments before. Two-Face sat with a smile on her small cat face, calmly watching the monster cat coming toward her.

Lenny hollered, "Two-Face, look out!"

Just when the lion got to where she was sitting, it shook its mane and lay down, rolling onto its back and pawing at Two-Face with long claws showing. Two-Face calmly leaned closer and rubbed her body against the lion's mane, the way she normally rubbed against Lenny's pant leg. Russell and Lenny clung to each other up in the tree limbs while the two cats nestled together like old friends. A purring sound rose up from Two-Face, and the lion let out deep belly groans.

Lenny noticed movement off in the woods and saw an old man walking toward them.

*"Look out,"* Lenny yelled, *"there's a lion on the loose!"*

The old man froze in place, but instead of looking for a lion, he seemed to be searching the trees for where the voice had come from.

Lenny called again, *"Look out, mister, there's a lion over here!"*

That time, Lenny's voice drew the old man's attention in his direction. The old man smiled and called back, "It's okay, he's my lion!"

Lenny and Russell watched in shock as the older fellow walked straight toward the lion and knelt down, rubbing its thick mane like a kitten.

"Come on down from there, young man, Caesar is as gentle as a lamb."

Lenny didn't budge. The old man stood up, looked up into the tree, and laughed. He had fuzzy white hair and a beard that encircled his face, reminding Lenny of the lion's mane. His blue eyes twinkled and he calmly asked, "Is that your cat?"

"Yes, that's Two-Face. She has a litter of kittens up in our barn."

The old man laughed again. "No wonder I haven't seen her lately.

"What do you mean?" Lenny asked.

"She used to come over and visit Caesar every day. She would slip through his cage bars and cuddle up with him and take a nap. I hadn't seen her lately and wondered why. Caesar somehow got out of his cage and it appears to me that he headed out looking for his little friend, Two-Face." The old man laughed a friendly belly laugh and it brought a chuckle out of Lenny.

"I'm really sorry my lion scared you, young man—and who is that you have up there with you?"

"This is Russell, my dog."

"And you are?"

"I'm sorry, I should have said, I'm Leonard Gingerich. Most everyone calls me Lenny. You must be the professor?"

The old man was still smiling, his blue eyes twinkling.

"Come on down, Lenny and Russell, I want to meet you properly and so does Caesar."

Lenny started to shinny down to a lower limb.

The professor suggested, "Here, let me take Russell. It will be easier for you to get down out of there."

Lenny pulled Russell out of his shirt and handed him down. Russell went to him readily but didn't seem to be in any hurry to leave his arms as he focused on the huge lion. When Lenny got both feet on the ground, he hurried over behind the professor, trying to keep the small old man between him and the lion.

"I'm Professor Mann, but most people just call me Adam," he said, and held out his free hand to shake Lenny's.

The big cat sat like most lion statues—on his belly with his front paws out in front of him. His massive head followed the professor and Lenny as they walked over toward him. Caesar looked past the professor and his steely eyes pierced into Lenny's. The younger man stayed behind the older. The professor leaned close and rubbed his hand in the lion's thick mane again.

"You're a kind old lion, aren't you, Caesar?"

Russell was dangerously close, but he kept his face turned away from the beast and didn't make eye contact with it at all. Lenny noticed Russell's strategy, and decided that was probably wisdom from the animal kingdom and followed suit.

The professor seemed to understand their fear and tried his best to convince them. "Caesar has been around humans his whole life. I believe that he is so sure of his superior strength and power that he doesn't feel any need to try and prove it by killing us, or dogs."

"I guess that makes me feel better," Lenny said quietly.

"I really enjoy seeing the cat and the lion together," the professor continued. "It reminds me of a human in the presence of God. You know, the Bible says that we are made in God's image, and when I saw this cat nestling next to this lion, I understood that concept for the first time in my life."

"Huh, that is really interesting," Lenny answered and gathered his courage enough to reach around the old man and touch the lion on his head. He had seen lions on TV and knew they were big, but it wasn't until he saw how small his own hand looked as he rubbed Caesar's head that he could really comprehended how huge.

"What do you feed him?" Lenny had to know.

"I have a wildlife refuge. The state brings me creatures that need a home, and they also bring Caesar deer that are killed on roads in Iowa. We keep him well fed."

"That's probably a good idea," Lenny said, laughing.

The old professor spoke a few words in German. Lenny knew it was German, but he didn't understand what it meant. He looked at the professor with a questioning brow.

Professor Mann said, "I usually try talking to my Amish friends in German. Even though you speak a different dialect, most Amish can understand me and I can understand them."

"Oh, I'm not Amish," Lenny explained.

The old man looked Lenny up and down and asked, "Are you sure?"

Lenny chuckled and said, "Well, actually my uncle tells me that I'm a frog." He looked at the professor and saw that he had his attention fully engaged.

"He means that I'm amphibious. My dad grew up Amish and moved to town. I grew up in town and moved out here to live with my Amish relatives. I'm not sure which world I fit into."

The old man continued rubbing his hand in Caesar's mane, and Two-Face continued rubbing against the lion's chest. The professor looked at Lenny and narrowed his eyes.

"You have been given a blessing very few people receive, and I would not take this opportunity lightly. You should do some deep soul searching before walking away from this lifestyle."

Lenny looked away from the professor and realized he was staring into the eyes of the lion. Caesar's massive head was fixed in his direction and his golden eyes with piercing pupils seemed to gaze right into his soul. An unmarked period of time passed before the professor finally spoke.

"Caesar, we should be heading home before you scare another person." He passed little Russell back into Lenny's arms. The lion stood up and walked beside the old man through the woods. The professor called to Lenny, "Bring Two-Face and come and visit us sometime!"

"I'll do that!" Lenny shouted through the woods.

Lenny set off hurrying home; he couldn't wait to tell Noey about the lion. He thought he saw Noey and hurried toward him, but it turned out to be Junior, Herbie's dad. The Abraham Lincoln-looking man walked through blowing leaves across the yard and toward the barn. His dark Amish clothes and black hat were similar to what honest Abe wore. His wrinkled kind-looking face, dark beard and bushy eyebrows were exact replicas of America's greatest president. When he spoke, Lenny felt sure his voice held the same warm, sincere tone.

"Hello, Leonard—are you and Noey getting your soybeans picked?"

"We are getting along fine. Noey says that you have agreed to trade us corn for part of our beans."

Junior smiled, but his dark eyes still seemed sad and heavy laden. His voice perked up a little as he spoke again. "Leonard, I picked up another horse at the Bulltown sale barn the other day. Why don't you bring Misty over to meet him?"

"Oh, I guess I could. Isn't it a little too late in the fall?" Lenny was careful not to be too specific, knowing that was the Amish way.

"Well, otherwise you'll have to wait until next June and lose a whole year," Junior explained.

Lenny didn't want to say too much or accidentally mention Laidlaw's big horse. "I will probably bring her by soon."

Junior smiled and asked, "Where's Noey? I should talk to him about our trade."

"He's up in the machine shed cleaning up his pull-type combine." Lenny searched for words to encourage the kind older man.

"I'm planning to go up to see my parents sometime soon. I am going to find Herbie and talk to him about coming back home."

By that time they had reached the barn and walked inside. Junior leaned against Misty, who was tied and standing quietly. Junior took off his hat, ran his hand through his dark hair, and then put his hat back on.

"I'm afraid I was too hard on Herbie when he was growing up."

"Oh, no, I'm sure that's not it!" Lenny said, shaking his head. "Herbie never complained about anything like that to me."

"I always made my sons work hard. They were never permitted to talk back or express their feelings, and I worry that might have driven him away. I'm learning to be more patient with my children, but maybe it's a little too late for Herbie."

"I really don't think that's it." Lenny looked in Junior's sad eyes. "Herbie seemed so happy, and he always spoke about you and Ruby with a smile. The only thing I ever heard from him about leaving was his interest in being a mechanic."

Junior eyes twinkled. "Thanks, Leonard, but that is something that he mentioned to me and I shut it down, because I wanted him to be a farmer. I should have at least talked to him about other possibilities."

That evening Lenny sat with his aunt and uncle in their living room, warmed by crackling firewood. A sweet scent of smoke mixed with that of their kerosene lantern. Noey read to them from a little paperback devotional written by ministers from Amish communities in neighboring states. The message for the day was about Christ being the exact image of His Father.

Lenny told them, "I learned something about this today. Remember Fanny Ella telling us about a professor that owns a lion? Russell and I were checking the fence and we went down to the river. While we were there we ran into that lion."

"Loose out in the woods?" Ruth gasped.

"Yes, but it turns out that it's a really gentle lion. Russell and I climbed a tree when we saw it, but Two-Face walked right up and rubbed against its mane. I thought the lion was going to kill her, but they acted like old friends. The professor came along to get his lion and told me that Two-Face comes to his place, cuddles up with her big lion friend, and takes naps."

Noey and Ruth shook their heads in disbelief. Noey asked, "What were you going to say about that being an example of our devotional?"

"Oh, yeah," Lenny replied. "The professor said that seeing a cat and a lion together reminded him of humans being made in the image of God. I'm guessing he means that we are like God in a small way, with God still being so much more powerful than us."

Ruth said, "Yes, and Jesus is like that lion. So powerful, yet so gentle."

Noah added, "I always liked the verse in Revelations that says, 'Behold the Lion of the tribe of Judah. I looked, and there stood a lamb....'"

# CHAPTER 8

## Amish Wedding

Noey, Ruth, and Lenny all dressed in their best Sunday clothes. It seemed odd on a Thursday morning, but Ruth said, "Thursday is wedding day in our community. Some do have Friday weddings, but Thursday has been a long tradition." Ruth had purchased a black broad-brimmed hat for Lenny to wear on Sundays or other holidays and weddings. It fit well and Lenny was happy when he got to use it. Ruth also made a black lapelless coat for him to wear over the black vest he wore to church in the summer. It was made of heavy material and kept him warm on a cool fall day. They visited cheerfully on their way to the wedding, which seemed different from going to church. Nevertheless, when they arrived at the Yoder farm, everyone seemed to have on a church face.

Lenny had been at this ordinary Amish farm before. Everything was painted white—barns, house, outbuildings, and even fences. However, fall had turned their farm into a brilliant wonderland. Golden leaves made trees near the house look like huge bouquets, crisp against white paint. Bright orange trees could be seen near the huge white barn and along the edge of a lush green alfalfa field. Cornfields were a brown backdrop, making the acreage appear as a colorful island of life in the middle of a dying countryside.

Lenny dropped off his aunt and uncle near the house and drove Smoky down into a pasture, where a long rope was stretched tightly between steel-wheeled tractors as a makeshift hitching rack. A long line of dark horses with shiny black harness stood tied on both sides of the rope. Everyone seemed happy to be gathering for a wedding. The service was very much like an ordinary Sunday meeting, except that the young couple getting married sat on a bench close to the ministers. While everyone sang hymns, the young bride and groom followed the ministers out of the room.

David explained in a whisper. "Ministers give counsel and advice to the marrying couple."

Lenny could only imagine what a scene that would be: old ministers talking soberly about marriage in a spare room upstairs, while four-part harmonies floated up the stairwell.

After several songs, the ministers and couple returned to their places in the center of the room.

Leah had mentioned earlier, "Amish brides don't wear white; instead, they often make a dress out of more colorful material than usual."

This young woman was wearing a crisp rust-colored dress that matched fall leaves visible through windows behind her. The bride and groom had each chosen a standup, her sister and one of his brothers. The men were dressed in black as usual, but the groom had a shirt that matched his bride's dress.

Lenny realized that if he leaned slightly to his left, he could almost see Leah seated among the women in the next room. He strained to see her without crowding David who was beside him. He couldn't look away from Leah's sweet glowing face.

A woman in front of her partially blocked his view. Lenny leaned forward and studied her crisp white prayer covering, imagining how her light-brown hair must be tied or twisted to fit under it. He knew she had long flowing ringlets, as he had accidentally caught her and her sisters brushing each other's hair a few summers back. He smiled to himself remembering how stunningly beautiful she looked. He had a thought at that moment about how much he liked the Amish tradition of a husband being the only man to see his wife with her hair down. A happy, warm sensation filled his heart as he thought about Leah being his wife and he alone seeing her pretty hair.

He looked at her face, which could barely be seen. He wondered why she was continually looking down to one side and smiling a sweet, angelic, glowing smile. The woman who was blocking his view leaned forward for a moment and revealed that Leah was holding a baby—a tiny bundle wrapped in a soft pink blanket. Lenny could tell the infant was looking into Leah's eyes from the way she was quietly communicating with expressions, raising her dainty eyebrows. Lenny's eyes were fixed on her, drinking in the sight. She must have felt that someone was staring at her, because she suddenly looked up at him. Even though they were separated by a distance and in the middle of a large group of people, their eyes held them close. Her sweet brown eyes, her glowing face and slight smile seemed to be shouting to him through the crowd, *I want to marry you and have a family!*

The woman in front of Leah leaned back and obscured his view, but the image was permanently imprinted in Lenny's memory. He knew he would never forget that moment even if he lived to be one hundred. He thought of how Aaron Burr had not seen his wife for over forty years. He remembered Aaron Burr saying, "I can only see her in my memory as a young woman, just the way she looked before I went blind."

## Wedding Meal

After the service, everyone filed out. Lenny gathered with a circle of young unmarried men under golden trees. They stood visiting about how harvest was going and how many bushels of corn or soybeans they were getting per acre. Others told stories of problems they had run into with equipment breaking down or with their horses. There were a few, like Lenny, who only listened, afraid of revealing what they didn't know.

Some of the older bachelors seemed to know when it was time to head over to the meal. Lenny followed his group of peers as they strolled closer to a long white building. It appeared to be a machine shop that had been cleared out and cleaned thoroughly for a wedding day meal. Tables were set. The wedding party, consisting of the bride and groom and their chosen stand-ups, sat at a corner table.

Leah had explained to Lenny that the bride and groom's table would be set in a corner—the man on the right side of the corner and the woman on the left. Her stand-up would have a chosen boy who sat between the bride and her "maid of honor." The "best man" would have a girl that accompanied him and sat next to the groom. That way the bridal party would be boy–girl–boy–girl. Older couples related to the bride and groom sat as couples for the wedding meal. With every other Amish service Lenny had been to, men and women were segregated. Likewise, the younger men and women were also divided by gender. It wasn't clear to Lenny if this were by choice or by tradition. Waiting on tables were young, unmarried people, chosen by the bride and groom. Leah was one of those asked to help and she served at Lenny's table. He suspected she made sure it worked out that way.

Leah's dimple was sunk into her cheek throughout the whole day. She couldn't seem to get the smile off her face, and the other single girls all appeared to be almost as happy. The young men and boys tried to act indifferent to the whole thing, but Lenny could tell they were enjoying themselves. They ate a hearty meal of roasted chicken, mashed potatoes, plenty of vegetables, bread, and a variety of dishes they called "Jell-O Salads." Everyone visited quietly, yet with an overall happiness that made it difficult for Lenny to be in a bad mood about being Amish. He wasn't sure if he was trying to talk himself into becoming Amish or out of it. The food alone made him think that he could endure other less desirable things about that lifestyle.

Leah came by with a pitcher of water. As she poured some into Lenny's glass, she spoke quietly, "Do you think Noey would let you use his four-wheeled open buggy tonight?"

"I guess I could ask him. Why, isn't my two-wheeled cart okay?"

Leah looked around to see if anyone might overhear her and then explained. "Two-wheeled carts don't ride as nice; they bounce as your horse trots. A four-wheeled buggy rolls so much smoother. I just thought it might be nice on a night like tonight."

"Oh, I guess you're right! I'll talk to Noey."

During the meal, the other guys mentioned that they would all be heading back to their homes for chores. David told Lenny he shouldn't eat at home, though. "There will be more food served to us young folks before the Singing."

Families began to leave one by one. It was easy to tell who belonged to whom because of their matching dresses and shirts. The family nearest to him had lime green matching dresses for their little girls. Two of them were very young, and they wore shapeless dresses and tiny white coverings. Six and eight-year-old sisters had more adult-type clothes, but still really small in that same green.

Lenny and Perry sat for a long while visiting about horses. "I hope to farm with horses when I have my own place," Perry announced.

"Really?" Lenny smiled at his cousin. "That's what I'm thinking, too!"

"Are you going to stay on here for sure?" Perry asked.

"I haven't decided yet for sure, but if I do, Noey and I are going to farm with horses. His farm is so close to the river, it doesn't drain well, and it is so much easier to get in the fields with horses. Besides, the main reason I want to stay Amish is for the horses." After he said it, Lenny wished he hadn't. He knew the real reason should be about his faith.

Perry smirked. "It doesn't have anything to do with a certain special friend, does it?"

"Oh, that, too!" Lenny felt his cheeks heat up and hoped they didn't turn red.

Perry continued talking about his dream of farming with horses while Lenny watched families leave the wedding. Trying to make Perry feel heard, Lenny made an effort to add to the conversation, yet he was seeing something that was speaking to him on a level he didn't understand.

Young Amish couples gathered their little children like tiny flocks of lambs. Daddy brought up the buggy, mama holding an infant in her arms while herding toddlers. If there happened to be a sister around the age of ten, she would be toting a younger sibling on one hip. Little girls around the age of five would often be seen holding a child who was almost as big as she was. They appeared to be such happy little families. It was clear that mothers had hand-sewn matching dresses for their daughters and used the same material to make shirts for their husbands and sons. As families drove off, they were crowded in their buggies—a few children sitting on laps, one or two standing on the floor watching their horses trot. Lenny smiled when he saw how many of the daddies let their younger children hold the driving lines. The dad's large work-worn hands held on right behind a smaller set as they headed off toward their bright futures, growing farms, and adventures awaiting them.

## Chores

Noey walked out with Lenny to get their buggy. He said, "Ruth is planning to help with cleanup and food. We will go do our chores and come back and join Ruth for the evening meal. You may want to bring Smoky and your own cart when we return, so you can stay for the young folk's doings … and take home a special friend." He didn't look at Lenny when he said it, but Lenny glanced at his uncle and saw a smile on his face and a twinkle in his eye.

"Noey, would you ever be willing to let me drive your four-wheeled open buggy? If you didn't want me to, I'd understand."

"Sure, you could use it. Four-wheeled carts are a little nicer to ride in, especially if you're giving someone a ride home," Noey teased in a friendly way.

Chores started out simple. All that Lenny had to do was feed horses and throw some small square bales down to his cattle. He planned to feed cattle first, because it was a little early for the horses and he knew his steers weren't too time-sensitive. The goal was to get them fat, and Lenny's job was to make sure they always had a full plate. He climbed into the mow and opened a large wooden door, through which he could throw bales down into a bunk below. He had already filled the further-out hay bunks the day before, knowing they wouldn't have time on a wedding day.

Lenny made a game out of throwing hay bales, trying to place them in a spread-out pattern, yet without breaking any of them. It actually didn't matter if they broke open, because after tossing them down he always took the twine strings off. Noey had explained, "If we leave those strings on, they end up on the ground and get covered with manure. Then when we're hauling manure, those twine strings get tangled up in the webbing of our spreader."

After Lenny finished tossing down bales, he usually looked out of the second-story doorway to check on his herds. He could see that his fat cattle were all lounging around—some eating, some resting and chewing cud. He leaned out a little further out to catch a view of his horses. He could see them gracefully grazing on the last of the pasture grass under yellowing trees, and then he noticed something odd: one horse was in a funny crouched position. He looked closer and could tell it was Nelly, but he couldn't figure why she was standing funny.

Lenny climbed down the wooden ladder as fast as he could go and ran out to see what was happening. He found Nelly trapped inside of a round wire bale feeder. She stood awkwardly with her head turned almost back to her side, cramped by the bale frame. One of her large hooves caught on the other side.

"Nelly, what on earth are you doing?" Lenny asked.

Nelly snorted and let out a warm nicker. Lenny stood for a short time evaluating the situation, wondering how he could get her out without hurting her. The metal frame was perfectly round, made to set down over a big round bale and designed to keep horses or cattle from stomping on or making manure in the hay. Livestock could reach their heads through the wire and eat hay without wasting any.

Lenny scolder her affectionately, "I can't imagine how you got in there, but please don't tell me—I don't want to know!"

He ran up past Noey's barn, into his shop, and grabbed a set of wire cutters. He hurried back and attempted to cut through the heavy wires that bound up Nelly's hind foot. He worked at it furiously, but wasn't able to get one wire cut. He ran back up to where Noey was milking Grace. He was all out of breath and Noey looked surprised when they met eyes.

"Whatever is the matter, Leonard, has there been an accident?"

"Not really, it's just that Nelly has herself in a tight spot again!"

"She will have to wait till I finish milking Grace. Where is she?" Noey asked, almost amused.

"She's caught in a round bale feeder. I tried cutting through a wire that's got her hind leg trapped, but I couldn't get it."

"No, those wire cutters aren't that sharp and those bale feeders are built heavy. You go ahead and finish feeding the rest of our stock and we'll figure something out as soon as we can."

Lenny rushed through his other chores and, by the time he finished, he was sweating. He met Noey heading down to where Nelly was still waiting patiently for them to rescue her. Noey brought a hacksaw and they cut through the wire, freeing her hoof. The uncle and nephew worked together, carefully pushing on the wire rings until they were able to flip the bale feeder over and off their horse. Nelly leaned her head into Lenny, as if in appreciation for his help. As they walked back up toward the barn, Lenny shook his head. "I don't know what is going on with that Nelly—she is constantly getting herself in trouble."

"Ruth thinks Nelly is doing it on purpose, because she misses all the attention you used to give her." He chuckled and added, "Maybe you better spend a little extra time brushing her when you do chores, to see if it helps."

"I can do that!"

They both laughed and headed in to clean up for the wedding-singing.

## Wedding Singing

Lenny drove Smoky on Noey's four-wheeled open-buggy. His uncle followed in a top buggy. Big Red seemed determined to try and keep up with the younger, faster horse. It didn't take long to get back to the wedding once they got going.

Amish folks could be seen everywhere when they pulled into a lane that was perfectly manicured. Even rocks in the driveway were in lines, having been neatly raked. Lenny drove Smoky down into a hayfield where all the horses were being tied at the very long rope stretched tightly between tractors. At least a hundred horses were tethered side-by-side along the full length, each with a black buggy or cart behind it. Smoky took his place in line and appeared to enjoy his chance to socialize with the other horses.

Lenny and Noey headed in for the evening meal, which was not that formal. People ate in shifts, instead of all at once. Apparently the women had already eaten their share. Men and boys returning from their evening chores all sat together and helped clean up leftovers from the afternoon meal. When they were all full again, the young men gathered in groups and visited near the barns and under the brightly colored trees. The sun went down in a bright display of reds.

Lenny walked with a group of other young men heading toward that long white building where a special Singing was to be held. Everyone was quietly visiting, each face with a smile. All the young single men began to form a line just outside of the long building. Lenny stayed near his cousins so he could follow them and do whatever they did, not being sure of the rules of an Amish wedding. All the young unmarried women were already inside. As the line moved along, Lenny could see into the door. Along the opposite wall inside, a long row of girls in brightly colored Amish dresses were visible. Lenny searched every girl's face, looking for his favorite one.

A middle-aged man stood at the door talking to each young man entering the room. After speaking to them quietly, he would call out a girl's name.

"What is going on?" Lenny whispered to David.

"You have to tell that man who you want to sit with. He will call out the girl's name and she will come over and join you."

Lenny nodded that he understood.

As they got near the front of the line, Lenny's heart was pounding. He felt self-conscious about revealing in front of everyone who he wanted to sit with. David went first, but Lenny was so nervous he didn't hear whom David said he wanted to sit with. All at once the Amishman was asking, "Leonard, who were you wanting to ask for?"

"Leah Yoder."

The man smiled and called, "Leah Yoder!"

The line of girls all looked at each other but nobody stepped forward.

The man quietly asked, "Which Leah? There are two Leah Yoders."

Before he even thought about how it may sound, Lenny answered, "The one with the dimple."

The Amishman smiled and said aloud, "Leah Yoder—with the dimple!"

Everyone laughed.

Leah was blushing when she met up with him.

"Sorry about that, Leah," Lenny whispered.

She didn't respond at first. Once enough time had gone by and everyone wasn't looking at them, she whispered, "You could have said, 'Harold's Leah.'"

"Oh, yeah, I didn't think of that."

As soon as they sat down and the next name was called, Lenny whispered, "Why didn't you step out when he said Leah Yoder the first time?"

"Because there are two of us. It would be prideful if I acted sure that you were asking for me."

During a regular Sunday evening Singing, boys and girls sat in alternating rows—a row of boys, then a row of girls; another row of boys, then another row of girls. At a wedding Singing, it was boy–girl, boy—girl, in the same bench. However, there was a section for boys who didn't ask a girl to sit with them and girls who didn't get asked. Leah explained that some of the boys asked for a sister to sit by them, or a cousin, or good friend. It didn't have to be a girlfriend or a date.

Lenny thoroughly enjoyed sitting with Leah and listening to her beautiful voice, singing like an angel. However, he hated for her to hear him singing. When sitting with a row of other boys, he could choose to follow tenors or bass. He wasn't used to singing parts.

## The Way Home

"I drove Noey's four-wheeled open buggy," Lenny was happy to tell Leah. She seemed pleased as he helped her up into her seat. Smoky lifted his head as though startled when Lenny untied him. "I think my horse was sound asleep." Lenny chuckled and it made Leah giggle. The tall gray horse walked a zigzag across the dark field where they had been parked, making Lenny think he was having troubles getting his bearings straight. Once he got onto the road, he acted normal again, trotting off into a dark night.

Stars were winking as the four-wheeled buggy floated smoothly between farm fields. At one point, they were in an extremely flat open area. The heavens above them looked like an upside-down bowl of stars.

Leah said, "I love riding in an open buggy at night—just look at the Milky Way!" A broad, creamy-looking band of stars formed an arch a million miles overhead. They rode together in a blissful silence, sharing a perfect moment.

"Lenny, which of my dresses is your favorite?"

"Your gray one."

"What? I begged my mother to let me make my yellow dress—isn't that your favorite?" She stared at him until he felt self-conscious.

"I do think you look really pretty in the yellow dress. Maybe it is my favorite." He looked her right into her eyes to convince her.

She shook her head. "No—when I asked you, you didn't hesitate but said right away, 'Your gray one.'"

"I'm sorry, Leah, I just like that dress. What can I say?"

"You're a funny guy. I don't think any Amish boy would choose that dress. And I know that no English boy would think it's pretty. I guess English boys think all Amish dresses are ugly?"

Lenny didn't know what to say but he knew he needed to come up with something.

"I don't know what other English guys think, but you are the prettiest girl I've ever seen."

"Don't say that!" she scolded.

"What, why shouldn't I say that?"

"It's vain to be caught up in looks. If you tell me that I'm pretty, I might be tempted to be vain." She folded her arms and looked at him, daring him to say something more.

He smiled at her. "Well, I hope this doesn't make it worse, but you're even cute when you're mad."

She tried to give him an angry look but couldn't keep it. "Well, I'm glad you like how I look, anyhow." She smiled coyly and looked more beautiful than ever.

## The Swing

At Leah's place, they tied Smoky and stood under the stars for a few moments.

"Come over and push me on the swing for a little while, Lenny."

"Really, you want me to push you on the swing?"

She nodded like a little girl. "It's such a pretty evening, and cold weather will be here soon. Let's take advantage of this nice evening."

She was already running toward the swing before he could answer. When he got there, she was sitting on the wooden seat taking off her shoes. He pushed her for a few minutes and while he did, he thought about his plan to propose. He wondered if this would be the perfect moment.

"Why are you being so quiet?" she asked.

"Oh, I don't know, I was just thinking."

"About what?"

"Nothing."

"Spin me, Lenny," she whispered.

That was all he needed to put his plan into action. He wound her up tightly and then twirled her in the opposite direction. As she giggled, he forced himself to say what he had planned.

"Leah, I'm going to ask you something and I'm not going to stop spinning you until you give me an answer."

She came to the end of spinning in one direction, but he quickly started her going the other way again until her ropes began to twist the other way.

"Will you please...."

"Stop, Lenny!"

"Nope, I won't stop until...."

"Stop! ... Stop! ... Stop! ... My fingers are caught!" she cried.

Lenny quickly stopped and unwound her. She stayed seated but hunched over, holding one hand with the other. Leah blew on her pinched fingers with a set of quick short breaths. Finally, she calmed down.

Lenny knelt down in front of her swing seat, took her hand, and kissed her fingers. "I'm so sorry, Leah! You know that I would never want to do anything to hurt you?"

"I know, Leonard." Her voice sounded normal again. "What were you going to ask me?"

"Oh, nothing...." He knew it was no longer a good time to ask after pinching her fingers.

"Lenny, tell me what you were gonna say!" she begged.

"I think I was gonna tell you that I wouldn't stop spinning you until you promised to kiss me."

"That's silly—you don't have to trick me into kissing you."

He laughed. "I know—I was just being silly."

Smoky trotted away from Leah's house under twinkling stars. Lenny told his horse, "After a day like today, I'm feeling really good about being here and staying Amish." Lenny could see Smoky's ears turning back in the moonlight.

They came down the hill and passed Web's place. Lenny prayed a short prayer: "Dear Lord, please help Web, he doesn't have anyone in the world. Please let someone show up in his life, a family member or someone who will make him feel that his life has purpose and meaning."

Lenny relaxed on Noey's four-wheeled open buggy, which rode smoothly and was comfortable, having a seat with a back. His mind drifted off, recalling the whole long day. He thought about seeing Leah holding the baby during the wedding and how sweet she looked with a baby in her arms. He smiled.

A moment later he woke up and realized he had nodded off. He shook himself and spoke to Smoky. "Good horse ... I'm glad I have a horse that stays on the road when I drift off to sleep." Lenny sat up on the seat for a while until he felt sure he was awake. He leaned back and got comfortable again. It was a little chilly, so he pulled the lap blanket up a little higher.

# CHAPTER 9

## Hauling Soybeans

Lenny looked straight into the lion's piercing pupils. He wasn't afraid, until he woke up in darkness unsure of where he was. He slowly concluded he was sitting on Noey's four-wheeled open-buggy and had the lap blanket pulled up to his chin. Lenny quickly sat up and stared at a huge round object in front of him, but couldn't think what it might be. He looked from side to side frantically, hoping to see something in the darkness that would give him a clue about his location. He could make out other large round objects here and there, nearby. All at once, he decided that they were big round hay bales.

"Smoky, are you eating hay? I fell asleep and you pulled us into someone's hayfield and started eating hay, didn't you?"

He got off the buggy seat and walked up next to Smoky to make sure his harness was on right and that nothing was amiss.

"I'm going to rein you up a little higher, Smoky. We need to get home before it gets light out."

Lenny tightened the strap that went from the top of his horse's head, down to his harness at the base of his neck. Lenny had learned that keeping a horse's head up high would encourage it to move faster. Smoky obediently made his way down a slope and back out onto the gravel road.

As it was really dark, it took the young man a few minutes to figure out exactly what road they were on. All at once, he saw a familiar bridge up ahead.

"Oh, good, we're not that far from home! Good job heading in the right direction, Smoky." He clucked and his horse set off in a quick gait, head held high. Lenny didn't have a watch with him so he rode along trying to guess what time it was. As they came down the last hill in front of Aaron Burr's place, Lenny could see a faint pink light on the eastern horizon. Smoky tried to turn into Junior's place out of habit, since he had lived on that farm for most of his young life. A few birds started waking up and chirped halfheartedly. He quickly unharnessed his horse and let him out to pasture.

Lenny slipped into the house and tiptoed upstairs. Every footstep creaked a little, even though the young man had learned which steps to avoid. There were two of them that were really loose and moaned loudly if they were used at night.

When the young man stepped into his room, Russell sat up and jumped off the bed as though Lenny was getting up.

"Shhh, Russell, I'm not getting up, I'm coming to bed."

Lenny had no more than stripped off his clothes and snuggled between the warm covers when he heard a "Cock-a-doodle-do." He lay still, hoping it was a false alarm.

Freddie the rooster was quiet for about ten minutes after Lenny lay down, just enough time for him to drift off into a comfortable sleep. Freddie crowed again and Lenny sat up.

"Rats, there is no sense in me trying to get to sleep now!"

He found his work clothes that Ruth had washed on Wednesday afternoon, knowing they would be wearing church clothes to the wedding on Thursday.

As they walked out to do morning chores, birds were singing their fully awake morning song. Lenny felt as if he hadn't slept at all, even though he knew he had been sound asleep for hours in the hayfield. He staggered through morning chores, eyes half closed. Mr. E stood perfectly still while he was being brushed. Lenny could almost imagine how good a currycomb felt as it scratched gently over the colt's neck, back, and hips.

He told his horse, "I've decided to tell Noey that I'll stay on here. I love this farm; besides, I could change my mind later. I could probably even sell the farm to some other Amish guy if I decide to leave." Suddenly Mr. E stomped at a fly or something, startling Lenny.

Lenny stopped in to check with Noey who was still milking Grace. He tried to think of how to tell his uncle that he decided to stay, but couldn't think of the right words. Noey was partially hidden by Grace, but he looked around past her tail enough to make eye contact with his nephew.

"Did you have some troubles last night?" Noey asked.

"Not really," Lenny hesitated to say more, not being sure if he should tell Noey what happened.

"Ruth thought she heard you come in just before the rooster crowed."

"Oh, that." Lenny shook his head and tried to act nonchalant. "I fell asleep driving home."

"Where?" Noey wanted to know.

"This is kind of silly, but I woke up in some farmer's hay field. Smoky was eating from a big round bale. I'm not sure how long I was there, but it must have been most of the night."

"I'm glad he didn't take you into a ditch, or run off." Noey's face seemed serious as he thought of other possible endings to Lenny's story. Suddenly, he chuckled. "I fell asleep one night on my way home from a Singing. I had left Ruth's house late after a long week of shocking oats. It had been so hot that whole week, and your grandpa had pushed Alvin, Jake, and I for days to get our oats shocked. I was hoping for a long Sunday afternoon nap, but that didn't happen because we had company over for lunch. By the time I left Ruth's that night, my eyelids felt like they weighed a hundred pounds each. I was driving an old horse named Charlie. He was such a good old horse we used to ride him without even using a bridle. We could just push on one side of his neck and he would turn that way. Push on the other side of his neck and he'd turn the other way. I knew he wouldn't run off with me, and I also knew that he could find his way home, so I let myself drift off." By that point in his story, Noey had finished milking Grace and stood up holding his bucket of milk.

"What happened, did Charlie take you home?"

"Not exactly," Noey replied, laughing. "I woke up to a funny noise. I sat up, looked around, and I was in my buggy on someone's front yard. A man was lifting up his garage door to get in his car." Noey hoisted up his bucket as he described the man opening his garage door. Milk splashed out and down his pant leg and onto the floor. Barn cats scrambled to lick up what had spilled. Noey chuckled and continued his story, as though nothing had happened. "That English guy stopped and looked at me and my buggy and called, 'Is everything okay over there, young man?' I scratched my head and answered, 'I think so?' I looked ahead at Charlie and realized he was grazing in the man's front yard. I was only a short way from Ruth's house. I must have fallen asleep right away and Charlie decided it was a good time to pull over and have something to eat." Noey and Lenny laughed together.

Lenny told his uncle, "I didn't have a good excuse like you. I was just kinda cold and I pulled my lap blanket up to keep warm. The next thing I knew, I was waking up in a dark place with some huge round thing in front of me. At first I couldn't think of where I was, or what that round thing could be. I slowly realized that I had been driving home and must have fallen asleep. It took a little bit before I figured out that I was in a hayfield. Smoky was reined up so he couldn't graze, but he could eat hay from a large round bale." Noey laughed again.

Lenny added, "I didn't know what time it was, but it started getting light as I got back here. I no more than got into bed and our rooster started to crow!"

Lenny and Noey laughed so hard that Noey spilled more milk, which made them laugh harder.

Lenny drove wagons with teams of horses and unloaded soybeans into Noey's grain bin. A corkscrew-looking object, called an auger, drew soybeans up into a log tube and dumped them into the top of their grain bin. The bean fields looked silent and dead until a person walked into them. Grasshoppers, crickets, and other bugs were everywhere jumping out with every step Lenny took. Grasshoppers sometimes leapt up as high as his face or arms and stuck until he brushed them off. Whenever the wind wasn't blowing, a rustling sound came from the dry beans, which Lenny discovered was the sound of bugs. As he drove horses back and forth with full wagons of soybeans, he kept thinking that one day this could be his farm. He looked at the little grandpa house, imagining Leah fixing a meal in the tiny kitchen. There was nothing he wanted more than to make this his home, Leah his wife, and stay in this Amish time zone.

Everything that had been green all summer faded to yellow or reddish brown. The center of Noey's soybean fields was first. If a person could have stood still for a few days, they would have witnessed a wave of color change. Like the stones Lenny had thrown into the river, sending ripples out in a circles growing until they reached the banks, so it was with the yellow in a bean field, spreading out until it reached the edges. By the time the whole field was yellow the center had turned rust-brown, and another wave began to grow. In a similar way, the clump of roots, visible at the base of Junior's cornstalks, turned yellow. That yellow climbed up the stalks, followed by a light brown. Those stalks had looked supple and green during summer months, but as time went by they became dry and crispy. If a person bumped against them, they crackled and broke. The odd part was that in a cornfield, the yellowing seemed to begin on the edges and move toward the center, exactly opposite of soybeans.

## Mystery Solved

Lenny led Misty under brightly colored trees between Noey's farm and Junior's. He walked into the lane about the same time as the milk truck arrived. Milkman Tom climbed out of his big white truck and waved to Lenny.

Lenny walked close by and said, "Hello, Tom, do you remember me from the summer I stayed at my Uncle Alvin's farm?"

Tom looked off to one side for a moment and then asked, "Are you the guy that took your Grandpa Jesse's horses to the horse pull?"

"Yep, that'd be me."

"You are from River City, aren't you?" Tom asked and Lenny nodded. Tom looked at Lenny's clothes with a puzzled expression. "Did you decide to join the Amish?"

"I'm thinking about it. I've been staying with Uncle Noey, who lives just beyond those trees." Just as he pointed, he noticed Two-Face heading toward him through the woods.

Tom took off his hat and slapped his leg with it. "Well, I'll be ... here comes Two-Face!"

"How do you know my cat's name?" Lenny asked with astonishment.

Two-Face ran up and began rubbing against milkman Tom's pant legs, while the friendly man petted the cat. By that time, Fannie Ella had joined them and listened to their conversation.

"I raised this cat from a kitten," Tom explained. "She accidentally got in my milk truck one day and came along on my route. She must have snuck out when I was picking up milk here. I asked all my milk customers, but none of them had seen anything of her."

Lenny laughed. "Well, she showed up at our place and we didn't know where she came from. Junior's little twin daughters, Edna and Elma, must have known her name because they saw her at my place and called her Two-Face. That's how I decided to call her that. I didn't know that they were trying to tell me that it was her actual name!"

Fannie Ella asked, "Is this the cat that had kittens in your barn?"

"Yes," Lenny answered. "Did you know that she belonged to Tom?"

"I never saw her," Fannie told them. "I knew there was a cat with kittens. If I would have looked at her, I would have known it was Tom's cat, Two-Face."

Tom looked really surprised. "So, she had kittens?"

"Yeah, she did. You can come and get them and take them all home if they are your cats," Lenny offered.

Tom shook his head. "No, Two-Face is smart. She must have been looking for a nice quiet farm home to raise her litter of kittens. Those kittens are better off here than in town, but when they get a little older, I might like to have one of the babies to keep."

"That would be fine," Lenny answered, "Come over anytime and pick one out. Several of them look exactly like their mother. There is a yellow one that I would like to keep, though."

Tom petted Two-Face and said, "That sounds great. Two-Face, you are a smart cat. There is no better place to raise a family than on an Amish farm."

They all headed back to work shaking their heads at the surprise information they had just learned. Misty clomped into Junior's barn and a loud whinny sounded. A huge black horse stomped in a stall, pawing straw and snorting. Misty noticed a pile of hay bales and pulled Lenny toward them by her lead rope.

Junior came in and asked, "What does Misty think of my new horse?"

"Eh, pretty hard to tell." Lenny looked at his filly munching on hay.

Junior put a lead rope on his big horse and led him out into the walkway. The big horse nickered at Misty. Misty seemed more interested in hay.

"Hum, maybe it is too late in the fall."

Sam came along and asked Junior, "Could you come look at a cow in our parlor? She is off feed and not milking too good."

"I'll be right back, Leonard. Keep an eye on these two."

When he came back he asked, "Didn't anything happen?"

"It might have. Fannie Ella asked me to help her pen up a loose calf, and so I was gone for a bit."

Junior shook his head and said, "We'll see what happens in the spring."

Lenny led Misty back through the trees. He thought about what happened a few weeks ago at Laidlaw's farm. He poured over the events of that night, remembering that he and his cousin, Perry, had thought they were just going to see if Laidlaw's big horse was the cause of Misty acting up. Laidlaw was a mean man, even though he had amazing horses. Lenny worried about the fact that Laidlaw charged huge fees for his big horse and that he wouldn't find it funny if he found out about what happened.

Lenny said to Misty, "How will I explain to everyone if you have a colt next spring? Maybe I won't be here to worry about it?" Misty pulled away from Lenny, but he held tightly to her lead rope and scolded her, "What's the matter with you?"

That evening Lenny told Noey and Ruth, "I have a great story for you two. You know that new cat that had kittens out in the barn?"

They both nodded and listened.

"I took Misty over to Junior's place today and their milkman happened to be there. Our cat came walking up and the milkman called her by name. I asked him, 'How do you know my cat's name?' He told me that it was his cat and he named it Two-Face when it was a kitten."

"What?" Ruth asked in bewilderment. "You both named the same cat Two-Face?"

Lenny tried to explain, "Actually, Junior's twins kept calling the cat Two-Face. I thought they were giving her a name; I didn't know they were telling me she was already named that."

Noey asked, "Did you offer to give the cat back to him?"

"Yes, but he said that Two-Face was smart to want to raise her family on the farm. He wants one of her babies when they get a little bigger. I told him to come by whenever and take his pick."

Noey, Ruth, and Lenny all laughed again and then headed off to bed.

Lenny couldn't get to sleep. He looked out through the curtains and noticed the moon hanging near the windmill. It had been full lately but it was starting to wane. He kept worrying about

Misty having a colt in the spring. For some reason the words of the plaque on Ruth's washroom wall kept coming into his mind.

*May the words of my Mouth and the Meditation of my Heart be Pleasing in Your Sight, O Lord, my Rock and my Redeemer.*

# CHAPTER 10

## Football Party

Saturdays were quiet on the Gingerich farm. Noey told Lenny, "My dad used to let us boys hunt or fish on Saturdays when we had our work all caught up. If you have anything you enjoy as a hobby, you should take time for that."

"Well, my favorite thing to do is working with horses. If you don't mind, I'd like to take Smoky out for a drive."

Noey laughed. "If that sounds fun, then by all means go take a drive."

Lenny couldn't believe how lucky he was. He had been trying to think of an excuse to get away for Justin's football party. He hurried over and picked Leah up at Beantown. The crisp air blew Smoky's mane and tail and Leah's covering strings.

"Do you think we should really be going to this party?" Lenny asked.

Leah nodded with an excited smile. "I can't wait to see Justin and his wife Barbie, and especially their baby boy. We don't have to stay long, but I really want to go."

"Okay. I just hope that we don't make trouble for ourselves by hanging around with these English kids. Justin is about as ornery as they come."

"Don't be so hard on him; he just wants us to see his new baby. After all, you are the one that talked him into marrying Barbie in the first place. If anyone asks us about being there, we can just say that we were going by and stopped in to see the baby."

Lenny nodded then asked, "Where should we say that we were headed? I mean, it's not that common for a couple like us to be headed anywhere together on a Saturday afternoon."

"I know there's an Amish fabric shop beyond Justin's place. We can tell them that I needed to get some fabric and you drove me over there. We can go there first and I'll run in and look at some material that I've been wanting to get anyway." Leah smiled, pleased with her idea.

"People will think that we were going to pick out material for a wedding,"

"And what would be so terrible about that?" All at once Leah looked put out. She folded her arms and leaned away from him. He tried to think of a way to explain himself.

"Everyone knows that I haven't made a decision about whether I'm staying on with Noey and Ruth. I haven't joined the Amish Church yet. What will people say if they see us buying fabric for wedding clothes?" As soon as he said it, Lenny knew he had made a mistake. Leah let out a sigh and refolded her arms like she was mad.

Smoky plodded on, clip-clopping on a dusty gravel road. Crisp cornstalks rustled with every breeze. The sound of multiple millions of cornstalks rustling almost drowned out Smoky's hoofbeats as they passed through a sea of brown cornfields.

Leah's cute voice asked, "Did you ever kiss Rebecca when you were dating her?"

"I wasn't really dating her!" he replied.

"Did you kiss her when you weren't really dating her?"

He could feel her staring at him with a look that meant he had better have a really good answer.

"Sort of…?" His voice trailed up like a question.

"Sort of? Either you did or you didn't! Besides, she told me that you did."

"Well, if she said that I did, why did you ask me?"

"I was hoping that she just said it to make me miserable. I guess she wasn't making it up after all?" She kept her glare going in his direction.

Lenny tried to think of what to say. Finally, he said quietly, "She asked me to kiss her and I thought that you were with Henry anyway. Didn't you kiss him?"

"No, I didn't kiss him because I liked you!"

"Why were you dating him if you liked me?" He thought he had found a way out of trouble, until he realized she was sniffling. He tried to look in her eyes, but she was turning away. He made an effort to console her. "It was only a half a kiss."

"What is that supposed to mean?"

"Well, when I went to kiss her, Tug and Train took the hayrack through some potholes in the road and she fell down."

She was quiet for a moment and then said, "At least I know that I can trust Tug and Train."

"Leah, you know you can trust me."

"Everyone was talking about you taking Rebecca to that wild party. Back when you and Noey were flooded in, everyone was talking about you and telling stories about all you had been doing."

"What?" Lenny turned and looked Leah in the eyes. "Who was talking about me?"

"Everyone!"

"Oh, great, what were they saying?"

Leah's body language told him that he was in trouble with her. She had her torso turned away from him and arms folded at her waist. He waited for her answer. "Rumors were going around that you took her to a party with English young folks and got her drunk."

"I didn't take her to that party. She went there on her own and I found her there and took her home!" He leaned over so he could see her face.

She unfolded her arms and played with her own fingers on her lap. Finally, she looked up at him and spoke kindly. "Leonard, you really shouldn't let people push you so much."

"Huh, what do you mean?

"You need to decide what you believe or want and stand by that. You let other people push you into doing things you don't want to do."

Lenny folded his arms and turned away from her. He looked across the quiet Iowa fields, wondering if she was right.

She spoke in a whisper, "Why didn't you just say 'I'm sorry'?"

"To Rebecca?" He asked.

"No, to me? Why didn't you just say, 'I kissed her and I'm sorry.'"

"Because I like you so much." He looked into her sweet eyes. "I didn't want you to think that I wanted to kiss her. I only want to kiss you. I'm sorry that ever happened, please forgive me."

"I guess it's okay."

Lenny told her, "Aaron Burr says that permission is for someone who didn't do anything wrong. Forgiveness is for those who did something wrong but ask to be forgiven. So don't say, 'It's okay' because it's not. Please just say, 'I forgive you.'"

"I do forgive you." She smiled and reached out and took his hand, squeezing it gently with her little fingers. When they were almost to the fabric store, Lenny pulled on Smoky's left line to turn him. Leah reached out and pulled on Smoky's right line, causing him to turn back onto the open road.

"Why did you do that? I thought we were going to stop at the fabric shop."

"I'm not going in there now ... I wouldn't want anyone to think that you decided to stay Amish or, even worse, that you might maybe want to marry me." Lenny laughed at Leah's cute pouty face and the way her voice lilted. She scolded, "I don't see any funny part about that!"

"It was just the way you said it and your accent."

"Oh, excuse me for being born Amish."

"Leah, please, we are almost to Justin's house; let's not go there mad at each other."

"Maybe you don't want your English friends to see you with such a plain girl."

"Look at me, Leah, I was wearing Amish clothes the last time I checked. Besides, I like you. I don't care what those kids think."

He had barely said those words when they found themselves pulling up to Justin's party. Music was blaring from Justin's big truck and Hawkeye football was on the screen. Lenny tied smoky to a telephone pole in front of Justin's house and the two of them awkwardly strolled toward a group of modern-looking people. At first nobody even seemed to notice they were there. They stood off to one side, watching two modern couples playing beanbag toss. They all held beanbags in one hand and beer cans in the other.

One of the girls noticed them and looked Lenny and Leah up and down, examining their attire. She didn't say anything. Lenny shifted his feet and Leah bit her nails. All at once Lenny heard a loud, "Lenny, you came!" Justin was right behind him and slapped him on the back.

"Hey, Justin! Do you remember Leah?"

"Yeah—hi, Leah, do you want to come over and talk to my wife, Barbie, and see our baby?"

Leah nodded with a big smile on her face.

They all walked over near the big-screen TV and looked at Justin's tiny baby who was decked out in Hawkeye black and gold. Leah tried asking questions about Justin Jr. but the football game was turned up loud and country music blared out of the big truck. Barbie pulled Leah by the hand and they headed away from the noise, obviously to have a conversation.

Lenny's focus was completely absorbed into the game. He hadn't seen a TV in a long time and Justin's was clear. The game was close and the Hawks were struggling to hang onto a lead. Lenny stood almost in front of the big screen, teeth clinched as his team fumbled the ball and somehow managed to recover it, barely escaping disaster. A timeout was called and instantly a commercial popped onto the screen with women in swimsuits. Lenny looked away quickly, not used to seeing all of that. He searched for Leah and saw that she was still over talking to Justin and his wife. Leah was holding Justin Jr. and had a sweet smile on her face. Seeing Lenny looking at her, she held the baby up for Lenny to see and smiled again.

Suddenly, the game was on again and Lenny sank back into it. The Hawks ran the ball several more times but came up a few yards short of a first down. Lenny glanced over at Leah and saw that Justin was talking to her and she was nodding her head. He wondered what in the world they could be talking about, but the game drew him in again. The Hawkeyes attempted a field goal and missed. They were ahead 10–7 and their opponents had the ball and two minutes left on the clock. All they needed was a field goal to tie the game, or a touchdown to win. Lenny stood still, unable to notice anything else around him as the Hawkeyes struggled. The other team moved the ball freely down the field. With only seconds left, they threw the ball into the end zone for a touchdown and win, but it was intercepted by a Hawkeye. Lenny jumped up and down and cheered with the other guys around him. They all gave each other high-fives and hollered. One of the guys tossed Lenny a beer and he caught it as a reaction. He looked over and Leah was standing quietly, holding the baby, watching him.

Lenny handed the beer back to the guy that tossed it and said, "Thanks, but I better check on my girlfriend." He headed over and said, "Leah, we should be going, shouldn't we?"

"We can stay longer if you want to." Her face seemed pale as she said it.

"No, I want to get out of here. I didn't know it was going to be such a party. I don't want anyone Amish to come by and see us here." He looked her in the eyes and Leah nodded.

She carried the baby over to his mother and said, "He is so cute! You must be so happy to have a new baby and everything."

Barbie smiled and said, "When are you two going to get married?" Leah shrugged and looked at Lenny as if he could answer that.

Lenny just laughed and told Justin, "Thanks for letting me come by and see the end of the game. It was a great one and I loved your TV, it's so big and so clear!"

"Thanks," Justin replied, smiling. "You two don't have to run off. Stay awhile and have a couple drinks!"

"Oh, thanks, but I need to get Leah back home before her family starts to worry about her."

Justin laughed and Leah's eyes got wide.

## An Awkward Ride

Lenny drove Smoky around the long way again, not wanting to drive past Noey's, Junior's, and Aaron Burr's homes. They rode along in silence, listening to rustling corn stalks.

Finally, Leah spoke, "You looked really happy when you were watching that TV game."

"Oh, that? I don't know why I get excited and act dumb when I watch a Hawkeye game, I don't really care that much about it."

"You looked like you really cared. You probably miss all of your old life, modern clothes, and music and all of that?" She sat with her hands folded in her lap and shoulders slumped.

"I guess I do a little," he finally admitted.

They pulled up to a stop sign where trees and bushes were near the road. Lenny had to stop Smoky to make sure no cars were coming and then clucked. Just as they rounded the corner, a horse and buggy appeared. It was Mose, the bishop, slowing down to turn.

"Leonard, Leah, how are you today?"

"We're fine," Lenny answered for the both of them.

"What brings you two out to this part of the country?"

Lenny tried to think quickly. "Leah wanted to go to the fabric shop."

"I see," Mose said with a smile and continued on his way.

Lenny and Leah rode on in silence, except for rustling corn stalks, until they came to Beantown where Leah's horse was waiting. As she crawled off the seat, she whispered. "Mose's sister owns the fabric shop." She quickly headed to her horse.

Lenny got off his cart to help her hitch her horse but she told him, "I can get this."

# CHAPTER 11

## Taffy Pull

Noey told Lenny, "There is no way we can feed up all these beans! Junior offered to trade field corn for some, but he doesn't need all of our extra beans, though. We'll haul some of them up to Yoder's and sell them, and use that money to buy more corn from Junior. He offered to sell us what he was going to take to Yoder's Feed."

It was fun for Lenny to drive Stone and Jim: they were beautiful dapple-gray horses and good-natured. Their hooves clomped along the road ringing out a merry song, followed by a deep rumbling of Noey's steel-wheeled wagon. Cornfields along the way were crispy-brown or already harvested stubble. Some of those fields had massive round bales of rolled up cornstalks useful for livestock bedding, serving as a reminder of cold winter days ahead. Once he finished unloading, Lenny hurried his horses back down the road, happy to reenter the quiet Amish countryside. He took a detour on his way home, stopping by Beantown to see Leah. Stone and Jim rested at the hitching rack, looking impressive. Tourists stopped to take pictures of them while Lenny went inside.

Leah pretended not to notice as he passed near her. Her dimple was sinking deep, giving away the fact that she more than noticed him. They tried their best to communicate without any Amish seeing it. She faced the shelves of dry goods and Lenny feigned shopping.

She asked him under her breath, "Are you going to the Hershberger's tonight for the taffy pull?"

"Didn't know about it," he whispered.

"Head over there about 7:00 this evening. I'll be there," she said, flashing her pretty eyes at him.

Lenny answered, "Okay." He headed over and picked up a Bulltown bar, paid for it, and headed out smiling.

## Left Behind

During lunch, Lenny asked his uncle, "Do you think I could try hitching up Mr. E with Misty this afternoon? I'd like to drive them together again."

"I don't know why not, they haven't given us any trouble when hitched with our older horses."

Winds continued blowing leaves in from the woods, pushing them across the newly harvested soybean fields. The leaves raced across the ground looking like a river, swirling in low spots and following the contours of Noey's field. Banks of dark, gray clouds marched in rows from the northwest, threatening storms.

Lenny pulled his jacket collar up and told his horses, "I wish I could wear a hooded sweatshirt, but for some reason Amish don't allow it."

A narrow river of small, gray birds flew over Noey's farm, reminding Lenny of a school of fish. The stream of birds flowed on and on and there seemed to be no end to their migrating flock. They moved together perfectly synchronized, yet not in a straight line but curving around trees, Noey's windmill, and barns. A solid V of Canada geese honked loudly as they winged straight south. A straggler flew a few hundred feet behind the large V, honking and flapping wildly as though fearful he might be left behind.

Lenny knew it was his last chance to flee before winter or make a choice to dig in and stay put. He thought about Leah and how sweet she looked holding a baby during the wedding, and how cute she smiled when he said in front of everyone that he wanted to sit with "Leah Yoder with the dimple." He looked at Isaac's grandpa house and decided to go tell Noey he would stay on permanently. He told Russell, "Maybe later in life, if we wanted to, Leah and I could leave the Amish. We could always sell this farm and use the money to start a new life in town, just like Justin suggested."

Russell sat and looked at Lenny with his head cocked, as though he couldn't believe Lenny would say such a thing.

Lenny hurried into the barn. He couldn't wait to talk to Noey, but stopped short. Hearing a strange voice inside, he stood still trying to make out who was talking. He strained his ears and listened closely.

"Of course he does, why wouldn't he want to be your partner? He's just sticking around here hoping to take your money. He probably wants to hang on long enough to get your farm, then he'll sell it and go back to the English."

Lenny's heart sank. He waited for Noey to reply.

"Leonard wouldn't sell this place, he knows that it was Isaac's farm and where my dad grew up."

The other voice replied, "I wouldn't be so sure."

It was quiet for a moment and Lenny thought maybe he should leave. Then the stranger added, "In the meantime, that guy is trying to take your farm and all of my inheritance. I'm just asking for a little money and you act like I'm trying to take everything you've got."

Instantly, Lenny knew that it was Davey W. talking to Noey.

Lenny headed back outside. He needed fresh air. He didn't want Noey or Davy to know he had overheard their conversation. He walked out to the cattle pasture and up the hill toward the little graveyard, with Russell at his heels.

They sat down together on the wooden bench for quite a while, before Lenny told Russell, "It is true what Davy said; I did think that I could sell this farm if I changed my mind about being Amish."

Russell looked Lenny in the eyes, listening. The little dog seemed to understand every word.

From the graveyard on the bluff, Noey's whole farm was visible. Lenny looked it over carefully, thinking about how attached he had become to the place.

"Is it bad of me to want this farm, Russell?" The little white dog cocked his head. His little black ears rose up a little as if trying to hear clearly. "I'm not trying to take everything away from Noey and Davey W., am I?"

## Swirling Winds

During the afternoon, winds picked up. Leaves raced along the ground, flowing like a river around Mr. and Misty's hooves. At times they swirled, dancing and rising up off the ground in tiny tornados about the size of a full grown man. Lenny's thoughts swirled within him as he thought about what Davy W. had said. He wished he could just run away; it was too hard to think everything through. At one point a gust of wind blew leaves sideways against Lenny and his horses. Some leaves flew overhead and Lenny realized they were birds, not leaves. A line of geese flapped past as Lenny watched. He said aloud, "I wish I had wings. I'd fly out of here with you, geese, and nobody would even know where I went."

Bringing in wagonloads of soybeans wasn't hard work, but it was made complicated by wind that never rested. It blew this way and that, covering over all sounds of birds or horses. Horse manes and tails lashed about. Lenny had to pull his hat down tight against his ears just to keep it from blowing away. His tight hat made it hard to think clearly. He thought about the lie he told Mose, about going to Mose's sister's fabric shop, and worried that may come up again. He looked at Misty and worried about how he would explain it to Noey if she had a colt in the spring. He unhooked an empty wagon and was heading over to hook onto a full one. Suddenly, without any warning, Mr. and Misty took off running. If he had been paying attention to what he was doing, he might have thought to seesaw their bits. As it was, there was too much slack in his lines.

Lenny began to shout, "Ho! Ho! Whoa!" but it appeared that his shouting startled the colts more than anything.

The young man felt a helpless sensation overtake him as he watched his horses gallop furiously toward a fence. His mind was racing enough that he had time to notice how impressively his colts moved, full of power and grace. In his panic, time seemed slowed down, and within seconds a multitude of thoughts crossed his mind. He thought of how much money he had been offered for his colts, and if they hit the fence, one or both of them could be seriously injured. He even thought that maybe if he died, he wouldn't have to make a decision about whether or not to stay Amish. Then he thought of Leah's sweet eyes and imagined her crying for him.

Lenny made one last attempt to pull the left line with both hands, a desperate bid to turn the runaways out toward the open field, his mind weighing out in a moment what he would need a lot of time to decide. Would it be better to hit a fence at this moment, or to drive his team out into an open field where anything could happen? He decided it was better to not hit the fence and let the rest play out. He yanked with all of his might on his left line and felt it give. At that moment he realized his driving line snapped. He felt himself falling backward, all of his weight instantly directed to the right line. Mr. and Misty turned right and pulled up to a stop just as Lenny fell back off his cart.

Unsure of what had just happened, Lenny got to his feet and heard himself saying, "Easy there, whoa. Easy there, Mr. E. Easy there, Misty!"

The colts stood in the corner of the field, where a north-south fence met up with an east-west one. Neither one of his horses had hit the fence; they stood there trembling. Lenny continued his soothing words. He was not sure if his colts would rear up and try to take off again, or if they might kick. He cautiously stepped near Misty's head, only because she was nearer to where he was. She raised her head a little as Lenny took hold of her bridle, and although he felt like shrinking back in fear, he knew he had to take that chance and held onto her. She reared up a second time and lifted Lenny's feet off the ground, but she came back down and stood calmly while he tied her to the fence. Mr. E also trembled as

Lenny took hold of his bridle. He didn't rear up, but sidestepped a little. Lenny smoothed his hand against Mr. E's thick black neck. It was difficult for Lenny to be sure if the trembling was in Mr. E's neck or in his own hand.

"Easy, Mr., easy."

Uncle Noey was standing right behind Lenny when he turned around. He no doubt saw the horses running away and came to help however he could. The older man spoke calmly, smoothing a hand on Mr. E's hip and unhooking the heel chains. Lenny followed suit and talked in gentle tones to Misty, while he reached behind her and disconnected her from the cart.

"What happened?" Noey asked his nephew.

"I'm not really sure." Lenny stood for a moment looking at his horses and then back at the field. There were divots in the bean stubble from horse hooves. He looked Noey in the eyes, searching for answers.

Noey wisely said, "Take a seat here for a moment, Leonard."

Lenny almost fell down as he sat on the cart. It all came back to him in reverse order and Lenny passed it on as he remembered it. "I know this: when we came close to the fence, I thought I've got to get these colts to head out into the open field or they are going to crash."

"Well, how did you happen to decide to turn them into the corner instead?"

"I didn't. When I pulled hard on my left line, it broke. All my weight then pulled on the right line and turned them into the corner of the field."

Noey shook his head in disbelief and tugged on his graying beard. He said, "I wouldn't have known that they would stop in the corner like that, but it sure worked out nice!"

Lenny didn't feel as positive as Noey, but he laughed and said, "I'm sure glad we didn't have Aaron Burr make us a new set of lines. If this old line hadn't broke, no telling what may have happened."

Noey nodded in agreement. "I've had lots of close calls where harness breaking seemed to save the day. Sometimes I wonder if new harness is a bad idea...."

They looked at each other and shook their heads at the same time. Noey asked again, "So, what happened that they ran off?"

"I'm not sure. I got a little careless seeing they have been working together so well. Maybe I wasn't paying attention like I should have been, but all at once they jumped and I couldn't gather my lines quick enough, and we were off to the races!" Lenny looked back at where they came from, hoping to see some clue to solve the mystery. "There were some dust devils kicking up leaves this afternoon, maybe one of those set them off?"

Noey nodded. "You have to stay alert whenever you're working with younger horses. They don't have the sense that older horses do and it's hard to tell what may spook them."

Noey's words hurt Lenny. He knew his uncle didn't say it to be mean, but he felt the last little bit of confidence drain out of his heart. He didn't want to be a horseman anymore. He didn't want to ever have to hitch up a horse again. They led Mr. E and Misty to the barn and took their harness off.

Noey told his nephew, "I guess you better head up to Aaron Burr's shop and pick up a new set of lines for your harness."

Lenny didn't care about the driving lines, but he felt it might be helpful to talk to Aaron Burr.

After putting his horses away, Lenny headed toward the house. He was just wondering if Davy W. was still around—when he met him coming out of the screen door.

"Hello, Davy!"

"I go by Dave now," was all he said and started walking away.

Lenny stopped him. "Hey, Dave, how's Herbie doing?"

"Why do you ask me?"

"Well, you guys went to River City together, didn't you?"

"No, I see him up in the city sometimes ... we didn't go up there together, though."

"Well, he left a note saying that you guys decided to move to River City together." Lenny examined Davy's face, looking for some kind of clue why he would lie about that.

Davy gave Lenny a disgusted glare and told him, "Well, your buddy is a liar."

Lenny watched Davy W. walk out toward the road in designer jeans and a shirt with the words, "Living the Dream."

## Taffy Fight

Smoky trotted quickly toward the Hershberger farm at dusk. Sunset was earlier than Lenny anticipated, because days were growing shorter as fall settled in.

Lenny's mind fluctuated between reliving a wild ride with runaway horses and pouring over the accusations Davy W. brought. Lenny told his horse, "I can't deny that I've been thinking about farming with Noey, but Davy W. made me sound like a real loser. I don't think I'm what Davy says I am ... maybe I am." Smoky picked up his pace. "I don't know what to think about what Davy said about Herbie. Davy pretty much told me that Herbie straight out lied." With those words Smoky broke into a gallop, which took Lenny by complete surprise.

"Easy, Smoky, easy." Lenny seesawed his driving lines, bringing his horse back to a trot. "I'm sorry, Smoky, I really need to pay attention to what I'm doing; my mind has been swirling lately." Lenny's mind went right back to the runaway with Mr. E and Misty.

Smoky trotted at a fast gait, clipping along at the same pace as leaves pushed by the wind. An open buggy was on the road ahead of Lenny's with three passengers. Lenny decided to see if Smoky could catch up with them. He kissed to him, "Get up, Smoky, let's catch that other horse!"

Smoky strode out with long steps and quickly shortened the distance between them.

Lenny was only hoping to test his horse against another. He was happy that Smoky was catching up, but when he realized it was three girls in the cart ahead of him, he wasn't as excited. As he drew nearer, he realized it was Leah and her sisters, sitting shoulder to shoulder on a small bench seat without a backrest. Their covering strings were blowing behind them, and long aprons strings flapped under little bows tied at their waist. Lenny smiled at how cute they looked. He let Smoky continue to shorten the gap between them. He realized Leah and her sisters were caught up in a conversation and that, together with the wind, kept them from noticing Smoky was right behind them. Lenny was laughing out loud when the sisters finally felt Smoky's warm breath puffing behind them. They all three jumped and let out a scream.

Leah scolded, "Lenny, what on earth are you doing?"

He couldn't stop laughing, his mind replaying how adorable they looked when they jumped and squealed. Ruby and Rachel looked back with smiles, but Leah's face was stiff. They pulled into a short farm lane lined with carts and buggies, horses tethered all along the fence. They tied their horses side by side.

Ruby said, "I like that Smoky. He is such a fast horse, but yet you can trust him."

Rachel agreed with a nod, "Yeah, most fast horses are high-strung and wild."

Leah didn't say anything. She picked up a sack of taffy-making supplies and headed on ahead of them into a white farmhouse. Lenny looked at her sisters and raised his eyebrows. They both smiled.

At the Hershberger's, Lenny was able to forget about his troubles. The house was full of young folks all talking and laughing. Young men stood in small circles having a conversation about picking corn. Lenny found his cousins, David and Perry.

He told them, "I just scared Leah and her twin sisters a few minutes ago."

They grinned and nodded for him to tell more.

"I came up behind them on the road with Smoky. He caught up to them before they knew we were behind them. You should have seen them jump when they finally did see his nose right behind them." They all three laughed, until they heard Leah's voice right behind them.

"It wasn't that funny." She said something more in Dutch about how dangerous it could have been, but Lenny didn't understand it all.

When she walked away, Perry asked, "What's wrong with her?"

"I don't know," Lenny said. "She has been grouchy lately."

The young women crowded in the Hershberger kitchen mixing up taffy. When they brought out big bowls of warm, gooey taffy, the young people got busy buttering up their hands to keep it from sticking to them. Leah took Lenny's hands in hers and made sure he had thoroughly buttered between his fingers.

Rosie commented, "Are you two holding hands or what?"

Leah blushed and explained, "This is Lenny's first taffy pull. Somebody has to help him know what to do."

Taffy-pulling seemed to be an opportunity for young men to almost hold hands with young women. A girl would hold her clump of taffy and a boy would pull from the middle of it with one hand. The young female would use her free hand to pull from between his hands, and he would use his opposite hand to pull from between hers. Lenny had to watch some of the others for a short time before he understood what he needed to do. The motion of it reminded him of the Scrambler ride at the State Fair. Once he got on to it, it was fun and they all laughed and visited while they pulled taffy. Boys lined up on one side, girls opposite them. Lenny noticed the guy beside him had rough hands with tractor grease in every crevice. After they had pulled a batch and put it together, the guy with dirty-looking hands said. "Hey, I had a Band-Aid on this finger, but now it's gone!"

Everyone laughed and one of the girls said, "We'll see if we can find it when we're cutting up the taffy."

Lenny's cousin Sam was pulling taffy with a girl at the far end of the room. Leah whispered to Lenny, "I think Sam and Barbara will get married soon. Do you see how they are looking at each other?"

"Huh, I didn't notice it," Lenny answered, and Leah scowled at him.

They all buttered up their hands again and started in pulling more taffy. Leah looked in Lenny's eyes without any expression on her face, no dimple in her cheek. The other young people were talking and laughing as they pulled taffy, but Lenny and Leah pulled like it was a job. They pulled more vigorously than needed, almost yanking it out of the other's hands. There was nothing said between them about it, yet a message somehow was conveyed. Lenny felt as though they were working out some kind of struggle on an emotional level and he wasn't even sure what it was. Leah didn't give in. She appeared determined to prove that she could hold her own and not back down. Taffy twisted and turned between them. Suddenly, Leah's sister Ruby spoke to them in a whisper, "This is supposed to be fun."

Leah didn't look away from Lenny as she asked, "Why?"

"You two look like you're fighting each other instead of having fun with it," Ruby answered.

When she said it, Leah let go of her grip on the taffy and slowly walked out of the room. Lenny handed his clump of taffy to Ruby. "Sorry about that, Ruby." She looked at Lenny with a questioning brow, and he shrugged his shoulders and headed for the door.

A girl spoke loudly, "Don't worry about that Band-Aid, I just found it in the piece of taffy I was eating."

Everyone laughed. Even though it was funny, Lenny didn't feel like laughing. He slipped out and headed for Smoky. He heard the door bang shut a second time and footsteps behind him. He stopped and let Leah catch up with him.

"What's the matter, Leonard?"

"Well, for starters, Mr. E and Misty ran off with me today."

"I guess I don't blame them."

"What is that supposed to mean?"

"They can feel what I'm feeling!" Leah paced for a moment then added, "Your heart and mind are somewhere else."

"That's not true."

"Leonard, tell me what is going on?" Her face wasn't visible in the dark night, making it easier for Lenny to be honest.

"Leah, I have to go see if I can find Herbie. I won't be able to have any peace until I find out what happened with him."

"What did you tell Noey?"

"I said that I need just a little more time to make up my mind."

"Lenny, you can't keep putting it off forever."

"I just need to talk to Herbie."

"That's not all, is it?"

"Did Fannie Ella talk to you?" he asked

"No, why? Does she know something I don't?

"Eh, no—she thinks she does. She thinks she knows everything." Lenny let out a chuckle to try and break the tension. Leah didn't laugh.

"Why don't you just say it, Leonard? Why don't you just tell me that you want to go home?"

"I really do want to talk to Herbie. I just have to know why he left." Lenny felt sure his explanation was enough.

Leah moaned, "Leonard...," in a long drawn out way.

"Now you sound like a catbird yowling in the summer," he teased.

"That's not funny! Don't try to be funny right now. I don't think you should go after Herbie. Ruby told me that he promised her that he would come back."

"Well, he's not coming back, though, is he? I'm tired of waiting for him and I'm worried about Junior's family and your sister Ruby."

"You're more worried about Ruby and Fannie Ella than me!" she shot out.

Lenny was stunned. He was just getting ready to ask more, but the house door slammed again and Ruby's voice called out, "Leah, are you out here?"

"Just a second, Ruby, I'll be right there," Leah called, and then turned back in Lenny's direction. "Just go … and don't bother to come back."

Lenny watched Leah disappear into the darkness before he headed over to untie Smoky. On his way home, his mind raced. Winds swirled around him, leaves spinning within those gusts. He couldn't stop thinking about what Davy W. had said. He wondered if Davy was right. Maybe after he joined the Amish, he would start wishing to be English. He didn't want Leah to leave her family. He didn't want to disappoint Noey and Ruth, but he was afraid that it would only get worse if he joined the Amish. He wanted to go home and just see what he thought of the English life one last time before he made his choice.

Lenny said to Smoky, "I wish I could run away in the night without telling anyone that I'm going!"

Just then a big gust of wind blew a limb from a tree and Smoky took off. Lenny held tightly to his driving lines and focused on keeping his big buggy horse between ditches as they rounded a curve. When the road straightened out, there was time enough to think of more than just staying on the road. Lenny remembered to seesaw his driving lines and at the same time spoke a firm

"Whoa!" He felt Smoky give his head and slow back into a trot. The young man didn't speak any reassuring words, nor did he chide his horse. Instead, he set his jaw and kept his lines pulled up tightly. He knew it was uncomfortable for Smoky but he didn't care, he was too frustrated with everything to worry about whether or not his horse was comfortable.

Smoky trotted briskly into Noey's lane. He puffed in deep breaths that billowed out like smoke in the coolness of a late fall evening. Lenny unhitched and unharnessed his horse without speaking one word to him. Instead of his usual ritual of grooming his horse after taking off the harness, Lenny turned Smoky out without currying him at all. He hurried through cold gusts and blowing leaves into the house. Noey and Ruth were already in bed. Russell followed Lenny upstairs and jumped onto the bed. As Lenny got under the covers, he whispered to his dog, "I don't think Leah likes me anymore." Russell's tail made a thumping sound against the blankets, but Lenny couldn't guess why Russell would wag his tail at those words. He drifted off to sleep, hearing Leah's voice, "Just go … and don't bother to come back."

# CHAPTER 12

## The Last Straw

In the morning, Lenny let in all of his horses like usual. He didn't bother to brush Smoky, Misty, or Mr. E. He didn't speak to them or even look at them. Instead, he fidgeted with Train's harness, making sure it was adjusted the way he liked it. He watched the kittens chase crickets. Mice and other creatures apparently thought Noey's barn would be a safe place to spend the winter, but several had already learned that they were mistaken.

Noey finished his chores and came to check on Lenny. He looked at the line of heavy-boned draft horses. "Which big team do you want to hitch your colts with?"

"I'm planning to use the four big horses."

"Tug, Train, Stone, and Jim?"

"Yeah, I just don't feel like messing with those colts today; I hope you don't mind. I'm tired of feeling on edge, like any moment my horses might be running away with me."

Noey was too nice to ask questions. He stood looking at the line of horses as though he may say something; however, after pulling on his beard for a while, he said, "Okay, I understand."

Lenny's four-horse-hitch pulled a loaded wagon of corncobs into Noey's corncrib. He called "Whoa!" and all four horses stopped and stood looking out of the open doors, watching cattle nosing through leaves that lay beneath empty trees. Lenny hooked his wagon box to ropes that were attached to a pulley system and he pulled a main rope, which hoisted the front end of his wagon up slowly. Corncobs began tumbling out of his wagon and down into a funnel-type shoot, drawing them toward a gas-powered elevator that took the cobs up high and dropped them into the corncrib. This was a noisy job, unlike most of what he was used to doing on an Amish farm. It was a relief every time the last cob fell into the elevator and Lenny could shut down the noisy motor, untie ropes that held his wagon's front end up, and drive his four-horse-hitch back out into wide open fields.

All morning Tug, Train, Stone, and Jim pulled full loads of corn to Noey's corncrib and Fannie Ella took wagonloads to Junior's corncrib with a tractor. Junior and his son Henry were both driving small tractors with corn-picking heads attached to their front end. Fannie Ella took wagons from Henry, who seemed to get his loaded faster. Lenny needed more time because he was driving horses and his corncrib was further away. Junior puttered along at a steady slow pace. Lenny ended up waiting on him at times. He didn't mind; he enjoyed watching the whole thing. All the fields were shades of browns and yellows that matched what leaves were left in trees beyond the field.

On his way out to Junior's cornfield and back, he crossed paths with Fannie Ella. She looked cute in her Amish dress, driving a small steel-wheeled tractor that was pulling a full load of corn toward Junior's corncrib. Lenny's next trip out into the cornfield, he got there and Junior didn't have a full wagon ready to go back yet. Lenny tied Train to a fence post and walked through crunchy corn stubble up to the highest spot of Junior's field. Canada geese flew overhead honking loudly. Yoder Towers stood off behind the geese, causing the young man to think of Leah, whose home was beyond that. Her words rang in his ears. "Just go … and don't bother to come back."

Junior's tractor sputtered, eating up two rows of corn at once. Three pointed cones attached to the front of the tractor pushed between cornrows, chewing cobs off and spitting them into a shoot that dumped them on a small wagon pulled behind. Something glimmered in the corner of Lenny's eye, drawing his attention to where he had seen Fannie Ella heading toward home with a full load of yellow corncobs. A strange heap of something lay with a wheel spinning. For a moment, it didn't mean anything to Lenny. All at once he hollered loudly, *"Fannie Ella!"*

Lenny's four-horse hitch raised their heads quickly as Lenny jumped up and down, waving his arms at Junior until he knew the man saw him, and then ran faster than he ever remembered running in his life. He never remembered unhooking the empty wagon or untying Train, but he must have because a wagon wasn't behind him as his horses galloped toward the road. Lenny's ears were still pounding from his mad dash to get his team, making everything else seem silent. His mind raced, trying to guess what may have happened with Fannie Ella. He somehow had time to notice that his four galloping horses reminded him of an old movie he had seen about firemen driving horses. Lenny realized he was still flapping his driving lines at their backs, even though they were racing at a full gallop toward an overturned tractor and wagon. He snapped himself out of a frenzy long enough to talk kindly to his horses as he drew them to a stop and heard his own voice say a deep, calm, "Whoa!"

Lenny rushed down beside the overturned wagon, stumbling over corncobs, until he could see Fannie Ella lying quietly under the tractor.

"Oh, dear God, please help! Please Lord let her be alive!" Lenny crawled on his belly to her and touched her shoulder, "Fannie … Fannie Ella … are you okay?"

She moaned and spoke in a pitiful voice, crying, "Herbie. Help me, Herbie, something hot is dripping on me."

Lenny immediately realized she was pinned down by the tractor. He dug his fingers in dirt, scratching his way back out from under the tractor and unwrapped the chain that was always looped under his cart seat. He quickly and carefully chose a place to hook his chain, jumped onto his seat, and called to his horses, *"Get up…! Get up!"*

He felt his cart jolt under his behind, flipping him into the air. As it happened, he knew instantly that he had not made sure his cart was straight away from the load as Grandpa had warned, "The power of the horses will flip a cart if it isn't straight away." He felt himself let out a, "Humph!" as he landed on his belly and face.

Lenny jumped up quickly, happy to find that his cart was still upright and his horses still attached to the tractor by his chain. He said aloud, "Well, now my cart and chain are good and straight to the load!" He gathered the lines that lay behind his horses, climbed on his seat, and called to them again, "Get up! Stone, Jim, Tug, Train ... get ... get ... get!"

All four horses dug hard. They all had years of experience with pulling big loads and they knew how to crouch and lean without losing their footing. They never did come up, but kept their bellies low. Lenny heard a deep moan from Stone, and he knew his horse was reaching the end of what he could do. Tug shook his mane and Train snorted. Lenny called one last, "*Get!*" before looking back and realizing the tractor was upright and had slid sideways a few feet onto the road.

"Whoa! Good job, guys!"

He jumped down and saw a man was running toward them from a big pickup truck. The man rushed down to Fannie Ella and began looking her over. He calmly told Lenny, "I'm a first responder. An ambulance is on the way. Maybe you better tie your horses before it comes racing up here with sirens blaring."

Lenny nodded and hurried to his horses, unhooking them from the tractor. He drove them quickly up Junior's lane and tied each of the four horses at a stout hitching rack.

Lenny raced up to Ruby's door and opened it, calling as calmly as he could, "Ruby, please come quickly!"

She must have noticed something unusual in his tone, because she came running with fear on her face.

"I think she's okay, but Fannie Ella had an accident with the tractor."

Ruby and her flock of daughters ran out of the lane as an ambulance came along crying loudly. By the time they all got close enough to see what was going on, Fannie Ella was on a stretcher and talking to the paramedics. Junior was with them. He looked at Lenny and said, "Maybe you paramedics better have a look at that young man while you're here."

Everyone looked at Lenny. Junior-Ruby asked, "What happened to you, Leonard?"

"Nothing—why?"

"Your nose is bloody and you're all dirty!"

"Oh, when my horses first tried to pull this tractor over, my cart jumped and bounced me off." He wiped his nose with the back of his hand and smeared blood.

They all stood and looked at the tractor and the place where Fannie Ella had been lying. Henry said, "It's real lucky that when you were pulling the tractor over, it didn't fall back down on her."

Lenny's heart started pounding in his chest. That hadn't even occurred to him. His thoughts swam around in his head and his stomach churned. He looked where Fannie Ella had been lying and imagined what that scene might have been if his horses had failed. He walked away. He didn't know where he was going, but he had to leave. He hurried over to where his horses were waiting and untied them. He drove through the field where he had been bringing loads of corn between Junior's and Noey's. When he was almost all the way to the barn, he wondered if he was supposed to have stayed and finished hauling corn. He couldn't think clearly. He wanted to go back and ask, but it was too late. He knew he didn't want to look Junior in the eyes after what Henry had said. "What if…."

Lenny walked out in the cattle pasture for a while, as though checking on his steers. He didn't even look at them. He thought about seeing the tractor upside down. He went over everything he could remember about what happened, between seeing that awful sight and when he pulled the tractor over with horses. He worked through all the scenarios of what he should have done and what could have happened if the tractor had toppled back over onto Fannie Ella. He spoke to himself aloud, "I should have waited until someone else came. I wish someone else had said, 'Pull that tractor off her!' Then, I would know that I did the right thing."

Lenny ran up the hill to the little graveyard. Wind blew through boughs of a pine tree. As Lenny passed by, it slapped him in the face, almost knocking him off his feet. He didn't remember climbing the fence—he found himself kneeling down by Grandpa's grave.

"Grandpa, I wish I could talk to you! I know you would have answers for all of my questions. I know God has the answers, but you are both in heaven and I'm stuck here on earth."

Lenny stood up and said, "I'm going back home."

He climbed over the fence and started edging his way down the hill. He slipped and tumbled the rest of the way down, crashing into a few tree trunks. He didn't feel it, or care. He made his way to the house and Ruth met him at the door.

"Oh, Leonard, come in here! Let me clean you up a little." She took his arm and pulled him toward the washroom sink. She dabbed a towel into water and washed his face. "I heard you were a hero this afternoon and pulled a tractor off Fannie Ella."

"I shouldn't have done it! What if the horses couldn't pull it over, I might have killed her!"

"What are you talking about? You pulled the tractor off and she's safe. We got word from the hospital already, and she is safe!"

"After it was all over, Henry pointed out that I'm just lucky the tractor didn't come back down on her. Why did I think I had to be the hero and save her, what if I would've killed her?"

Aunt Ruth looked Lenny in the eyes, "Now, Leonard, you can't do that to yourself. Don't ask, 'What if?'"

"Junior's family must all be thinking that what I did was really foolish. Why didn't I wait until someone else came and helped decide what to do? I'm not a hero at all. Like Henry said, I'm just lucky."

"I'm going to go get bathwater ready. You get some clean clothes to change into." Ruth's kind eyes made him feel worse, because he knew that he was planning to leave.

After a bath, Lenny got ready for bed. Russell climbed up and sat beside Lenny, with his chin on his paws. "I don't belong here, Russell. I'm not an Amishman, a farmer, or a horseman; I don't even know what I am." Russell scooched up by Lenny's face and licked his cheek.

# CHAPTER 13

## Penny for Your Thoughts

After morning chores, Lenny untied Penny and led her out of the barn. Russell followed them as they headed through the woods between his home and Junior's farm. When he passed the chicken shed, he saw Herbie's beehives. Two white boxes sat perfectly still—no sound, no movement.

He told Penny as he walked, "I'm going to ask Fannie Ella to take care of you while I'm gone. I know that if she is around you even a little bit, she will fall in love with you." Penny's dark eyes looked at him, as if she hoped he was right.

Fannie Ella's six and eight-year-old sisters were pushing a wagon across the yard. Lenny stopped to speak to them. "I'm going to be gone for a little while. I'm planning to ask Fannie Ella to watch my pony while I'm gone. I know she can't do it yet, but will you girls take care of her until Fannie Ella feels better?"

The little girls took Penny's lead rope and smiled. Both seemed more than happy to take care of a pony. Blue and Tick didn't bellow the way they used to. They did jump off the porch and lope toward Lenny, sniffing his pant legs. Russell ran in circles around them and under their long legs.

"Russell, you stay out here with Blue and Tick while I go in to see how Fannie Ella is doing."

Lenny knocked on Junior's door. His little twin daughters came running and opened the door. They jabbered out Dutch phrases that Lenny couldn't understand. He tried to speak to them in his own broken version of Dutch, but he couldn't tell if they understood him or not. Junior was in his chair reading from his paper.

"I came to check on Fannie Ella. How is she doing?"

"She seems to be fine, thanks to you, Leonard."

"After everything was over, I wondered if it was bad that I tried pulling the tractor off her with my horses. If the tractor had come back down on her ... it could've been bad." Lenny said and watched Junior's face to see his reaction.

"When trouble comes, we react. You did what you felt was best at the time, and God honored your intentions by giving you success."

"Did you think it was a mistake?" Lenny had to know what Junior really felt.

Junior took his paper and folded it neatly before giving an answer. "If I had been driving that team of four horses, I would have done exactly what you did."

"Thank you, Junior, I've been worrying about it."

Ruby came into the room wiping her hands on her apron. "Why don't you go upstairs and say hi to Fannie Ella? She is getting along fine and might even enjoy some company."

"I don't need to bother her. I'm just so happy she is okay and wanted to check in with you all."

"Go ahead, Leonard." Junior's voice was calm and firm. "Go and talk to her for a few moments. That will cheer her up."

"Okay."

Lenny headed up the steps, listening to each one creak as he went. Fannie Ella's door was open, and Lenny could see her lying under her covers looking out the window. He knocked anyway.

"Come in," she said matter-of-factly.

"Hi, Fannie Ella. How are you feeling?"

"Fine," she said without much expression.

"You really scared me, Fannie Ella. I can't lose you—I've already lost my best friend Herbie, and you are about my next best friend."

"What about Leah?" she asked quietly.

"She is my special friend, that's different." Fannie Ella looked toward the window. Lenny changed the subject. "Did you know that when you were pinned under the tractor you called me Herbie?" Lenny chuckled, hoping Fannie Ella might find it funny, too.

"You looked like him. It must have been the teardrops in my eyes," she answered soberly.

Lenny felt bad that he had said anything about it. He didn't think she would remember that moment. He walked to the other side of her bed and looked into her eyes.

"Fannie Ella, I'm leaving in the morning to go talk to Herbie. I have to try to talk him into coming back to the Amish."

She didn't respond, but lay looking beyond him toward the window. Finally she whispered, "I'm afraid Herbie won't come back, and…."

"Don't worry, Fannie Ella. I will try to convince Herbie to come back, even if I stay there." He looked at her even though she didn't look back at him. A teardrop rolled down her cheek, but she didn't move.

"I brought Penny over here. Will you take care of her while I'm up in River City?"

"I guess so," she said without emotion.

"I know you can't take care of her right away, but I asked your younger sisters to watch her until you can get on your feet again. I will pray that you get better real soon. Will you pray for me and Herbie?" He watched to see some kind of answer. She didn't turn her head, but wiped the tear off her cheek with her nightgown sleeve and nodded her head slightly.

Lenny walked back downstairs and Fannie Ella's mom said, "I'll bet she was happy to see you?"

"I don't know. She seems so sad. I don't think I cheered her up too much."

Junior looked at Lenny with his dark serene eyes. "I'm sure she was happy to see you, Leonard. Thank you for stopping by."

Lenny walked slowly back through the trees between Junior's place and Noey's. There were almost no leaves left above him; they were all underfoot. Every step crunched loudly. He clomped up the porch steps and peeled off his coat. Ruth was in her kitchen stirring something that smelled wonderful. He asked, "What is it with these girls? I don't understand Leah or Fannie Ella."

"Today's little girl is tomorrow's woman. Today's woman was a little girl yesterday."

"What does that mean?" He watched Ruth stirring a pot on the stove.

She set down the spoon and wiped her hands on her apron. She looked Lenny in the eyes. "A few years ago Leah was playing with dolls; a few years from now she will have babies of her own. It's the same with Fannie Ella. She seems like a little girl to you, but inside she is growing up."

Lenny looked at her; his face must have given away that he still had no idea of what she was talking about.

"Fannie Ella has feelings for you."

After supper, Lenny went back out to the barn to be alone for a while. He sat on a bale of hay, watching little Lion tormenting his sisters. The little male kitten stalked and pounced on the smaller females, biting them until they yowled. It usually made Lenny laugh, but he didn't even smile. Two-Face rubbed her sides on Lenny's pant legs and meowed. He didn't bother to reach down and pet her. He took his lantern and headed toward the house through cold wind and blowing leaves. He could see the dark forms of horses just beyond the barn, but he didn't look in their direction or speak to them.

When he stepped into the house, little Russell jumped off the couch and ran toward Lenny, his little dog toenails clicking on kitchen linoleum. Lenny popped open the porch door and let Russell out to take care of business one last time before going to bed. When they climbed onto his bed, Lenny whispered, "I'm going to the English world tomorrow, Russell. I doubt that I'll come back." Russell's little white body was curled up, but his head was facing Lenny. It was too dark to see his face and eyes. "I'm sorry, Russell. I will miss you something terrible, but you need to stay here and keep Noey and Ruth cheered up."

Wind whistled through tree limbs and moaned through cracks in the windows as Lenny tried to sleep. He kept hearing Leah's words. "Don't bother to come back." He almost got up and lit his lantern to see if she was in his room—her voice sounded so clear.

# CHAPTER 14

## River City

Big Red walked slowly, and Noey did nothing to change that. Normally Noey would have at least clucked and shook his driving lines. If Red didn't respond to those cues, Noey often spoke to his horse with a chiding voice and said, "Red, step up there!" Lenny expected his uncle to do one of those things at any moment, but it never happened. The sky was filled with billowing gray clouds that seemed to grow taller and darker as Big Red neared the bus station. Lenny thought he heard his uncle muttering, and then concluded that there was a deep rumbling in the clouds. When Noey pulled his horse to a stop at the bus depot, he did speak.

"Tell Jake and Susan that Ruth and I said 'Hello.'"

"I will," was all Lenny could force out of his tight chest. He wanted to hug Noey and promise to return in a few days, but he doubted it would turn out like that.

"You better catch your bus," Noey told his nephew.

"Okay. Thank you for everything, Noey."

"Thank you, Leonard." Noey looked older than usual.

Lenny had planned to say more but he was afraid to speak or tears might have followed. Finally, he took a deep breath and blew out slowly in an effort to calm himself enough to talk. "I'm going to do everything I can to encourage Herbie into coming back home."

Noey nodded and tilted his hat so that Lenny couldn't see his eyes, and then walked back to his buggy.

Lenny found a seat in the bus—near a window—and watched Big Red pull his uncle's buggy through the streets of Bulltown. Raindrops streamed down the windows, making it hard to see out, and eventually covered the glass, blurring everything. The bus lurched forward. Through his foggy window, Lenny could see Noey's buggy leaning, lopsided with only one passenger. Wind blew harder, causing a pelting rain that clicked as it hit, which drew a shudder out of Lenny, imagining a cold buggy ride. He nestled back into the comfortable bus seat and smiled as heat blew through the vents. When Noey could no longer be seen, Lenny watched the last few Amish farms disappear into the distance. He felt a sadness, and at the same time a relief. He thought, *No more runaway horses in bad weather, no more worrying about my lie to Mose, and no more worrying about explaining about Misty and Laidlaw's horse.*

Modern music jingled softly. Lenny didn't recognize the song but enjoyed hearing drumbeats and guitars. He drifted in and out of sleep. At one point he heard Leah say, "Don't bother to come back." He sat up and looked around before realizing it was only a dream. The next time he drifted off, he could see her sweet smile and dimple. Finally, he sank into a deep sleep.

Deep mumbling rumbled and Lenny felt himself waking up. He didn't open his eyes right away, but listened. Someone with a very low voice was speaking and Lenny tried to make out if the words were in Dutch or English. He couldn't comprehend what was being said. He sat up abruptly and looked around. An old lady in the seat across the aisle was looking right at him and spoke, "We are having quite a thunderstorm for this time of year." Lightning flashed, followed by a sharp clap of thunder. Lenny jumped and then looked around to see if anyone had noticed. A college-age couple were behind the old woman, passionately kissing. Lenny did a double take—he hadn't seen any such thing in quite some time. He leaned back on the comfortable seat and looked ahead at the road. It was dark and rain soaked, winding like a river. Cars and trucks flowed along ahead of them, kicking up a mist as they sped forward. Windshield wipers clicked rhythmically.

River City rose up from the horizon as the bus drew near. Gray clouds hung just above the tallest buildings and rain drizzled over concrete parking lots. It seemed the rain would wash everything off, but instead it left a dirty film. Puddles had brightly colored rainbows of purple, blue, and green, which looked pretty at first, but the colors were an indication that gas and oil were everywhere. Lenny had forgotten that River City was such a concrete fortress. He stepped off the bus and walked through the quiet streets. As a boy he thought it was a long way between downtown and home, but after checking fence all summer, he realized it was a short walk.

Lenny clomped up the steps of his parent's house and caught himself ringing the doorbell. Ashley came to the door.

"Lenny, why are you ringing the doorbell? Come on in!"

"Hi, Ashley, did you know that I was coming home?"

"Yeah, Mom said that you were coming home today. It's so good to see you!" By that time, Lindsey and his mom had come into the room. They both gave him big hugs and said, "You sure do look Amish."

His sisters asked a million questions; before he could fully answer one, they were already asking another. Lindsey asked the big one: "So, are you actually thinking about staying Amish?"

"Well, I was considering it. Uncle Noey and Aunt Ruth are really kind people and they want me to stay on with them. Noey offered to make me a partner in his farming operation and … that was really nice of him."

"We hear you have a girlfriend," Ashley said, looking through her blond curls that hung on her forehead.

"There is someone special," Lenny said. His sisters smiled at each other. "That's a big problem, though. I don't want her to leave her Amish family behind, and she wouldn't anyway. So, if I want to be with her, I'd have to become one of them."

Lindsey brushed her dark hair out of her eyes, "You don't want to be Amish, Lenny. There are lots of cute girls here in River City who would be willing to date you. If I were you, I'd talk to Herbie about why he left the Amish. There must be something bad that made him leave."

Lenny's mom gave him a look she used to have when he had done something wrong. "Leonard, I really want you to talk to Pastor Jeff. Please don't make a decision about joining the Amish without at least talking to him."

"Okay, Mom, I'll talk to him."

"Would you mind talking with him this afternoon?"

"I'm not in that big of a hurry." He shrugged as he said it.

"I called him and mentioned that you were going to be in town. He told me he has an opening in his schedule this afternoon. He'd like to talk to you."

"When's his opening?" Lenny asked.

"In fifteen minutes."

## Pastor Jeff

Lenny followed Pastor Jeff into his office. The pastor took a seat behind his large mahogany desk, a wall of books behind him. The younger man sat and surveyed the library. He noticed university diplomas framed and hanging as credentials; one was inscribed with the words "Master of Divinity." On the pastor's desk were pictures of him with his wife and children, taken on a beach vacation somewhere exotic. Pastor Jeff put his hands together, fingertips touching fingertips, index fingers on his chin. With a look of concern, he asked, "Lenny, you're not really thinking about becoming Amish, are you?"

"Well, I guess I did think about it."

"Oh, Lenny, I can't even imagine why you consider doing that! Do you even comprehend what their theology entails?"

"No, not really ... I mean." Lenny hesitated a second and the pastor interrupted him.

"No, I'm sure you don't. With a thorough education of systematic theology, I see their religion as very problematic. They have a completely law-based relationship with God. Do you know what I mean by that?"

"I think."

"They are attempting to gain God's favor by works. Salvation is by grace, through faith, we receive the gift of God because of believing in Christ. Jesus paid for our sins when he died on the cross and we can't add anything to what he did by how we dress, or what kind of vehicle we drive. Do you understand that?"

"Yes, I get that, but...." The pastor's phone vibrated and he looked at it for a moment. "Eh, Lenny, I'm getting a text message from my son—do you mind if I quickly text him back?"

"Oh, no, that's fine." Lenny sat quietly listening to the pastor clicking in a message to his son.

Finally the pastor looked up and said, "Lenny, I must say I'm very concerned about you."

"Well, I just have one question, though." Pastor Jeff looked so intelligent behind his desk Lenny wished he hadn't said anything. He had opened his mouth, so he felt he had to speak. "Is there something bad about Amish clothes? I mean they are modest—surely God has no objection to them?"

"Of course, he does. Those clothes are works, and Amish people are attempting to earn salvation by what they wear. That, in itself, is more offensive to God than immodesty." Pastor Jeff's face was red and upset.

Lenny thought of Grandpa, his kind eyes and gentle wisdom. He looked down at his black Broadfall pants that Aunt Ruth had made and the suspenders that held them up. Pastor Jeff was confident and it didn't seem possible that there could be any argument Lenny could win with him. The younger man nodded and said, "Okay, Pastor, thank you."

"I'm glad we talked, Lenny. If you want to know anything more come to me—I will be happy to explain everything to you. Please excuse me now, I need to give my son a call—our car is giving him troubles."

"Okay; thanks again."

"You're welcome, Lenny."

Lenny and his mom rode toward their home in silence. He couldn't stop thinking about what Pastor Jeff had said about Amish clothes being works. As he was trying to sort it out, his mom spoke and changed the subject.

"Did you know that Herbie goes to our church now?"

"Herbie Gingerich? My friend Herbie from Bulltown?"

"Yes, that Herbie—do you know any other Herbies?" she asked, laughing.

"Ah, no, I guess it just surprised me."

"When he came to our house to get the title for your old car, we invited him in for supper and we had a long conversation. He really likes you, Leonard."

Lenny nodded. "Yeah, we got to be really good friends before he left the Amish. Did he say why he left?"

"No, I guess we just assumed he wanted to be free of all those strict rules."

Lenny nodded again. "I really want to talk to him—do you know where he lives?"

"I sure do," Susan replied, smiling. "He lives a few blocks from our house with Nate and Brian and some other guys from our church."

"Nate and Brian?" Lenny asked with his nose crinkled up. "Those long-haired guys with a Christian rock band? They're both covered with tattoos, and their whole world is skateboarding"

"Well, don't judge them for their looks; at least they are Christians. You should be happy he is hanging around with boys from our church."

"I guess?"

## Skateboarders

After supper, Lenny told his mom, "I think I'll head over to Nate and Brian's place. I want to talk to Herbie."

"Great! Maybe if you move back here you can spend time with those Christian boys. I'm sure that would be a nice group of friends." Susan seemed sincere as she spoke. Lenny didn't say anything; he only nodded and went to his bedroom. He looked at his old clothes hanging in the closet and then at his suspenders and broadfall pants. He thought about changing but didn't quite feel comfortable with it yet.

Nobody was home at Nate and Brian's place. Lenny walked on a few more blocks until he came to the skate park. Skateboard wheels rumbled each time one of the daredevils zipped past. He searched their faces and recognized the guys who went to his parent's church, but he didn't see Herbie. One shaggy-haired young guy took more chances than the others, impressing Lenny with his skateboarding skills. He flew through a tunnel type area and then up a ramp, flipping his board in the air at the top of his jump. During that jump, Lenny noticed the shaggy-headed guy didn't have any shoes on even though it was late fall. Instantly Lenny realized it was Herbie.

Loud clattering noises snapped Lenny out of his shock. Herbie overshot a jump and his skateboard sailed one way while he somersaulted the other, rolling head over heels and ending up on his feet. All the other guys cheered and Herbie calmly picked up his skateboard and walked toward Lenny.

"I can't believe you're hanging out with these guys, Herbie!"

"They told me that they were your friends."

"Yeah, they are, but beware: these guys will push you to get a tattoo if you're not careful."

Herbie laughed. "No, don't worry I wouldn't do that."

Just then the other guys came over and one of them said, "Hey, Herbie, did you show Lenny your new tattoo?" They lifted up the back of Herbie's shirt, revealing a windmill tattoo. The frame of the windmill doubled as the A in the word "Amish."

The crowd of guys all cheered and one of them explained it to Lenny, "Herbie has a trademark skateboarding move; we all call it the Amish Windmill."

"Why Amish windmill?" Lenny asked.

"Well, Herbie is an Amish guy and he jumps and spins like a windmill."

"I'll have to see that sometime," Lenny told him. When the other guys returned to their skateboarding, there was an awkward silence. Lenny took a deep breath and dove in. "Did you know about Fannie Ella's accident?"

"Yeah, my mom called me."

"Really? Does your mom know your phone number?"

Herbie laughed. "No, she called me at work. I sent a postcard, telling them that I work at Bud's Auto. I guess she called information or something and got the number."

"What did she tell you about it?" Lenny bit his lip while he waited for Herbie's answer.

"She told me about you being a hero and pulling the tractor off her with your horses. And she told me that Fannie Ella is okay and everything."

"Well, I'm no hero. I should have waited until someone else got there to help. I'm just lucky that my horses pulled it all the way over, or...." Lenny looked down at his work shoes.

Herbie reached over and pulled one of Lenny's suspenders and snapped it. "You worry too much, dude!" They laughed together like they used to.

"So, Lenny, are you going to stay Amish?"

"I don't know. It's a tough decision. How about you, Herbie, are you gonna stay English?" Herbie shrugged his shoulders and laughed. Lenny nudged him, "Poor Ruby has been awful sad without you."

"Well, like you said, 'It's a tough decision.'" They laughed a little and then stood without talking. They both stared at their feet and smoothed gravel in the driveway.

After a few minutes Lenny asked, "Do you ever see Davy W.?"

"Yeah, Davy has a girlfriend now. Did you know that?"

"Yeah, I heard. Is she a nice girl?"

"I guess so. She is one of those hipster girls, if you know what I mean. She has tattoos, a nose ring, dyes her hair black, and smells like a bowling alley!"

Lenny laughed. "Smells like a bowling alley?"

"Yep, kinda." Herbie wrinkled his nose. His phone chirped and he stared at it. "Oops, looks like I'm getting a snap."

"A snap?"

"Yeah, don't you know about Snapchat? People can take short video on their phone and send them to each other. " Herbie grinned and held up his phone.

"Oh, yeah, I know about it. I guess I'm just a little surprised that you are getting snaps and everything."

"Check this out—it's a snap from Davey W. right now." Herbie held up his phone and Lenny could see a video of a worldly-looking girl with a Dalmatian puppy. Herbie said, "That's Davy W.'s girlfriend. It looks like they got a new dog."

"So you guys get together sometimes?" Lenny asked.

"Yeah, Davy works at a gas station not far from here. Over on the corner of Friendship Avenue and 5th Street."

"Oh, I know where that is. Maybe I'll head over there and talk to him for a bit."

## The dog and boy

When Lenny walked in, Davy said loudly, "Hey, you're the first Amish customer I've had since I started working at this gas station."

"Hi, Davy, how are things going for you in the city?"

"Okay I guess, but call me Dave. Are you going to move back up here, too?"

Lenny bit his lip, trying to think of what to say. "I came home to figure things out. It's a tough decision."

"Not for me, it wasn't." Davy's face was covered with a huge smile. "This lifestyle is so much easier and now that I met Courtney, I wouldn't go back for anything."

"Hey, Dave, I felt bad about how that all went with Leah Yoder."

Davy W. laughed out loud. "Don't think twice about it, Leah can't hold a candle to Courtney.... Oh, I guess I shouldn't say that ... are you and Leah dating?"

"We were, but things weren't going that great. When I told her that I was coming up here, she really got out of fix." Lenny tried to change the topic. "I heard you and your girlfriend got a Dalmatian. Those can be really nice dogs."

Davy W. looked out through the plate glass windows of the gas station. "Yeah, the best dog I ever had was a Dalmatian. Well, it wasn't actually mine. You see, I found a lost dog. It was the kind I really wanted and we hit it off right away. I called him Spot and he followed me everywhere for several weeks. It was a strange feeling, like we already knew each other somehow. Dad made me put an ad in the Bulltown News, saying, 'Found, Dalmatian, contact Noah Gingerich, Route 2.' For a few days nobody came by, and I thought I was gonna get to keep Spot for sure. Until some old geezer showed up one day wearing bib overalls, a ponytail, and beard. He called my dog over to his side and Spot ran right up, tail wagging, and jumped in his truck. The guy laughed and told us, 'I'm gonna have to beat some sense into that dumb dog.'"

Lenny listened quietly, even though he had already heard Noey and Web tell the same story. Davy seemed strangely sad, considering it was all about a dog he only knew for a few weeks. Then he added, "I didn't know it at the time—that bum was my real dad."

Lenny felt his own eyes almost pop out of his head before he caught himself. He tried to calm his facial expression. "How did you find out that Web ... I mean, that he was your dad?"

Davy's temper flared, "I didn't say Web—who told you that?"

"Eh, nobody told me ... it's just that Noey had mentioned that you found that dog and it turned out to belong to Web. And when you told the story, I put two-and-two together."

Davy looked perturbed and set his face, stubbornly refusing to talk anymore.

"Davy—I mean Dave—I had a conversation with Web a few weeks ago. He told me that he has cancer. I didn't have any idea that he was your real dad at the time, but he asked me to tell you that he was sorry about taking that dog away from you. I thought it was strange how sad he was, but now I get it."

"What does he care?" Davy's face seemed bitter. Lenny wanted to try and help if possible.

"Web has changed!"

Davy looked at Lenny with a skeptical smirk.

Lenny repeated, "No, really, I believe his being sick has made Web think about things differently. He told me he was sorry for what happened with my dad and mom."

"Why? What happened with your dad and mom?"

Lenny shrugged, knowing he couldn't get out of explaining. "Just that he had sorta tricked them into getting together when they were young."

"Oh, great, just one more bad thing my dad did."

"Really, Davy, he told me he was sorry. Besides, if he hadn't done that, I wouldn't have been born."

Davy nodded but didn't seem too convinced.

"Hey, here she is now!" Davy pointed out the window and there was a hipster-looking girl, just as Herbie had described, with a Dalmatian puppy.

Lenny introduced himself as he walked out, "Hi, I'm Davy's cousin, Lenny."

"Oh, yeah, I've heard about you."

"I hope it was good," Lenny said, and Courtney just laughed. A whiff of bowling alley passed by, reminding Lenny of Herbie's description. He had to cough to keep from cracking up. He gathered himself and said, "You really should go meet Davy's parents, Noey and Ruth. They are about the best people you will ever know."

She looked surprised. "You mean Dave's parents? He doesn't say much about them."

"Yeah, Dave's parents. Sorry about that, I'm used to calling him Davy W."

## Sisters' Help

That evening, Lenny lazed around on the couch. His sisters asked him questions.

"What is this Leah like?"

"She is pretty and sweet. But she is really mad at me right now."

"Why? What did you do?" Ashley looked at her brother out of the corner of her eyes.

"First off, I didn't ask her to marry me. And then to make matters worse, I told her that I wanted to come up here to River City."

"Did she say that she was mad because you didn't ask her to marry you?" Lindsey asked.

"No, but she kept hinting at it and I pretended not to notice. I didn't know what to do. The last thing she said to me was, 'Just go … and don't bother to come back.'"

"She didn't mean it," Ashley told her brother. "She was just frustrated because she likes you so much."

"I don't know. I think she meant it. Anyway I need to figure out why Herbie left the Amish before I can decide about where my future is headed; maybe there is something I need to know."

Lindsey asked, "Is it possible that Leah knows why Herbie left the Amish and that's why she didn't want you to talk to him?"

"Ooh, I never thought of that. I wanted to ask him. I just couldn't make myself pry into his business that way."

"Maybe you could hint around; like ask him, 'Do you know any reason I shouldn't become Amish?' and see what he says."

"Good idea, but I don't know if I can trust Herbie. He lied to me about Davy and my car, he said that he left the Amish with Davy W. and Davy told me they didn't leave together."

"Do you believe that Davy?"

"Good question. But, today Herbie told me that he wouldn't ever get a tattoo, and then his buddies pulled up the back his shirt to show me his new tattoo right after he lied to me about it."

Everyone headed to bed. Lenny was comfortable in his old bed, and he even turned on some music to listen to while sleeping. He couldn't help but think about what his sisters had suggested. Maybe Leah knew something about why Herbie left the Amish and she was hiding it from him.

# CHAPTER 15

## Windmill

Around noon the house phone rang. Ashley answered it and called, "Lenny, it's your friend Rick. He wants to talk to you!"

Lenny took the phone. "Hello."

"Hey, Lenny, I heard you were back in town. I'm going out to the mall, do you want to ride along and hang out for a while?"

"Yeah, sure, that'd be great to talk to you, and I haven't been to a mall lately."

"I heard about that," Rick said, laughing. "Well, it won't take you long to get back with normal life."

Lenny chuckled along with him. "All right, when are you going?"

"In about an hour. I'll pick you up on my way"

"Okay, thanks, Rick. See you soon." Lenny told his sisters, "Rick wants me to go to the mall with him. I want to go, but I don't want everyone to see me in these suspenders," he announced, snapping them.

"Put on some of your old clothes. Nobody here cares anyway," Lindsey suggested.

"Yeah, I guess you're right." Lenny headed to his closet and found a pair of jeans and a Hawkeye T-shirt.

"Now that is more like it," Lindsey said, smiling, and pulled her long dark hair back into a ponytail.

## The Mall

Crowds of shoppers filled the mall. A stream of people flowed like traffic, those on the right going one direction, those on the left the opposite way. A colorful and modern-looking crowd coiled around a center fountain. Bright lights and background music created atmosphere. All of Lenny's friends gathered in an open food court area where there were numerous fast-food options available. They all chose exactly what each one wanted to eat. When everybody sat down, Lenny bowed his head out of habit, and then caught himself and looked up. Everyone else had already torn open their prewrapped food and started eating.

Rick was well known and liked, and soon a whole group had gathered around their table, talking loudly about college, sports, and music. Shelly, Lenny's neighbor while growing up, asked, loud enough for all of them to hear, "So what's this I hear about you becoming Amish, Lenny?"

"What are you talking about?" He felt his face get hot. "No, I'm not gonna be Amish!"

"Well, look at this." She held up her phone and showed everyone a picture of Lenny in Amish clothes.

"Who sent you that?"

"It's going around; everybody has seen it." He looked at the others to see their reaction, and they were all laughing.

After that Lenny sat off to one side while his friends texted other people, oblivious to what was going on around them. They occasionally laughed and nudged a person next to them to show them something funny on their phone. Lenny quietly watched a crowd of modern people walking past. He felt alone even though he was in a crowded place with all of his old friends. He was surprised when he noticed a couple of Amish women in the stream of English people. He watched to see what they were up to, or if he knew them. The women stopped by an ice cream shop and purchased cones. They looked so old-fashioned and out of place with their long dark dresses, black shoes, and stockings. He caught himself feeling sorry for them.

All at once, Lenny realized they were standing with his sisters. Ashley called, "Lenny! Hey, Lenny, we're looking for you!"

Leah and Ruby followed his sister as she walked straight toward Lenny and his friends. He glanced around for a place to hide and tried to stand behind a large trash receptacle to keep the Amish girls from seeing him in his modern clothes. He wasn't sure if he was more embarrassed being seen by Leah and Ruby in his old clothes, or of Leah and Ruby's Amish clothes.

The Amish girls stood back awkwardly. Ashley and Lindsey headed into the pool of visiting young people. Lenny hid behind a few of the other guys, feeling naked in his T-shirt and jeans. Leah and Ruby averted their eyes, as if embarrassed. Ashley stepped near Lenny and whispered, "Your girlfriend and her sister came to our place looking for you. They are so cute!"

"Well, maybe we should take them back to our place," Lenny suggested. His sisters nodded in agreement. Lenny told his friends, "Hey, guys, I think I'm gonna take off with my sisters."

Shelly stood up and gave Lenny a big hug. "It was so good to see you again, Lenny! Give me a call sometime."

The others all chimed in, "See ya around, Lenny!"

Ashley and Lindsey talked casually as they walked through the mall, but the Amish girls lagged behind, especially Leah. Her face looked pale and her ice cream cone began to melt, dripping over her fingers. They pushed through the current of English people and passed a clothing store with a huge picture of a scantily dressed woman. Lenny did a double take, surprised by the picture. He glanced at Leah, who had a pale, expressionless face.

Lenny whispered to Ashley, "We need to get these girls out of here—they don't need to see all of this."

As they were getting near the car, Ashley whispered to Lenny, "So, I suppose you want to drive?"

"No, go ahead, you can drive."

"What—really?" Ashley looked at Lenny to see if he was serious. He tried to give her a look that said, *Don't ask any questions.*

Lenny and Leah rode together in the back. She leaned against her door and looked out of the window. Without turning toward him, she asked quietly, "Who was that girl that gave you a hug?"

"Oh, that was just Shelly. She lived across the street from me when I was growing up."

## Awkward

When they got home, everyone went inside quietly. Lindsey turned on the TV, obviously not sure of what else to do, to break an uncomfortable silence. Ruby and Lenny's sisters were soon caught up in a *Lifetime* movie.

Lenny and Leah kept meeting eyes awkwardly until he finally suggested, "Let's play a game of Ping-Pong."

The Ping-Pong table was in an adjacent room where they could almost be alone. At first they focused on the game, with him showing her how to play and explaining the rules. He slapped the ball hard, bouncing it against one wall. As he went to pick it up, it rolled near Leah's feet, and when he stood up to hand it to her she was staring into his eyes with a pleading look. "Please, Leonard, come home." The corner of each eye held a teardrop, and her lower lip was trembling.

"I will." He instantly knew that his words sounded unconvincing.

Leah turned and hurried out of the room. He followed and watched her hurry up the steps, obviously heading to Lindsey and Ashley's room.

Ashley followed Lenny back into the ping-pong room and asked, "Is Leah okay?"

"Huh, Leah?" He knew what Ashley was asking but he needed time to think of an answer. Ashley nodded, waiting for him to speak. "Well, not really."

"Lenny, don't lose her. Leah is so sweet. It's crystal-clear how much she loves you, and what a doll!"

"I'm just so mixed up right now. I wish these girls wouldn't have come up here to River City!"

"Lenny, they came to get you and Herbie."

"I know." Lenny headed out into the other room and asked, "Ruby, can I talk to you for a minute?" Ruby stood up right away and followed him into the Ping-Pong room. "I suppose you are wanting to go see Herbie, huh?"

Ruby's face lit up in a flash, and she nodded.

"Okay, I will take you over there this evening, but in the meantime, could you do me a favor?" She nodded again. "Could you please talk to Leah … tell her that everything is going to be okay?"

"Are you coming back then?" Ruby smiled excitedly.

"Well, maybe." Ruby's face turned as pale as Leah's had. He told her, "I'm really going to try and talk Herbie into it."

"You did talk to him already, didn't you?" she asked with pleading eyes.

"Yeah; for a little bit—yesterday."

"Did you encourage him to go back home?"

"Well, I asked him about it, but…." Ruby rushed out the way Leah had and hurried upstairs. Lenny headed out into the living room and found his sisters with tears in their eyes. "Now what's the matter with you girls?"

Lindsey blew her nose and said, "Oh, we were just watching a movie about a guy that leads a girl to believe he is going to marry her, then disappears from her life."

"Oh, great!"

## Supper Time

Lenny's mom came home from work with a large sack in her hands. She said to Lenny, "Ashley called me and said that your girlfriend and her sister showed up here. Do you think they will stay long?"

"No, I'm going to try and send them back home as soon as possible. Their parents are probably not happy about it, and they have no business in town anyway."

Susan's eyes open wide as she looked at her son. "Leonard, why would you say that? They have you and Herbie here, maybe they're thinking about leaving the Amish. The least we can do is to make them comfortable here and hopefully they will decide to stay in River City."

"I guess you're right. Maybe I should be happy they are here. I was just thinking that they came to try and guilt me and Herbie into going back."

"Maybe they did, but we can always try and encourage them to think about staying around here," she whispered and winked at Lenny. "Now, call upstairs and tell the girls to come down and eat. I brought home some Chinese food. Your dad should be here any minute."

Everyone sat around the table quietly, except for Lenny's mom who tried to keep a conversation going. "Have you girls tried Chinese food before?" They both shook their heads and nibbled at a little rice. "I'm sorry if you don't like it, my family always thinks of it as a treat. Do you young people have any plans for this evening?"

Lenny answered for them, "I'm going to take them over to Herbie's place after supper. We want to stop in so they can see where he lives and find out what he has planned for this weekend."

"I know what he has planned," Lenny's mom got excited as she talked. "One of his roommates is getting married! Leonard, you know Kenny Smith from church? I'm sure that all of you would be welcome to go to his wedding. I am on the committee that is providing the meal!"

"What, Kenny is getting married? You have to be kidding me—I didn't think that guy would ever get married."

All of the women looked at Lenny as though offended. Susan scolded him. "Leonard, why would you say that?"

"He's just such a punk. He's one of those skateboarding guys with all those tattoos and everything."

"He is a Christian, Leonard. Don't judge him by his clothes and hair," his mother chided, and then asked Leah and Ruby,

"You girls would enjoy going to a wedding at our church, wouldn't you?"

The Amish girls' eyes lit up for the first time all day as they nodded. Both Leah and Ruby started eating Chinese food as though they were hungry.

"This Chinese food is actually really good," Leah said.

When they had cleaned up the last of the rice, Lenny suggested, "We should have an after-meal prayer; that is something we do in Amish homes." Lindsey and Ashley looked at Lenny as though he was speaking Dutch. Jake and Susan bowed their heads, being familiar with that tradition.

## PlayStation

Lenny drove, and his female Amish guests rode quietly in the front seat of his parents' car.

"I'm not sure what things will be like at Herbie's apartment. I don't know his cell phone number, so I couldn't call him and tell him that we are coming over." He looked over at Ruby and she was glowing for the first time in months.

Lenny found Herbie's house and parked near a driveway full of cars.

"Do you girls want me to go to the door first and tell him that you're out here?"

"No, I think we should surprise him," Ruby said, laughing.

"We will," Lenny agreed.

They all three stood at the door in their Amish clothes and Lenny knocked. A guy with dyed black hair and a nose ring opened the door. He quickly pushed it back shut and they heard him holler over thumping music, "Hey, Herbie, I think your family is here to get you!"

A few moments later, Herbie appeared in the doorway scratching his head.

Ruby smiled wide and said, "Hello, Herbie!"

"Oh, hi. Come on in, we're having a bachelor party, but you all can come on in for a bit."

It was dark inside as the visitors stepped into the room, except for a blue glow emanating from a large screen TV. The strange light flickered on a group of guys sitting in a semicircle around it, their faces made to look alien. Music, gunshots, and occasional explosions came from speakers encircling the room.

Ruby asked, "What is this, a movie?"

"No, it's a game. That's a PlayStation," Herbie explained.

They all watched while a musclebound man shot bullet holes into an SUV. Another of the game's characters was a scantily dressed woman who ran around with her hands outstretched, pointing a gun and shooting at everything that moved. Every now and then she fell or bumped into something and let out a "Humph!"

Lenny was struggling to make any sense out of what he was seeing. Leah and Ruby watched with horrified looks on their faces, until Lenny called them aside.

"Do you girls want something to drink?"

They both nodded and followed Lenny into the kitchen. Half-empty pizza boxes were sprawled out on a table, and pop cans were everywhere.

Herbie stepped into the kitchen with them and said, "You can have some of that pizza if you want!"

Leah and Ruby looked around at the mess and shook their heads. Ruby picked up a can of pop and opened it with a loud snap. "So, this is where you've been living?"

Herbie answered, "Yeah, I signed a yearlong lease with these guys."

"Does that mean you have to stay here for a full year?"

"Yeah, unless I find someone to take over my place on the lease."

Lenny noticed Ruby looking at Herbie's English clothes and shaggy hair. Loud music and gunshots from the other room made things even more awkward. Lenny pointed toward the TV and said, "These girls don't need to see all of that."

Herbie looked into Ruby eyes. "I'm really happy to see you, but I have to stay here. A bachelor party is an English wedding tradition and I'm in the wedding. You all can come to the wedding tomorrow if you want." Herbie turned to Leah and Lenny, "We could all hang out together there!"

Ruby's eyes lit up. "Okay, we'll see you there!"

The three Amish visitors passed back through the living room just as a huge explosion erupted and a fireball lit up all the English boys' faces. The guys glanced up awkwardly but didn't say anything.

As soon as they drove away, Leah said, "Lenny, don't treat us like little girls."

"What are you talking about?"

"You are trying to keep us away from everything. We want to see what it's like to be English, and we can't do that if you're trying to shield us from it." They rode along in a silent glow of dashboard lights, until Leah suggested, "Turn on your music if you want." Lenny pushed the radio knob and drumbeats thumped out and a female singer's voice filled the car. Lenny was embarrassed about how suggestive her words were and he quickly shut it off. Leah scolded, "Leonard, we are not little girls."

Ruby said quietly, "I'm worried about Herbie." No one spoke for a few moments and then Ruby added, "I don't think those boys are a good influence on him."

"They're not," Lenny agreed. "Did you know that they talked him into getting a tattoo?"

Leah asked, "What kind of a tattoo?"

"A windmill, on his back, and the frame of the windmill is the A of the word Amish." The girls didn't say anything more and Lenny wished he hadn't told them.

# CHAPTER 16

## English Wedding

A sound woke Lenny out of a deep sleep. He rubbed his eyes and felt around his feet for Russell, and then remembered that he was not at Noey and Ruth's. He lay still wondering what it was that woke him up. He felt himself drifting back into his dream where he left off—sitting on Noey's steel-wheeled manure spreader. Tug and Train were in front of him, Misty on the right of Train, and Mr. E on the left of Tug. Lenny admired his massive horses for a moment and then looked up at Noey and Ruth's house. A light twinkled in the window and Lenny missed Aunt Ruth. His dream shifted and he realized the twinkling light was coming from the little grandpa house. Smoke rose up out of its small chimney and Lenny could almost smell the hickory. He clucked to his team, but they didn't move. Lenny wanted to get to the little house more than anything. Something deep inside his heart was pulling him—he wasn't sure what. He couldn't believe that his horses weren't obeying his command. He shook his lines and kissed to them again. This time he woke to his own kissing sound and felt his arms moving to shake the lines. He sat up on the edge of his bed laughed at himself.

Leah and Ruby were excited about going to the wedding. They both came out wearing their nicest Amish dresses, crisp and clean. Lenny wasn't sure what he should wear. After talking to Pastor Jeff he was planning to wear his modern clothes, but with Leah and Ruby along, that didn't seem right. He came out with his Amish Sunday suit. Leah and Ruby didn't seem surprised. His sisters' eyes popped and they scrunched up their noses.

Lindsey whispered, "Do you have to wear that suit?"

## Wedding

Organ music filled the church with a wedding song. Herbie was the first groomsman and he walked down the aisle in a sharp tuxedo. A pretty bridesmaid in a strapless dress held onto his arm and they made it about halfway to the front before his bridesmaid stumbled in her high heels. Everyone gasped as Herbie caught the girl before she hit the ground. The bridesmaid was laughing and leaning on him as she regained her composure and continued down the aisle. Lenny looked past Leah and saw Ruby watching without expression, and then she looked down at her apron and smoothed out a wrinkle. Several other couples followed with fancy tuxedos and strapless dresses. The couple to be married both had long dyed hair, his black and hers blond. Her lacy white wedding dress didn't cover her shoulders or tattoos.

Pastor Jeff stood in front of the church with a wedding party all lined up, bridesmaids on one side and groomsmen on the other. The pastor's voice boomed out through speakers and echoed.

"Marriage is an example of Christ and the Church. In the beginning, 'The Lord God said, "It is not good for the man to be alone." So the Lord God caused the man to fall into a deep sleep; and while he was sleeping, he took one of the man's ribs ... then the Lord God made a woman from the rib he had taken out of the man, and he brought her to the man.'" Genesis 2:18–22

"In a similar way, the Church came from Jesus side. Adam's deep sleep represents the death of Christ, and like Adam, Jesus' side was pierced and blood flowed out. Through that blood, God has fashioned a bride for his Son."

Lenny looked over at Leah and she was completely focused, listening to the sermon. Lenny was thinking about how worldly the bride and groom looked with their modern clothes, dyed hair, and tattoos. He heard Pastor Jeff say, "Don't let anyone judge you about what you wear; we are under grace not law," Pastor Jeff said. "You who are trying to be justified by law have been alienated from Christ; you have fallen away from grace." Galatians 5:4

Lenny picked up a Bible from under the bench in front of him and found the passage. He read it for himself, and felt even more confused. As soon as the service ended, Leah and Ruby went directly over to talk to Pastor Jeff. Lenny took a sip from the drinking fountain and watched from a distance. After what Pastor had said a few days ago about Amish clothes, Lenny couldn't help but be embarrassed for the girls. They looked so out of place with their coverings, long dark dresses, and aprons. While they talked, Jeff's wife came over and joined them. Lenny was embarrassed about her short hair and slacks as she visited with Leah and Ruby.

He could only imagine what the girls thought about a pastor's wife dressing like that at a wedding.

He slowly walked closer and overheard Pastor Jeff ask, "So why do you wear those white bonnets?"

"The Scripture says, 'Women should have their heads covered when they pray,'" Leah answered matter-of-factly.

Pastor seemed stumped for a minute. He regained his confidence and said, "The old law is done away with by the new Covenant."

Ruby reminded him, "The verses about coverings are in the New Testament."

Pastor changed the subject, "So, Lenny, are these girls your cousins?"

"Um ... no ... they are from the Bulltown area though."

"Oh, one of these two must be your girlfriend?"

Lenny felt his face get hot when he saw Leah blush. He didn't know how to tell Pastor Jeff that it was a subject not openly discussed among the Amish.

Ruby changed the topic again, "We really enjoyed your sermon. It was quite different than what we're used to ... but it was really good and helped me understand some things that I always wondered about."

When they all got back into the car, Lindsey told her brother, "We girls want to go back to our house before the wedding reception. We want to...," she hesitated and then said, "freshen up a little."

"Is there time?" Lenny asked.

"Of course there is. We won't need a lot of time, just stop by our house."

## Wedding Reception

Lenny didn't want to change out of his Amish Sunday clothes. He liked his black pants and vest that Aunt Ruth had made for him, and they seemed more fitting than anything else he owned. He waited patiently for the girls to get ready, lounging on an overstuffed sectional couch and watching football on TV. Someone walked into the room quietly, causing Lenny to look away from football. The woman had long, flowing hair and a little black dress. He was initially stunned to see an extremely gorgeous woman standing in his parent's house smiling at him—and it took him seconds before he realized he was looking at Leah.

"Do you think I look pretty?"

Lenny didn't know what to say. The last thing in the world he wanted to do was to encourage her to dress English. He couldn't deny that she looked pretty—"pretty" would be an understatement. He remembered sitting in Amish church and thinking he would be the only man to ever see her with her hair down. His heart ached knowing he was about to lose that.

"Leah, I wish you would just wear your own clothes—I'm wearing my Amish clothes."

"Don't you think I look pretty in this?" Her face had been lit up, but turned sober. He knew he had made a mistake, yet he wasn't exactly sure how to respond. He stood up to tell her that she looked beautiful in everything she wore. Just as he did, the other girls came walking in, all dolled up for a wedding. Ruby was wearing a bright red dress and matching lipstick.

"Ashley, Lindsey, what are you doing? Don't you have something these girls could wear that isn't so tight?"

"What are you, a bishop?" Ashley asked, and all four girls laughed.

Lindsey added, "Come on, Lenny, you know they look drop-dead gorgeous!"

He nodded but didn't even want to crack a smile. "Okay, let's go."

Leah sat up front with Lenny as he drove to the reception. He couldn't help but think of what life might be like if they did decide to stay English. Lindsey, Ashley, and Ruby talked and giggled together in the backseat, contrasting the silence up front.

"Why are you two so quiet up there?" Ruby questioned.

"I'm focusing on my driving."

Lenny used the excuse to keep from having to explain how much his thoughts were swirling as he tried to sort out his feelings. He felt confused about everything that was happening around him, as though he was being pulled by an undertow. They waited at a stop light. When it turned green, Lenny started to go.

Leah screamed, "Lenny, look out!"

Just as he got stopped, a SUV blew through the intersection without even slowing at the red light.

"I thought you were focused on your driving?" Lindsey quipped.

Lenny let out his breath slowly. "I guess people are as unpredictable as horses."

Leah said, "I trust horses more than people."

Everyone was enjoying a nice meal with soft background music in the reception hall. There were quiet conversations and an occasional tinkling of spoons on glasses, encouraging the newlyweds to kiss. When they gave in and met lips, everyone cheered. Lenny watched Leah's sparkling eyes and deep-dimple reaction.

Mrs. Blodgett, an older lady from Lenny's parent's church, stopped by and asked, "Who is the girl you're with, Leonard?"

"This is Leah Yoder."

"Hello, Leah, where are you from?" Mrs. Blodgett asked.

"I'm from down near Bulltown—have you heard of that?"

"Oh, yes! Isn't where all the Amish are from? I love your strong accent! What is your background?" Mrs. Blodgett exclaimed.

Leah looked at Lenny with an expression that shouted, *You lied to me about my accent!* Then she said politely to the woman, "Actually, I am Amish."

Mrs. Blodgett looked down at Leah's dress and stammered out, "Th ... the rules must have changed a lot since I last visited Bulltown."

"Okay, it's time for the first dance!" a loud voice boomed out of a PA system.

Lights were turned down and everyone watched the bride and groom slow-dance. Herbie had to sit at the head table with the other groomsmen and bridesmaids, including the girl who fell into him on her way down the aisle. Champagne was served and Lenny could see that a number of people were starting to feel the effects. The whole bridal party danced next, each with the partner they walked in with. Ruby watched and bit her lip.

Emboldened by drink, Lenny's friends came by talking to Leah. "Lenny, where did you find this knockout?" one asked.

Leah smiled shyly, which made her even prettier.

Another buddy said, "If you're not gonna dance with her, can I?"

Shelly, Lenny's neighbor growing up, came by and took Leah by her hand and pulled her to her feet.

"Look at you, girl, you look amazing! Come out on the dance floor with us and have some fun!"

Ashley and Lindsey took Ruby's hands and tugged her to her feet. "Yeah, let's all go dance!"

Lenny sat alone at the table dressed in his black Amish clothes. He couldn't help but notice that Leah and Ruby were adorable as they awkwardly attempted dancing for the first time. Lenny looked away. He sat staring at a dark wall off to one side, but he could still see their dancing shadows reflecting from colorful flashing lights. He put his face down into his arms, folded in front of him on the table, trying to block out everything.

"What's the matter, Lenny?" Rick came over and asked. "Are you all right?"

"Yeah, I'm just a little confused right now. I'm trying to decide if I should go back to college or become Amish."

"For real?" Rick met eyes with Lenny, and asked, "What would you do for a living?"

"Farm with horses. My uncle wants me to become his partner in his farming operation."

"Do you mean with Clydesdales, like the Budweiser horses?"

"Well, he has Percherons, but it's the same idea—huge draft horses."

"Awesome!" Rick's eyes lit up. "Man, that has to be about the coolest job ever! But isn't that a little scary? I mean can you trust them?"

"I think you can trust horses more than people. I bought a team of colts and I've been working with them. We hitch up six horses that weigh a ton apiece and pull plows and other farm equipment." Lenny looked at Rick to see if he wanted to hear more. Rick was totally captivated. Lenny continued, "It's pretty sweet living on an Amish farm, all you can eat homemade food. We cut our own firewood, pull wagonloads of hay with horses to feed our cows, and spend the rest of the time hauling manure with horses."

"And you have a good-looking girlfriend who is willing to live that lifestyle with you?" Rick pointed out to the dance floor where Leah was trying to dance and looking pretty. Lenny smiled and nodded. Rick asked, "Can that girl cook, too?"

"Can she cook? Oh, man, she makes pies that melt in your mouth."

"I bet your uncle is an old grouch though?" Rick looked at Lenny as if he finally thought of a real reason to not stay Amish.

Lenny shook his head, "No, actually my uncle is about the nicest man I know, and his wife, Aunt Ruth, is super sweet."

Rick shook his head. "I don't get what the question is—what do you want to do, stay in River City and be a mailman?"

"Being a mailman would be a cool job!" Lenny perked up at the idea.

Rick shook his head. "Lenny, my dad is a mailman. He says it's a tough job in bad weather, and the bosses get after ya if you don't make your numbers."

"You're right, Rick, I don't know what the question is. Living on an Amish farm is as good as it gets on this earth."

One song ended and another began. The girls came and sat near Lenny again, so he straightened up and tried to look happy. They were all excited talking and laughing.

Ruby called to Lenny above the music, "These girls have an apartment!"

Lenny nodded, wondering what that had to do with them.

Leah added, "There is an extra room and they told us we could move in with them. The rent is cheap and they know where we both could get jobs as waitresses." Leah's face was beaming, her dimple sinking in while she spoke.

Lenny wanted to smile, but a cold sick feeling was growing in the pit of his stomach.

Leah whispered in his ear, "This music is pretty loud—let's go outside where we can talk."

The two of them stood up and started for the door. Shelly's voice rose above the music, "Ooh, where are you two headed?"

Everyone else chimed in, "Oooooh!"

Lenny and Leah stepped outside under glowing neon lights. Lenny searched the sky looking for stars, but only a few were bright enough to compete with city lights. Leah shivered.

"Maybe it's too cold for us to talk out here. Is there somewhere else?"

Lenny answered, "Yeah, there's a coatroom we could try."

They headed back inside and found the coat room. Lenny sat on a small table and Leah stood in front of him, smiling.

"Ruby and I have been talking. We decided that we're gonna jump the fence." Lenny put both hands over his face and she reached out and tugged on his wrists. "Listen to me, Lenny, I thought you would be happy. What's wrong?"

"I don't like you here!"

"You don't like me here?" Her face contorted.

"Take an Amishman for what he means, not for what he says."

She asked, "What did you mean?"

"I was trying to say that I don't like to see you here dressing English and everything."

"Lenny, I'm really confused. When we were Amish all you could think about was going back to your English life. You didn't like our Amish clothes or music. Now that we are here, all you can think about is going back to the Amish."

"What makes you think that I didn't like Amish clothes or music?"

Leah looked down at high heel sandals. "Justin told me," she whispered.

"What? When did Justin talk to you?"

"At his football party. He told me that you wanted to go back to the English, but you didn't think that I would go with you. Well, here I am. Why are you still not happy?"

"First of all I never told him that, and if I ever did feel that way, I don't anymore. Just seeing you in these clothes makes me feel bad. All I can think about is your parents."

"That's what I figured," she said, her face pale and sober. "You want to be English but you think I should stay Amish."

"Leah!"

"So, it's true, isn't it?"

Lenny tried to think of how to explain himself. "I have been struggling to know if I should stay Amish, but all along I've been sure that you shouldn't leave."

"Oh, I get it. You want me to be that little goodie-goodie Amish girl you dated once, and you can return to your modern world without me."

Lenny shook his head. "I had a dream last night."

"About me?" Leah smiled coyly.

"Well, kinda. I dreamt I was out in Noey's field hauling manure with Mr. and Misty."

"What—how was that about me?"

"Well, I stopped my horses and looked off at Yoder Towers. I can see them from Noey's field and that sight always makes me think of you … because I know you live just beyond those towers."

Leah smiled. "That's sweet, I guess." Lenny felt his face lose expression. She must have noticed because she said, "I'm sorry, Lenny, was that it?"

"I dreamt that I could see Noey and Ruth's house, with smoke coming out of their chimney, and I could also see smoke coming from their little grandpa house's chimney. I saw lantern light shining out of its little kitchen window."

"Lenny, what's that supposed to mean?"

"Well, in my dream I got this warm happy feeling, because I've never seen light in that window before. I knew right then that is where I belong."

"In a grandpa house?" Leah's face took its turn losing expression. She stood there with a blank look for a little while before speaking. "I don't know, Lenny, what about what Pastor Jeff says about the Amish?"

"Pastor Jeff says a lot of good things, but when it comes to the Amish, I'm not sure he knows what he's talking about. Think about it: my grandpa, Aaron Burr, Junior, Noey, your dad. Those men all are true believers, aren't they? They are the kind of men that I want to be like. I would rather be like them than Pastor Jeff."

Leah's face showed surprise. "Why do you say that?"

"Well, I tried to tell Pastor about Grandpa and Noey and their faith, but he wouldn't even listen to me. He just got angry and told me about how they are caught up in works, but he's wrong. Okay, maybe some Amish are caught up in that, but not Noey and Ruth or your parents, do you think?"

Leah looked away as though thinking hard. After a moment she said, "But everyone here is so nice." She pointed in toward the wedding reception.

"Leah, they're not nice, they're drunk! People always get all friendly and say nice things when they're drunk, but believe me those girls that asked you to move in with them are not nice!"

"Lenny, couldn't we just put off our decision for a while and see how things go?"

"I know what I want."

Leah drew silent and Lenny wondered if he had said too much. They headed back into the reception hall and sat quietly. Music was blaring and Shelly called over the noise, "What did you say to your girlfriend, Lenny? She was having so much fun till you talked to her!"

On the way home Leah sat beside Lenny while he drove. Laughter came from the backseat as Ruby, Lindsey, and Ashley talked about the wedding dance and how much fun they had. Leah whispered to Lenny, "I can see us living up here in River City and I could get used to this life quickly. Everything is so easy: laundry, dishes, cooking. People just jump into a car, turn a key, and go." She clicked on the car radio: drumbeats and music filled the air.

# CHAPTER 17

## Herbie's Secret

Lenny looked right into the lion's piercing pupils; he wasn't afraid until he woke up. He sat up and looked around the room trying to figure out where he was. He quickly remembered he was in River City, at his parent's house. He nestled back under his covers and thought about the lion. His mind took him back to those first days on Alvin's farm, when Grandpa taught him how to work with horses. He felt an urge to brush Tug and Train again—they were such magnificent creatures. He thought about when he saw Leah down in Alvin's field. How sweet she looked with that wide-eyed innocent face.

His memories took him back to Noey's barn during the flood. He remembered how messed up everything had become and how kind Noey was about it all. He smiled as he thought about riding Train out into the floodwaters to rescue Mr. E. He smiled as he thought about the following Sunday when he gave Leah their first kiss under the oak tree, and then pushed her on the swing.

He knew it was chore time in the Amish time zone. He imagined Aaron Burr and Suzanna starting their day. He thought of Harold and Mildred and how distraught they must be with Leah and Ruby gone. That made him think of Junior and his wife Ruby and how sad their whole family had been since Herbie left. He imagined Noey and Ruth doing their morning chores alone. He wondered if Russell was following Noey or babysitting for Two-Face's kittens. Lenny felt a burning desire to go back and see everyone, and to see Leah in an Amish dress again.

Lenny got dressed and paced back and forth like a caged lion. He wanted some kind of chores to do, but there was nothing that needed done in town at this time of the morning. He crept through the house and went outside. He took a deep breath, but it wasn't as sweet as farm air. He walked down the street and looked at houses in his suburban neighborhood. Nobody seemed to be awake yet. He walked a few blocks and came to where Davy W's gas station sat on the corner. Lenny watched a few cars zipping past. He walked on toward the skate park. He longed to be in an open field, somewhere out in creation. Most of the skate park was filled with concrete ramps and jumps, but at the far end was a huge old oak tree. He ran until he was directly under it and stood looking up through its outstretched limbs. A bright red cardinal was twittering a clear call.

He told the bird, "Mr. Cardinal, you don't know what you're missing by living here in town. If I were you I'd move to the Bulltown area and live on an Amish farm."

Suddenly, it hit him: he knew that if he stayed English, every time he felt a connection with nature, he would be filled with sorrow and a longing for Noey's farm and Amish life.

He looked up into the heavens and cried out. "Lord, forgive me for not trusting you. I wanted to leave the Amish for worldly pleasure even though I knew you wanted me to stay, that you sent me there in the first place. I'm sure that I am called to be Amish. Please forgive me for not taking Aaron Burr's advice. I jumped into this river to try and save my friend, even though he warned me about that. Leah and Ruby jumped in to save me and now they are drowning. Please, Lord, save us."

## Mom and Dad

As Lenny walked back home he thought of Smoky, remembering the last time he drove him. He had put him out to pasture without brushing him. He felt awful to think he had done such a mean thing to such a good horse. Lenny also remembered Two-Face and her kittens. He could imagine them playing in the barn chasing each other. He smiled when he thought of little Lion and wished he could see how much he had grown. Mr. E and Misty also came to mind; he knew they were inexperienced and young, yet he had lost his patience with them. He wanted to make it up to them somehow.

A few cars passed and Lenny noticed that every driver had a cell phone pressed to their ear. It seemed that English people couldn't put down their phones long enough to drive a car or have a simple conversation with a friend. He thought about how he could walk onto any Amish neighbor's farm and whole families would stop everything they were doing to visit with him. His hands ached to hold driving lines again. He thought of wood-burning stoves, hay in the barn, the sound of catbirds in the spring; even the mewing sound in July was better than listening to sirens blaring in town. He reminisced about working out in wide-open fields and watching the sky brilliantly light up in a blazing red display of sunset, clearly proclaiming the glory of God. He remembered the Amish wedding and seeing Leah holding a tiny baby in her arms.

Lenny turned and ran as fast as he could toward his parent's house. He popped the door open and found his dad and mom sitting at the kitchen table.

"Dad and Mom, I've decided that I have to go back and join the Amish."

"Really?" his mom asked with a surprised expression. "I thought Pastor Jeff talked to you about that. Are you sure?"

"Mom, you know that Grandpa and Noey are real Christians, don't you?"

"Yes, but is that really the best thing for you?"

"I'm not sure that it is for everyone, but I feel that I'm called to live there. What do you think, Dad?" Lenny looked at Jake.

His dad didn't speak right away. Jake wiped his hand across the table as though sweeping off crumbs that didn't exist. Susan and Lenny watched until he looked up. "It would make me really happy if you would choose to go back to the Amish."

Lenny couldn't hide his excitement. "Really, Dad?"

Jake nodded. "I've always been sorry that I left. I have a good life here with your mother, and I'm too old to go back to that way of living now. I've gotten too soft and used to everything modern. But if you go back, it will feel like part of me returned."

Susan's eyes were wide open. "Really? You've never told me that!"

"I didn't want you to take it personally."

Susan looked at her husband. "What about the religion part of it, will that be okay for Leonard?"

"Yes, he's right about my dad and my brothers. They're good Christians, and so are Leah's parents and Junior's family. I believe the Bulltown Amish community is a good one—they are serious about their faith."

"Good," Susan said, as though her husband had convinced her. Then she looked at Lenny with a furrowed brow. "I hope you can talk Leah into going back with you."

Lenny sighed. "Pray for us."

Lenny's mom looked out of the kitchen window for a few moments, as though she could see a memory out through the glass. She laughed softly and began to share what she was remembering.

"Leonard: when you were only about two or three years old, we took you to Bulltown. We stayed at Noey and Ruth's home for a couple of days." Lenny's mom looked at him and smiled. "You went right to Ruth and she held you the whole time we were there. She had several stillborn babies and wanted a child so badly. I almost hated to take you away from her, she seemed so attached to you." Lenny looked out of the window, feeling awkward and afraid he might get a tear in his eye. Susan said, "Noey played with you, too. It was so cute: every time he held you, you would grab his beard." Susan laughed and wiped a tear from the corner of her eye. "I think it would be really nice if you stayed on with them."

"I agree," Lenny's dad added. "I hope you will let me come and help farm with horses sometime. I miss that."

"That would be awesome!" Lenny said, smiling.

## The Decision

Leah and Ruby came out dressed in Lindsey's sweat pants and T-shirts, both joining Lenny in the living room. They looked at Lenny as though expecting him to read their minds. He almost could.

"I'm going back to the farm today," he announced.

"Why?" Ruby asked, and so did Leah's eyes.

"Well, I came here to find out why Herbie left the Amish, and he won't tell me. I can't trust him anyway—he lied to me about leaving the Amish with Davy W. and about his tattoo." Lenny glanced at Leah: she looked sad. He added, "I know where I belong … it's not here with the English."

Ruby surprised Lenny, "Herbie's tattoo isn't real."

"What do you mean? I saw it."

"I asked him about it at the wedding. He told me that those guys held him down and drew that windmill on his back with an ink pin, because he refused to get a tattoo."

"Oh, man, and I accused him of being a liar."

Ruby smiled. "And I'll tell you why Herbie left the Amish."

"You will?"

"Yeah, he told me that I can tell you now if I want to." Lenny stared at her waiting. "He did it for you and Leah."

"What are you talking about?" Both Lenny and Leah asked at the same time.

"Last summer—the night when someone came up to our house and hit our buggy with a car, Herbie was there. He saw a car pull into our drive and crash into a buggy. He told us right then, 'I think that was Lenny's car, but I know Lenny would never do anything like that." Leah and I asked him who it could be. He said, 'I think I may know.' When Leah went to bed, Herbie told me, 'I think Davy W. did it to make Lenny look guilty. He wants Lenny to get sent away.' Herbie told me then, 'I'm going to take the car and leave for a while so that nobody can blame Lenny. I will come back home soon.'" Ruby looked at Lenny as though pleased to shine light on Herbie's character, and then continued her story. "I asked him, 'Why don't you just tell everyone that it was Davy?' He said that Noey had been hiding Davy W. in his corncrib, and he didn't want to bring that out in the open."

"So he left the Amish to keep me from leaving?" Lenny asked.

"Yes. I told him that Leah had special feelings for you, and Herbie said, 'That does it! We have to clear Lenny's name so he stays. Lenny is my best friend and Leah is your sister, we have to do anything we can to help them stay together.'"

"Herbie did that for us?"

"Yeah. You're his best friend, and Leah is my sister."

Lenny shook his head. "And I got mad at him and accused him of lying. Oh, boy, do I feel like a fool!"

Leah's face went as pale as the kitchen curtains. Lenny looked at her.

"What's the matter, Leah?" She didn't speak right away; she only sat looking at Ruby.

Ruby asked, "Leah, what is it?"

"Ruby, I'm so sorry."

"For what?"

"You knew it all along—that Herbie left to help Lenny?"

Ruby smiled. "I knew that it would help you, too, Leah." Leah covered her face with both hands. Ruby hurried over to her sister and sat beside her. She pulled Leah's hands from her face. "Leah, what's wrong?"

"I'm so ashamed of myself." She looked at Ruby in the eyes, her lower lip trembling. "You did that for me to help me keep Lenny around. Then when Lenny wanted to go get Herbie, I tried to talk him out of going. All I thought of was myself. I'm so sorry, Ruby."

"It's okay! That was different: Lenny was English; if he would've left, he may not have come back." She smiled and looked at Leah tenderly.

A tear dripped from Leah's eye and landed on her hand. She brushed it off and touched the corner of her eye. "No, it's not okay. I should have thought of you, Ruby. I should have wanted Lenny to go get Herbie, but all I thought of was myself. Please, forgive me?"

"I forgive you." Ruby smiled and brushed Leah's few strands of hair that were loose on her forehead.

Lenny stood up and headed for the door. Leah asked, "Where are you going?"

"I'm going to see my best friend and tell him that I'm sorry. And then I'm going to try and talk him into going back home."

Leah looked at Lenny with a serious face. "I think we should stay here. Ruby and I have decided to stay."

Lenny pulled the door open. "Well, I need to go talk to Herbie."

## Herbie

"Herbie is still in bed," his roommate told Lenny as he let him in the house.

Lenny laughed. "That's okay, I'll wake him up." He stood near Herbie's bedroom door and let out a cock-a-doodle-do as much like a rooster as he could muster up.

Herbie came stumbling out pulling on his shirt. "Sounds like I better get up and do chores, eh?"

They both laughed, and Lenny said, "Thank you, Herbie, for what you did for me and Noey."

"What are you talking about?"

"I just found out that you left home to protect me and Noey. That is so amazing that you did that for us. I have to say that I'm sorry I ever doubted you."

"Awh, you would've done the same for me."

Lenny said, "I came up here to River City because I wanted to know why you left the Amish. I thought maybe you knew something bad about the Amish that would help me decide what to do. Now that I know what it was, I'm ready to go back. I still want to know why you want to stay here?"

Herbie scratched his head. "When I first got here I was lost, I couldn't wait to get back home. I talked to your parents and they got me connected with Pastor Jeff. He really wanted to help me cut my ties to the Amish and all of their man-made rules and everything. I guess I didn't see that coming and I started thinking maybe I should stay here after all."

"Herbie, when Fannie Ella had her accident, I was the first at the scene. I crawled down beside her under that tractor and I heard her crying for you." Herbie got a serious face, and Lenny continued, "I decided right then that I had to find you and make sure you really want to be English." Lenny watched Herbie, searching his face for clues about his feelings. Herbie stared out of the window and didn't look like he planned to give any answer, which drove Lenny to try harder. "Herbie, you had so much. How can you walk away from your family, friends, and Ruby?"

"Ruby is here now." He glanced at Lenny but didn't make real eye contact.

Lenny continued his speech. "Herbie, look around you: do you see where you're living? Is this really the kind of life you want and what you want for Ruby, and maybe your children someday? I grew up here, Herbie, and I know I don't want to raise my family like this ... not when there is a better option. We have been given a great gift to live in an Amish community like Bulltown. A place with sincere Christian people who care about each other. In Bulltown everybody knows you and cares; here you are just another guy alone on the street. Up here electronic gadgets rule people's lives and keep them from living the way they should. It makes me sick and I can't take it anymore. Besides, I'm so bored without chores to do and real work!"

Herbie chuckled. Then he asked seriously, "What about the faith vs. works message Pastor Jeff preaches?"

"Well, I can't speak for all Amish everywhere, but seriously, Herbie, you know as well as I do that your dad and my uncle Noey are not trying to earn their way into heaven by works. They follow the rules of their church about clothes, but at the end of the day those are just clothes, they don't even think about them. I know that they are real believers; their only goal is to serve the Lord that saved them."

"I feel free here, though, and nobody is watching every step I make."

"That's because nobody really cares. I hate to tell you this, Herbie, but I know it's true from when I lived here. Noey explained it to me like this, 'Deer seem to have freedom to go where they want and cattle don't, but fences are there to keep cattle from wandering into danger. Deer have to search for food, but farmers provide for their livestock.' Being Amish is like that. Our bishops and ministers set up guidelines that are meant to help us stay away from things that harm our walk with God. They search the scriptures to share with us nourishing truths. There was a time when leaving the Amish may have been reasonable, not now."

"Why do you say that?"

"The way everything is nowadays, like movies, magazines, TV. The world is so messed up and Amish people have found a way to stay out of all that. I know everything isn't perfect about being Amish, but it's better than living like the modern world, don't you think?" Herbie averted his eyes and stood looking at his own hands. Lenny continued his sermon, "Being Amish is like living in the old days. I want to raise my family in an old-fashioned community, and I believe God is okay with that; in fact, I believe He wants me to!" He looked at Herbie, trying to read if he was winning him over. "Even in Pastor Jeff's church there are homeschool families. Some of them give up TV and things to keep their lives more simple. That's not works, is it? The Amish in Bulltown are similar to those homeschoolers."

Herbie sat quietly. Lenny stood up to leave. "Maybe I've said too much? I care a lot about you, Herbie, and I just want what is best for you and Ruby." Lenny reached out to shake his hand.

Herbie stood up and said, "I think I'm probably gonna stay here, but thanks for being honest about how you feel."

"If you come back, I'll let you have Smoky," Lenny winced as he said it and Herbie laughed.

"Thanks, Lenny, I don't want to take your horse away from you, though." He followed Lenny to the door and asked, "Are you going back then?"

"Yeah, I know where I belong."

They didn't say good-bye, which was normal for two Amish young men from Bulltown.

## Never Give Up

Lenny bit his lower lip as he drove his parents' car back into their garage. He felt like crying. He let the automatic garage door shut behind him and sat alone in a dark car for a few minutes. He hit the steering wheel and said through clinched teeth, "Great, I failed to change Herbie's mind, and now Leah and Ruby won't come back with me either." He stared at the dashboard in the dark.

Lenny closed his eyes and, as if having a vision, he could see Grandpa's horses. Tug shook his mane and snorted, which spurred Train on, causing him to arch his massive neck and pull. Both horses surged forward, muscles rippling, refusing to give up. Lenny shouted out loud in his parents' car, "Tug and Train, never give up!" He jumped out of the car and ran inside. He found Ruby in the TV room with his sisters. "Where's Leah?"

"She went upstairs for a minute. She'll be right back down," Ruby answered.

Lenny heard someone coming down the steps. He popped the door open, took Leah by her hands, and pulled her into the Ping-Pong room.

"Please, come talk to me for a minute." She followed him in without speaking. He was beside himself with frustration, "I don't know how to say this … but…." He paced back and forth and covered his eyes with his hands. Lenny dropped to his knees and held Leah around the waist, with his cheek against her stomach.

"Please, I'm begging you, Leah, please come back with me. I don't know how Amish boys say this … but I want to marry you. Please, Catbird, I'm going back to the Amish and I want you to come back with me and be my Amish wife." He buried his face in her tummy and cried.

Leah didn't speak. Lenny looked up, slowly, afraid to see what her expression was. Her soft brown eyes were looking into his, tears streaming down her cheeks. She nodded her head and used her pretty fingers to swipe tears from her cheeks. After a moment she whispered, "Don't you see what I'm wearing?"

Lenny stayed on one knee and looked at her through his tears. "You're wearing your Amish dress!"

She pulled a hankie from her apron's waistband, blew her nose, and laughed, "Okay, I'll be your Amish wife. But I probably won't always be singing like a spring catbird. Sometimes I might yowl like a catbird in the summer."

Lenny took her hand and kissed it. Looking into her eyes, he said, "I won't mind. When I hear a catbird yowling in the summer, it reminds me of how beautiful they sound when they are singing!" She smiled and her dimple sunk into her pretty wet cheek. He stood up, held both of her hands, and looked at her clothes with a smile. "You're wearing my favorite dress, too!"

"I brought it along because you said it was your favorite. I was planning to use it to help talk you into coming back home." They both laughed. She furrowed her brow and stated, "I still don't get why my gray dress is your favorite?"

"Because you look like a Catbird in it," he said with a smile.

She pushed him away from her, laughing. "Oh, you make me mad! I thought it must make me look pretty and now you tell me it just makes me look like a catbird!"

"I don't want to make you vain, Leah, but you would look pretty in rags. It doesn't really matter what dress you're wearing."

She smiled, her eyes sparkling. "Okay, stop with all of that if we are going to be Amish."

Lenny looked Leah in her eyes and said, "*Eich liebe deich*." Leah giggled and he asked, "What's funny about that?"

"That is kind of a German way to say it. Most Amish would say, '*Eich glache diech*,' which is to say, 'I like you.'"

Lenny explained, "I got it from the song *Got isch de liebe*. I wanted to say more than 'I like you.'"

Leah smiled. "That's a German song, but I like how you did that, Lenny—I love you too!"

He gave her a kiss, and then said, "Leah, you've got to help me talk Herbie and Ruby into coming back with us."

She shook her head. "I don't think we can."

Lenny put his hands on his head. "I thought I was big stuff when I tried to pull that tractor off Fannie Ella with my horses, but if they had given up while the tractor was half over, it could have killed her. And as if that wasn't bad enough, I thought I was so smart coming here to get Herbie. If I fail to convince him now, he will probably never come back."

Leah frowned. "Ruby wants to stay here. I don't think she will help us talk him into coming back home."

They headed out to the living room. They were surprised to find Herbie standing there with Ruby.

"Are you wearing your Amish clothes, Leah?" Ruby asked.

Leah looked down at her clothes and back up at her sister, nodding. "Will you come back with us, Ruby?"

Ruby smiled coyly. "It wouldn't be much fun here by myself."

"What?" Lenny looked at Herbie. "Are you coming back home?"

"You'll make a good Amish preacher someday, Lenny—you talked me into it."

"I'll give you Smoky back, just like I promised!" Lenny shouted.

Leah looked at him in shock, but before she could say anything, Herbie said, "I'm not gonna take Smoky away from you. I'll buy another horse. I sold the old Impala to Davy W. and as part of the deal, he agreed to drive us all back to Bulltown."

# CHAPTER 18

## Snow Tunnel

Lenny's whole family gathered around by the door.

Leah said, "Ashley and Lindsey, you girls were so good to me and Ruby. Thank you for taking us in and showing us what life is like in River City. Now you two need to come visit us so we can show you what life in Bulltown is all about."

Lenny's sisters both nodded and seemed excited about the idea.

Lenny's mom hugged Leah and Ruby.

"Thank you, girls, for coming up to see us. Your parents did a great job raising you, and we're happy we got to know both of you."

Leah and Ruby only smiled in response to her words.

Jake spoke to them in Pennsylvania Dutch. Lenny wasn't sure what he said exactly, but it was something about keeping an eye on his son. Herbie and the girls laughed. Jake added in English, "Well, the moon is growing, so it should be a good time to begin a new phase of life."

Lenny looked at his dad for a moment, surprised at how much he reminded him of Uncle Noey. As they walked out toward the car, Lenny called back to his family, "Come and visit us real soon!"

## Changing Time Zones

On the way home, Lenny and Leah rode in the back together. It seemed odd to Lenny riding as a passenger in his old Impala, and even stranger to be riding in the backseat.

Leah asked Davy, "Couldn't your girlfriend come along?"

"No, Courtney has to work tonight."

"What kind of job does she have?" Leah questioned.

"She works at a bowling alley."

When Davy. W said it, Herbie looked at Lenny and raised his eyebrows. Lenny had to fake a sneeze to conceal his laughter.

After they had been riding for a while, Leah's head began to nod. Lenny told her, "You can lay your head on my shoulder if you want."

She smiled and leaned against him. Moments later he could hear her breathing change to that of deep sleep. Davy W. drove fast, just as he always had when he drove Lightning, his horse. Ruby and Herbie rode up front with Davy because they couldn't both fit in back and there were three seatbelts up front.

Lenny spoke up, "Hey, Herbie, maybe you could get a job at Hershey's garage? They are always so busy they could use another mechanic."

"No, I got that mechanic thing out of my system. I have another idea."

"What do you have in mind?" Lenny couldn't wait to hear his answer.

"My grandpa offered to let me take over his harness shop. I think I'll do that."

Lenny wanted to jump up and shout, but Leah was sleeping on his shoulder. Instead, he whispered as loud as he could, "That's perfect, Aaron Burr will be so happy! He was just telling me that he didn't know what to do about his shop."

For a stretch of time everyone rode along in silence

After a long nap, Leah began to stir. Lenny watched her pretty face. He didn't get a chance to study her features very often and now relished the opportunity. Her dainty eyebrows furrowed and her face contorted as though having troubling dreams. All at once she opened her sweet eyes and looked right in Lenny's.

"I was having a strange dream," she said. Lenny didn't speak, but looked into her eyes, listening. "I dreamt that we were down by the English River, you and me." Lenny nodded and gave her the *Tell-me-more* look. Leah continued, "I don't know what we were doing there, but you wanted to get in the river and I kept begging you, 'No Lenny, don't go in there,' but you did it anyway. All of a sudden I realized you were drowning and I came in after you. I couldn't seem to get you out and then I started drowning and you were trying to save me. Finally, I felt myself get to that stage we talked about, when a drowning person starts to be in a bliss and they don't mind that they are dying. I could see myself underwater but smiling and you struggling to pull me out. You pulled me onto the shore and put your mouth to mine. I thought you were going to kiss me, but instead you breathed life into me and I woke up."

"You woke up in your dream?"

"No, I woke up and I was looking into your eyes riding in this car."

"I'm so glad you're here with me, Leah. Thank you for trying to rescue me, and even more for coming back home with me."

"Thank you for pulling me out of the English River." Leah's eyes sparkled and her dimple sunk in deeply.

"Leah, were you really thinking about staying English without me?"

She smiled softly and looked into his eyes. She shook her head slightly, but just enough that he could see it.

He asked, "Well then, why did you let on like you were going to?"

"Because I thought you were just going back to the Amish for me, and that if I told you that I wasn't going back, you wouldn't either."

Lenny took a deep breath and let it out very slowly, the first full breath he had taken in days. "Well, you sure did scare me."

She looked into his eyes and asked, "So, were you really going to go back to the Amish without me?"

Lenny laughed. "I don't know what I was going to do. I hadn't thought it all through." Leah didn't smile. She continued looking him in the eyes, as if she wasn't satisfied with his answer. Lenny stopped smiling and said, "This is what I wanted—more than anything."

"What is?"

"You and me going back to the Amish together." Leah's dark brown eyes glistened. He added, "I knew we were going to stay together somehow. I just didn't know how I was going to talk you into coming back with me." She smiled and her lips were so pretty he wanted to kiss her, only not with Herbie, Ruby, and Davy around.

Leah whispered, "I'm really nervous about going back home. I'm scared to face my dad."

"Harold? I think he will be super happy to have you and Ruby home again."

"We left home without telling anyone where we were going. Mom and Dad must have been really angry with us when they realized we were gone."

"Didn't you even leave a note?" Lenny asked. Leah didn't speak but shook her head slowly. "Leah, you should have."

She looked at her hands, "Well, we knew that everyone would know where we went. Now I'm afraid they will be angry."

"If Harold isn't happy to see you, then I was wrong about him, Noey, Junior, and everyone." After he said it, Lenny wished he hadn't been so sure of himself.

A light, wispy snow began to fall on the Impala's windshield. Lenny watched as snowflakes appeared out of nowhere and seemed to be flying straight at them. Davy W. continued to drive fast and recklessly even with snow coming at them. The highway looked like a tunnel, drawing them back in time toward the Amish world. Lenny couldn't wait to get back home to Noey, Ruth, and Russell. However, he realized he was biting his lower lip as he tried to imagine what Harold's response would be.

Amish farms began to come into view, peaceful and cozy under a pristine blanket of fluffy snow. Gray smoke billowed from chimneys and a scent of firewood seeped in through the Impala's heater vents. The carload of young people were silent, each one of them nervously anticipating how they may be received. Lenny wished the Impala would go as slow as a buggy horse so he would have more time to prepare a speech for Harold. He started worrying again about Misty having a colt, and about his lie to Mose, the bishop.

Davy W. broke the silence as they came up to the place where the road split two hills and Alvin's farm was in plain sight.

"I guess we will take these girls' home first?"

"Yeah, that's the right thing," Lenny agreed.

They turned down the road that crossed Old Man's Creek and Web's place came into view. Neither Davy nor Lenny said anything, but it seemed obvious they were both thinking the same thing. Davy drove slowly up the hill toward Harold's farm, which reminded Lenny that Davy had a reason to be nervous about going to Harold's also, having crashed the Impala into one of Harold's buggies.

Leah spoke up, "Davy, you could just drop us off at the end of the lane … since it's snowing." Everyone in the car knew she was trying to let him off the hook.

Davy W. stopped at the entrance to Harold's lane and said, "Okay."

Leah and Ruby drew their shawls around their shoulders tightly and looked each other in the eyes nervously.

Lenny said, "I'll come up there with you."

"So will I," Herbie told them.

They—all four—climbed out of Davy's car and slowly walked through swirling snow. Herbie and Lenny tilted their Amish hats downward to keep the snow out of their eyes. Ruby and Leah had their black Amish bonnets on over their white prayer caps, which looked like parka hoods, offering protection from the blinding snow. Lenny had imagined they would all stand at Harold's door and knock, but before they even got halfway up the lane, a door on the barn slid open and Harold came running out to meet them. Having never witnessed an older Amish man running, Lenny stopped in his own tracks, stunned and unsure of what Harold was going to do. Herbie hesitated with Lenny. Leah and Ruby began to run through snowdrifts toward their dad and all three of them met in a big hug.

The young men stood awkwardly watching as Harold and his daughters cried. In only a moment, Mildred appeared out of nowhere and joined them. Powdery snow continued falling on the little group, who didn't seem to notice. Finally, Harold looked up at the boys.

"Leonard, Herbie, I'm so glad to see you both! Come on over here!"

Harold shook Lenny's hand and looked him in the eyes, "Thank you for bringing Leah home—thank you!"

Lenny couldn't speak, he just wiped the corner of his eye and nodded.

Harold took hold of Herbie's hand and shook it vigorously also. "Thank you for bringing Ruby home, Herbie!"

Mildred dabbed her eyes with a corner of her apron. "You young men better get home to your families as soon as possible. Everyone will be so happy to see you!" she said, smiling.

Harold made a point of walking partway back out the lane toward the Impala. He waved and smiled at Davy W., obviously in an effort to let him know that everything was forgiven. Davy W. returned the gesture. Lenny and Herbie brushed snow off themselves and got back inside the Impala.

Lenny said from the backseat. "Davy, why don't we stop off at Web's? I'll go inside with you."

Davy didn't say anything, but he turned into Web's lane and parked near the windmill.

"You two take your time," Herbie told them. "I need to think about what I'm gonna tell my parents."

Lenny and Davy laughed at him as they climbed out the Impala. Lenny knocked on Web's door and noticed that Davy W. seemed to be setting his face with a hard exterior, maybe to protect himself from being disappointed by his dad one more time. The house door opened and there stood Web looking ten years older than the last time Lenny saw him.

"Come in, Lenny. Come in, Davy." Web's voice sounded hoarse, and he coughed. "Would you like to sit down for a minute?"

"Herbie is waiting for us in the car," Davy spoke gruffly without making eye contact. Web had been heavyset when Lenny first met him; at this point, his bib overalls hung as if on a hanger. His eyes looked hollow, yet sincere, as he reached out a hand toward Davy. He didn't shake Davy's hand but held it and said, "I'm sorry I took your dog away from you." A big fat tear rolled down Web's cheek and Davy watched it drop but didn't speak.

Web attempted to clear his scratchy voice and spoke again. "You know that you are my son, don't you?" Davy glanced up at Web and nodded. Web wheezed out, "Davy, I'm glad Noey and Ruth raised you—they're much better people than I am." He coughed again and it was obvious that he was working hard to get out his words. "But ... I wish I had done the right thing and married your mom...." Web's voice trailed off, filled with emotion. The sickly old man sat down and covered his face and cried.

Lenny took a quick glance at Davy to see his expression. Davy's face remained stiff, but tears were streaming down both his cheeks.

Web gathered himself and stood back up. "Davy, I'm not gonna be around for long. I want you to know you're my only son, and I've put you on my will to own this place." Davy looked surprised. Web continued, "It's not much of a farm, but it'll be yours." He looked at his son and asked, "Do you have a woman in your life?"

"Yeah, I live with my girlfriend—"

"Don't be like your old man, Davy: put a ring on her finger."

Davy laughed and said, "Okay."

"If you're not too embarrassed of me, bring her by to meet me before I die." Web said and began to cough again.

"I'm not embarrassed; I'll bring her by real soon." Davy's voice sounded different.

The two younger men walked toward the door and Web spoke to Lenny. "Thanks for bringing my son by here to see me, Lenny."

"No problem."

"And, I'm awful sorry about the trouble I've caused you, too."

"It all seemed to be part of God's plan, in some mysterious way." Lenny surprised himself by saying it.

Web grinned and his eyes looked bright for a moment. "I think maybe you are right. And you should marry that Leah girl you're in love with, too!"

"I just might do that!" Lenny said and they all three laughed.

## Herbie's Homecoming

When the Impala pulled into Junior's lane, a lantern was visible out in the dairy barn and another in Ruby's kitchen.

"Looks like they're finishing up their milking chores," Herbie announced.

"It won't be as hard as you think." Davy actually seemed to be kind as he spoke.

Lenny tried to encourage Herbie as well. "Your family is going to be so happy to see you. Just let them know right away that you are planning to come back for good. Then all will be forgiven."

Herbie nodded that he understood and agreed with Lenny's theory. "Will you walk up with me, Lenny?"

"Okay, I'd be happy to if that will help." Lenny looked at his friend.

Herbie seemed unusually serious and said, "If you are there, they won't yell at me right away."

"Really, Herbie, they aren't gonna yell. If you had accidentally shot a cow they might holler at ya, but this is too big a deal for yelling. Your dad is a good man, like Harold; he just wants what's best for his children. If they think you are just coming home for a visit, they may be quiet and not sure what to say to you. I believe that as soon as they know you are home for good, they will only be happy."

"I hope you're right!"

Lenny and Herbie climbed out of the car. Davey W. rolled down his window and said, "I'll wait here for you, Lenny. We can go back to Noey and Ruth's together."

Just as they stepped away from the car, a group of Amish men emerged through falling snow. One of them held a lantern that swung at his knees as he walked. He hoisted it to head height as they drew closer, creating an orb of light. Junior's bearded silhouette appeared with Henry and Harvey's younger-looking faces. They all stood studying each other's features.

Lenny broke the silence. "Herbie and I have come home to stay if everyone will let us?"

Junior didn't speak, but lowered his lantern which lit a glowing path toward the house and up the steps. They all clomped inside and Ruby came through the kitchen doorway bringing her lantern with her. She held it up, shining light on the circle of men. Lenny watched her face change like a woman who has seen a ghost. She stepped back and sat in a chair, holding the lantern up as though afraid that if she looked away Herbie would disappear. Nobody spoke.

Lenny thought he should help break the ice. "Herbie and I want to come back and stay for good."

Ruby set down the lantern on the floor beside her feet. She held her apron up to her face, clearly trying to keep back her emotions.

Junior spoke calmly, his voice as smooth as honey, "This is what we have been praying for." He hung his lantern in the center of his living room and Herbie's sisters gathered around their brother and stared. They looked him over as if checking to see if it was really him or if their minds were playing tricks on them. Fannie Ella let out a little snicker, and everyone looked at her. Her face was glowing and she began laughing out loud. The next thing Lenny knew, the whole family was roaring with laughter, as if with a joy that was so full they couldn't contain it. Even Herbie busted out into his hearty laugh that Lenny had longed to hear for months. Lenny sat watching them all with a big smile on his face. He got a tear in his eye when he noticed the twins, Edna and Elma, were holding hands and giggling. Blue and Tick howled from the front porch.

Junior took Lenny's hand and shook it. "Thank you, Leonard, for going after Herbie. Please go tell Noey and Ruth that you are home. I don't want them to suffer another moment!"

Lenny glanced at the corner where Herbie usually sat at the table. His place was set, waiting for him. Lenny hurried out past the howling dogs and jumped into the car.

"What was so funny in there?" Davy W. asked.

Lenny tried to think of how to put it into words. Finally he said, "Junior's family is so good-natured they used to laugh all the time. It just hit me, but the whole time Herbie was gone they stopped laughing. I guess now they are just overcome by happiness seeing Herbie again their laughter came back."

Davy W. stared at Lenny to see if was pulling his leg.

Lenny told him again, "No, really, that was it!"

## Lenny and Davy W. Return

Lenny got nervous when he thought about the fact that Ruth had stopped setting Davy W.'s place at the table. He tried to guess if his own place would be set and what would happen if it was and not Davy's. They pulled into the drive and before they climbed out into the snowy night, Noey and Ruth were coming out of the house. They didn't hug the boys like Harold and Mildred had hugged their daughters, but they seemed every bit as happy to see them. They all stepped inside the warm porch to talk. Lenny started taking off his black coat that Ruth had made for him, but Davy kept his worldly coat on.

"Won't you come in, even for supper?" Ruth asked.

Davy W. was actually kind to Ruth as he answered. "Thank you so much for asking, Mom, but I've got to get home to Courtney. It's dark and snowy, and I have a long drive home."

"Are you sure you should be driving in this bad weather?" Noey asked.

"I'll be fine. Besides, I have to work tomorrow. I want to come back sometime soon, though. I am planning to bring Courtney here to meet everyone."

"That would be nice, Davy," Ruth said, smiling. Davy W. turned without saying anything more and headed out into the snow.

They all three headed into the kitchen. Lenny looked at the table right off and noticed three plates set—Noey, Ruth's, and his. His heart swelled as he looked at the sight. He sat in his place and couldn't help but shed some tears.

"I'm sorry that I left like that, Ruth. I just had to go back."

"Oh, Leonard, don't be sorry. That is your home. You had every right to go back there."

All at once Lenny had a sick feeling in his stomach. "Where's my little Russell?" he asked.

Noey looked at the floor and Ruth looked Lenny in the eyes. "I'm so sorry, Leonard. He disappeared the day after you left. We haven't seen or heard anything of him since."

They all sat quietly around the table.

"I have some interesting news," Lenny told his aunt and uncle.

They gave him all of their attention.

"Remember I told you that Davy W. knows who his dad is?"

They both nodded.

"Well, I found out who. Noey, you told me about that Dalmatian Davy found, and how Web came and claimed him after you put an ad in the paper. Well, Davy W. was telling me the same story. Instead of telling me it was Web that came and took the dog, he told me that it was his dad. I accidentally let him know that I knew it was Web and then everything came out. He told me that our neighbor, Justin, told him that Web is his dad."

"Justin—the guy with the big red truck?" Noey asked with a confused look.

"Yeah, he is Web's nephew, and I guess Web told Justin about it, and Justin told Davy."

Ruth and Noey's faces turned white and their mouths hung open.

Lenny wondered if he had made a mistake telling them about it. He tried to make it better by telling more. "Web and I know each other. I talked to him when I was on my way to Harold's place a few weeks ago. He told me that he has cancer and doesn't have long to live. He brought up the story about the Dalmatian, too. He asked me to tell Davy he was sorry about taking the dog from him. I didn't know what a huge deal it was, until I found out that Web was his father."

Ruth lifted the corner of her apron and dabbed her eyes with it. She said, "No wonder that dog bonded so quickly with Davy W. Web and Davy probably have a similar scent, and a dog would notice that."

Noey added, "It's so sad; just think, that Dalmatian really should have belonged to Davy W. if he had grown up with his parents."

Lenny continued his story. "We stopped by Web's place on our way here tonight. Web asked Davy to forgive him for failing him as a child and for taking the dog away."

"What did Davy W. say?" Ruth asked.

"He cried and forgave him."

At this point both Ruth and Noey had tears in their eyes.

"Web also told Davy that he was glad you folks raised him, because he said, 'Noey and Ruth are better people than I am.'" Lenny paused while both his aunt and his uncle got out hankies and blew their noses. "Web told Davy that he plans to leave his farm to him. He also asked Davy to bring his girlfriend down soon to meet him before he dies. And Davy said he would." As an afterthought, Lenny asked. "What does Davy's middle initial stand for?"

"Webster," Ruth answered.

After supper they bowed their heads for silent prayer. Lenny prayed in his heart, "Lord, thank you for bringing me back home. I know I belong here. And more than anything, thank you that Leah came back with me, and Herbie and Ruby, too. Please be with little Russell wherever he is."

After Noey cleared his throat to signal they were finished praying, Lenny spoke up. "I think I will head out to the barn for a bit. I really want to see my horses."

Noey and Ruth didn't say anything, but they were smiling as they cleared off the table.

## Old Friends

Lenny lit a lantern and gathered his jacket off its hook. He looked at the jacket and smiled. It seemed extra nice because of the fact that his aunt had made it by hand. It fit perfectly and was warm and comfortable as he headed out into the snowy night. His lantern glowed in bright orbs of light that moved as he walked toward the barn. Fresh snow glistened like glitter on the ground under his feet. He unlatched the two half doors and hung his lantern on a hook made for that purpose. It continued to sway as Lenny walked under the warm, moving glow. He opened the oats bin and Two-Face jumped out and rubbed her calico body against his legs.

"Hello, Two-Face, how's that litter of kittens getting along?" She purred and her little face seemed to be smiling. Lenny reached in to get a scoopful of oats and a little yellow kitty pounced on his hand and bit it. "Ouch, that must be my little Lion, huh?" He picked up the kitten and held him close. Lion's eyes stared straight into Lenny's with that same piercing look Caesar's had. "You really think you are a lion, don't you?"

Lenny slid open the big door and horses started clomping in one by one. They all had a thin layer of powdery snow covering their backs. He was sure Noey fed them at chore time but he also knew it wouldn't hurt to give them all an extra snack. Lenny tied them as they ate. He took a currycomb and started with Smoky, even though he wasn't at the top of the pecking order.

"I'm so sorry I was mad at you, Smoky. You are such a good horse and it was my fault you tried to run that night. It was my heart that was fearful and thinking of running away and I put that into you, and into Mr. E and Misty, too." He gave Smoky a hug around the base of his neck. Lenny was happy to see that Tug and Train were still on the farm. He looked into their eyes and they raised their eyebrows as if asking a question. "Tug and Train, you two inspired me to never give up. If you two hadn't taught me that, I might have failed to talk Herbie, Leah, and Ruby to come back home with me!"

Lenny brushed all of his horses and gave each one a big hug. "I'm here to stay now! We'll have to find a way to get along even when there is a subzero wind chill. I'm gonna be Amish and that is just part of our life."

After he turned his horses back out, they all gathered in a herd under the foreshoot. Lenny called out toward the English River, "Russell! Russell!" but the woods were silent under a blanket of snow.

Lenny walked back to the house and stepped inside. Noey was still up reading. He rocked his chair for a moment and then said, "Mose stopped by here the other day."

"The bishop? Was it about me?"

"Yes, he said that he saw you and Leah together the other day, and you told him that you had been to the fabric shop. He happened to mention it to his sister and she said you never came into her shop."

Lenny sat down and let out a long sigh. "Well, it's kinda hard to explain. Leah wanted to stop in the fabric shop, but I told her that people would think we were picking out material for a wedding. I guess that hurt her feelings, because she said, 'What would be so bad about that?' Then, when I stopped at the fabric shop, she wouldn't go in."

Noey laughed. "That is exactly what I told Mose! I told him that you probably were nervous about going into a fabric shop with a girl. Mose got a kick out of that and said that he felt the same way when he was your age."

Lenny confessed, "Well, I have to be honest with you, Noey. Leah and I had been at Justin's house for a football party. I didn't want to mention that to Mose, so I only told him the part about the fabric shop."

Noey sat quietly for a few moments and then chuckled. "You sure have a knack for getting yourself into a tight spot."

"Yeah, that wasn't the only thing—there was a little incident with Misty, too."

Noey nodded. "Perry already told Alvin about what happened with Laidlaw's horse. Alvin and I talked about it and we decided that it would be best to keep that to ourselves. Laidlaw is a bitter man and he wouldn't understand."

Lenny asked, "Perry told Alvin?"

"Yes. Perry said that it was all his fault."

Lenny let out another big sigh. "Well, it wasn't all Perry's fault, but I sure do feel better now that we talked about it."

"If I were you I would ask the Lord to forgive you," Noey said. Lenny looked down ashamed to meet Noey's eyes. Noey chuckled. "And then I'd forget about it. I think everything will blow over."

# CHAPTER 19

## Icing on the Cake

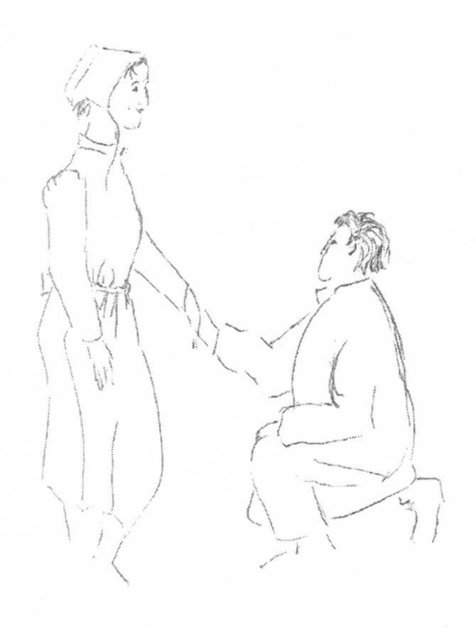

As soon as morning chores were done, Lenny took a walk out into the cattle lot to look at his fences. As he walked around, he noticed Big Red pulling a buggy out of the lane. He wondered where Noey was headed and why he didn't tell him where he was going. Wispy snowflakes sailed around him as he walked through a forest of leafless trees. For the first time Lenny could see straight through the woods, which took some of the mystery out of it. He could hear his own breathing and see his breath. He looked for birds and didn't notice any.

Finally he heard a lone bird call, a bright red cardinal perched on a limb up ahead. He said to the bird, "Mr. Cardinal, I guess you decided to take my advice and moved from town to live out here on an Amish farm." A blue jay also made a sharp cry through the crisp air, and then flew to a higher bough. "It looks like a couple of my favorite birds decided to stay here."

Tree limbs looked stiff, like a person who is really cold. The sweet smell of oak firewood drifted from Noey's chimney in a thin blue line of smoke and followed Lenny as he walked through the woods. Lenny decided that since Noey was gone, it would be a good time to head up the steep bluff and visit Grandpa's grave. His own rhythmic exhaling got louder, and he could see his breath billowing out into falling snowflakes. He slipped a little as he climbed up a steep incline, using tree trunks to pull himself forward by grabbing their rough bark as he went. His heart rate climbed and his breaths became more rapid. Finally, he reached the top and climbed the woven wire fence, entering his family graveyard.

He brushed fluffy snow off the face of Grandpa's headstone and read his name aloud, "Jesse Gingerich." He let his finger trace the engraved letters and then spoke.

"Grandpa, maybe you already know this … but I wanted to tell you that I'm going to stay Amish. You showed me what kind of man I ought to be. I want to be just like you, someday." Lenny looked at the headstone silently for a moment and then let out a soft laugh. "Grandpa, you'd probably be surprised to know that I asked Harold's Leah to marry me … and she said, 'Yes!' I wanted to tell you first. I know that you two were friends. She told me how you used to tease her about having a hole in her cheek. And that you used to let her ride along with you on the hayrack when her family came over to make hay. She said that you let her hold the driving lines and told her that horses teach us a lot about the character of those who are working with them. Thank you for taking time to be kind to a little neighbor girl even before you knew she would one day be your grandson's wife."

A horse snorted not far behind him and Lenny turned. A horse and buggy were tied about twenty yards away. He realized that Noey had walked up and was standing right behind him. After a length of silence, Noey spoke quietly. "I come up here every year on my son's birthday."

Lenny looked over at the tiny headstone and read, "Leonard Noah Gingerich." Lenny asked, "Today is his birthday?" and then reached over and brushed away the snow, confirming the date.

"When he was born, Ruth told me she wanted to name him Leonard," Noey said quietly. Lenny held his breath so he could hear what his uncle was saying. "You were only about five years old then. Ruth told me, 'There is something special about that Leonard, and I would like to have a son like him.'"

Lenny turned away from Noey to gaze on the little grave—and because he felt tears stinging in his eyes.

Noey said, "I doubt it's a coincidence that I overheard you saying that you are going to marry Leah and stay here like a son, and right on our Leonard's birthday. God works in mysterious ways." Noey was quiet and Lenny tried to keep from sniffling while he wiped his eyes with his coat sleeve. He was glad when Noey began to talk again.

"My grandpa, Isaac Gingerich, used to live in the little grandpa house there beside our house. When you were about two years old, your mom and dad stayed with us for a few days and I took you over with me when I went to talk to Isaac about something. He asked to hold you. Isaac was really old and I tried to tell him who you were, but he didn't seem to understand what I was saying. He held you on his lap and you looked at him and smiled. He put his hand on your head and blessed you." Noey's eyes twinkled like Grandpa's used to. "I can still remember what he prayed, 'Lord, give this child the blessing of feeling your presence with him as he farms this land, just as I always felt your presence with me as I farmed this land.'" Noey chuckled. "I remember feeling bad that old Isaac was confused and thought that you were my child. I guess the Lord knew what would be. Apparently, I was the one that was 'leaning on my own understanding.'"

Lenny stood up and shook Noey's hand and held it tight. Noey pulled him close and gave him a hug. "That was years before we knew that you were Jake's son and Jesse's grandson, and Isaac's great-grandson. Come and ride back home with me in my buggy.

Big Red trotted down the winding road off the bluffs, onto a flat river-bottom road that led back home.

"Leonard, let's put Mr. and Misty on the bobsled to haul hay out to the cattle," Noey suggested. Lenny didn't answer right away; he wasn't sure how that would go. "Don't worry, we'll load it up with hay and they'll have to work a little. By the time we get the cattle fed, they will be pretty relaxed." He chuckled as he said it.

Mr. E and Misty were frisky but well-mannered as Noey and Lenny hitched them onto a heavy wooden bobsled. Lenny clucked and they obediently circled around the barn with a full load of hay. As they came around a corner, they saw a young Amish woman with a black bonnet and cloak heading out toward them. He pulled up his horses.

"Leah, what are you doing here?"

"I wanted to see you."

"Really? Is something up?"

She reached under her heavy cloak. "I found something that belongs to you." She pulled out a little mostly-white dog with black ears.

"Russell, where were you?"

"I went out to do chores this morning and I found this little guy lying on your old ripped-up shirt in our rag pile." Russell jumped from Leah's arms into Lenny's and licked his face until he laughed.

"The shirt I was wearing when that old sow tried to kill me?" he asked.

Leah nodded, looking as pretty as ever.

Lenny said, "I was just getting ready to go feed cattle. Why don't you and Russell come along for a ride?"

Mr. E and Misty trotted out easily with a soft jingling from their harness. They romped over the small hill where Yoder Towers could be seen. Lenny pulled them up, "Whoa!" He pointed with his driving lines still in hand, "Whenever I'm in this part of the field, I stop and look at Yoder Towers and think of my little Leah Yoder. The Leah Yoder with the dimple."

Her dimple sank in as she looked away, obviously embarrassed.

Lenny had been wanting to ask her about something, and he forced himself to say the words, "Why were you so mad at me the night of the taffy pull when I snuck up behind you and your sisters with Smoky?"

Leah giggled. "Because I was just telling them, 'Lenny is never going to ask me to marry him.' I turned around and there you were! I was afraid that you heard me and I was embarrassed about it." She asked him quietly, "Did you really mean to ask me to marry you yesterday?"

"I don't know how Amish guys ask … did I do it wrong?"

"I don't know either how other Amish guys ask a girl to marry them, you're the first Amish guy to ask me." She smiled and looked into his eyes as if to see if he really was serious. She added, "You did it right if you really meant it?"

"I've never been more serious about anything in my life. But, if you need more time to think about it ... maybe you don't want a guy that grew up in town."

"I want a man who knows what he believes and is willing to follow his convictions no matter what anyone else says. You showed that you are that type of man over the past few days."

"Then your answer is still yes?"

"Yes!" Leah looked at the ground for a moment. Her brow crumpled a little and Lenny knew she was worrying about something. "You won't change your mind later about being Amish will you?" she asked and looked at him out of the corners of her eyes.

"No, I'm sure I won't. There is one reason I wish I was still an English guy right now, though...." He hesitated to make her nervous and added, "Then I could give you a great big kiss right out here and nobody would care!"

Her dimple sank in and she had that wide-eyed look that he had fallen in love with when he first saw her out in Alvin's field. He pointed up toward the grandpa house. "Do you think that little house will suit you okay?"

She gazed at it and smiled while Lenny gazed at her and smiled.

He clucked and his horses bounded off, causing her to fall back against him. The bobsled seemed to be floating over the smooth snow-covered ground.

"Lenny, this snow reminds me of white frosting, like Noey's farm is a big cake."

"A wedding cake?" he teased and they laughed. "This is gonna be our farm," he reminded her. "I want to show you something in our barn."

"What?"

"Just something to prove to you that I was going to ask you to marry me." He looked into her sparkling eyes.

They tied their horses and climbed up the mow ramp. Lenny slid open the door and showed her the rope swing. "I put up this swing and thought to bring you in here and ask you to marry me. My very first memory of you was pushing you on a swing in Alvin's barn. And I pushed you on a swing the night of our first kiss."

"That's so sweet!"

"And that night after the wedding, you suggested that I push you on the swing at your place. I wanted to ask you to marry me right then. So when I was pushing you on the swing, I decided I was gonna do it right then and there. It seemed like the perfect moment, until I pinched your fingers in the ropes."

"Really? Is that what you were going to ask me?"

"Uh-huh. Would you have said yes?'" he asked.

"Oh, Lenny, I would have been so excited and very surprised!" She smiled at him, "And yes, I would've said yes!"

Lenny looked into her soft brown eyes and said, *"Eich liebe diech."*

She smiled and echoed, *"Eich liebe diech."*

They headed back out to finish feeding his livestock. Leah tossed off flakes of hay as Lenny circled his horses out through his cattle lot. At one point Russell jumped from the bobsled to chase a squirrel back up a tree. Leah helped Lenny unhitch and unharness his team while Russell watched with his head cocked to one side. They were heading out to her buggy when Ruth came out of the big house.

"Russell! Where did you find him?"

"Leah found him at her house. He was sleeping on my old torn up shirt, the one the sow shredded."

Ruth scolded Russell with a smile on her face, "You ornery little dog, you had us all worrying!"

"As soon as I found him, I told my parents that I had to bring him back home," Leah said, laughing. "I knew you all would be worried about him."

Ruth walked over closer and said, "Thank you, Leah, we are really happy to see you, too. Have you ever been inside our grandpa house?"

"No, I haven't," she answered.

Ruth smiled and led the way. They stepped inside the little kitchen and Leah's face was glowing. Lenny tried to keep his face turned away from Ruth—he didn't want her to see his big smile as they took the small tour. Ruth showed her around and then took her out to see the tiny porch.

"Noey and I loved to sit on this swing whenever the weather was favorable. Some of our best conversations were right here while eating popcorn."

Leah answered, "I can see why; it's a perfect spot with a lovely view of the pasture."

Ruth agreed. "Yes, and if we have mares with colts, we always put them right over there so we can watch the babies play."

Leah and Ruth were all smiles as they walked out toward the hitching rack. Before Leah could get onto her cart, a couple of buggies pulled into Noey's lane. Alvin's family came busting out and hurried over toward Lenny and Leah.

"We got word that you two came back home!" Aunt Lydia called as the crowd got closer.

Alvin hustled with the others as they all formed a circle around Lenny, Leah, and Ruth. Everyone was smiling, even the little girls.

Lenny choked out nervously, "I'm so sorry I missed church when you had it at your place."

"Don't worry about that," Alvin chuckled, "We'll be having it at our place often enough in the future. You will have plenty of chances to see that!"

Everyone laughed. Rosie asked with a smile, "Did you hear about our brother Sam and his special friend, Barbara, getting published?"

"Published?" Lenny asked.

"Yes, it was announced last Sunday that they will be married."

"You and Barbara are getting married?" Lenny looked at Sam. His face was beaming as he nodded. "When?" Lenny questioned.

"The weekend after Thanksgiving," Rosie answered.

"That is only a two weeks away!" Lenny let it show how surprised he was.

Viola piped up, "That's how Amish weddings are. You get published only a few weeks before the wedding."

"I can't believe you are going to get married, Sam"

"Hey, Leonard, maybe you should marry Leah?" a loud voice boomed out over the crowd.

Lenny knew immediately that it was Truman. Not only by his voice, but no other Amish person would make a loud suggestion like that in public. Lenny looked at Leah and her cheeks were as rosy as his own felt.

Truman repeated himself, "Maybe you should marry Leah!"

Lenny smiled and said, "Hello, Truman, it sure is good to see you."

"It's good to see you, too, little Jake!" Everyone roared with laughter at that.

Lenny asked, "So where were you all headed this time of day?"

"We came to see you, Leonard!" Lydia said.

"You came all the way over here to see me?"

"Of course we did, Leonard," Alvin confirmed. "We were so excited to hear that you and Leah came back home!"

Just then, a brown pony could be seen trotting toward them.

"Fannie Ella, how is your pony working out?" Lenny called.

"She's a really nice pony! Thank you so much for bringing her to me."

"Don't thank me, thank Perry—it was his idea."

Perry's face got redder than Leah's had, and he tilted his head so that his black Amish hat covered his face.

Aunt Ruth changed the subject, "I have fresh baked apple pie. Why don't you all come inside and have a piece?"

"One pie won't be enough for this crowd," Noey said quietly.

"I baked four of them this morning," Aunt Ruth said, her face glowing.

Alvin laughed. "It's a good thing you made four—here comes Junior's whole family!"

Aunt Ruth called to Junior's family, "Come on in the house, we are all having some apple pie! If I run out of apple pie, we'll bake some cookies."

Herbie teased her, "You better stir up the cookie dough right now!"

Everyone laughed and headed for the porch.

Lenny called to Fannie Ella, "You can tie your pony and come inside—or do you think she will climb these porch steps?"

"She may be willing to go up the steps," Fannie Ella said seriously.

Her mother, Ruby, scolded, "Don't you even think of taking that pony in Ruth's house!"

"I wasn't serious about that," Fannie answered.

Junior Ruby laughed. "I want her to climb our house steps first."

Everyone laughed and Russell barked.

"Where did you find Russell?" Perry asked, excited as could be.

He was in Leah's barn…," Lenny started to explain.

Alvin interrupted, "That little Russell is pretty smart. He figured, 'If I can find Leah, Leonard will be somewhere close by.'"

The little mostly-white dog barked when he heard his name and the laughter grew, which made Russell bark louder.

Leah blushed and picked up Russell, hugging him as she followed Lenny.

Everyone crowded into Noey and Ruth's home. Lenny started to speak and everyone got quiet.

"I just wanted to mention that both of my aunts have part of Psalm 19 on their walls, and Leah's mom has another part of that same Psalm on her wall…."

Everyone looked at Lenny, waiting for him to say more.

"Well, I just wanted to say Psalm 19 has become my favorite passage in the Bible. When I'm out working in the fields with horses, I can feel God's presence. I know that I belong here with all of you. This is where I learned what David meant when he wrote the psalm, 'The heavens declare the glory of God; the skies proclaim the work of His hands."

Alvin said, "That always was your grandpa Jesse's favorite verse."

Noey nodded in agreement, "Our grandpa Isaac said that it was his favorite verse, too."

Lenny smiled and looked at Leah. She smiled back at him and a crystal-clear teardrop fell from her eye, rolled down her cheek, through her dimple, and landed on her hand.